MURDER AT THE
NATURAL HISTORY MUSEUM

MURDER AT THE
NATURAL HISTORY MUSEUM

JIM ELDRIDGE

Allison & Busby Limited
11 Wardour Mews
London W1F 8AN
allisonandbusby.com

First published in Great Britain by Allison & Busby in 2020.
This paperback edition published by Allison & Busby in 2021.

A CIP catalogue record for this book is available from
the British Library.

10 9 8 7 6 5 4 3 2 1

ISBN 978-0-7490-2508-3

Typeset in 11/16 pt Adobe Garamond Pro by
Allison & Busby Ltd.

The paper used for this Allison & Busby publication
has been produced from trees that have been legally sourced
from well-managed and credibly certified forests.

Printed and bound by
CPI Group (UK) Ltd, Croydon, CR0 4YY

For Lynne, again and always

CHAPTER ONE

London, August 1895

Daniel Wilson and Abigail Fenton gazed at the pile of smashed bones heaped against the wall and exchanged puzzled looks. They were an interesting pair, contrasting in looks but of one mind in almost everything. Daniel, an ex-Scotland Yard detective in his mid-thirties, famed for his work on the Jack the Ripper investigations, was tall and well-built, his rugged features made more so by his slightly broken nose veering to one side. Abigail, an internationally renowned archaeologist, famous for her work on the Egyptian pyramids but who now concentrated on criminal investigations alongside Daniel, her partner in life as well as detection, was also in her thirties. She was tall, slim and elegant, her long reddish hair cascading down around her attractive, almost feline, face. To those who didn't know her, she could appear haughty, but she was as down-to-earth as the humblest porter on any of the digs she'd been on.

Lying amongst the bones was a piece of cardboard with the words 'BECAUSE OF HE THAT BETRAYETH' scrawled in block capitals.

'It's an iguanodon,' said Evelyn Scott, the curator of the Natural History Museum. 'Or it was before someone attacked it.'

They were in the museum's huge Grand Hall, shielded from the eyes of the general public by a series of temporary screens.

The rest of the Grand Hall beyond the screens was filled with skeletons of dinosaurs of all sizes, along with the fossilised remains of other prehistoric creatures, all part of the museum's recently opened 'The Time of the Dinosaurs' exhibition, which extended to two smaller rooms off the Grand Hall.

Evelyn Scott was tall, thin and pale-faced, her pallor emphasised by having her black hair pulled back into a knotted bun, and smartly attired in a long black dress. Behind the curator, the paunchy figure of the museum's maintenance manager, Herbert Sharp, resplendent in a large-checked purple three-piece suit, glowered angrily at the wreckage of bones, taking this outrage as a personal affront.

'I'm not sure why we've been called in, Miss Scott,' said Daniel. 'Our speciality is solving murders . . .'

'In museums, I know,' said Scott.

'But this isn't a murder,' continued Daniel. 'At best, it's a case of criminal damage, with possibly breaking and entering, or burglary if the people who did it broke in during the night.'

'They did,' said Scott. 'We discovered that a window at the back of the building had been forced. But our concern is not just what happened here with this, but that something worse might happen in the future. We have had threats, and it is possible this . . . this outrage is the result of those threats.'

'Threats from whom?' asked Abigail. 'And do they mention anything about betrayal, as these words do?'

'It reads like a quotation,' observed Daniel.

'Almost,' said Scott. 'In fact it's a misquotation from The Gospel of St John: "Which is he that betrayeth thee", and we have had a letter which threatens retribution.'

'Retribution for what?' asked Abigail.

'For not buying dinosaur skeletons from them.'

'We'll need to look at that letter,' said Daniel.

'If you come to my office I'll show you.' Scott gestured at the pile of bones. 'We left these as they were for the police and then for you to see. Some of the staff wanted to remove the wreckage immediately, but I do understand investigators prefer things being left as they are after a crime to possibly supply clues as to the perpetrators.'

Daniel nodded. 'That's true, and I'd like to make a close examination of the damage. Can I suggest that while I do that, you and Miss Fenton go to your office to show her the letter, along with anything else you have, and I'll join you once I've finished here? Then Mr Sharp can have things cleared things up and the screens can be removed.'

'Thank you,' said Scott gratefully. 'The screens have aroused all manner of curiosity from visitors, wondering what we might be erecting behind them.' She turned to Abigail. 'If you'll follow me, Miss Fenton.'

Abigail followed the curator towards the main reception area, while Daniel knelt down to examine the wreckage, watched by the angry Herbert Sharp.

'We've never had anything like this happen before,' said Sharp.

'The damage looks like it was done with a heavy hammer. Possibly a coal hammer,' said Daniel. He looked up at the maintenance manager. 'I'd like to talk to whoever was the first to find the damage.'

'That'd be the cleaners,' said Sharp. 'But they've all gone home now.'

'What time do they arrive in the morning?'

'Six o'clock,' said Sharp. 'The head cleaner, Ada Watson, has a key and lets them in. They work until 8.30 a.m., cleaning and polishing. The senior attendant arrives at 8.30 a.m. to make sure everything is in order, with the staff coming in at 9 a.m. The museum opens to the public at 9.30 a.m. Every day of the week except Sundays. Yesterday, being a Sunday, no one was here. It's also the only day the cleaners have off.'

'What time does the museum close?' asked Daniel.

'Five-thirty,' said Sharp.

'And who locks up?'

'The senior attendant, Brandon Walpole. He makes a last tour of the museum and then leaves at 6 p.m.'

'And he did that on Saturday?'

'Yes.'

'I'd like to talk to the cleaners who found the wreckage.'

'The best thing would be for you to call here tomorrow morning at about eight o'clock,' said Sharp. 'By then the cleaners will have done most of their work and will be free to talk. I'll leave a note for Mrs Watson telling her you'll be coming.'

'Thank you,' said Daniel. 'That would be good. Out of curiosity, how is the exhibition doing?'

'It's early days,' said Sharp. 'But that's often the way with a new exhibition. Things will pick up once word spreads about it.' He gave a proud, almost smug, smile as he added: 'We had Mr Bram Stoker himself here on Saturday, and I heard him tell Miss Scott how impressed he was and that he'd do his best to get Sir Henry Irving to come along. Once that sort of thing happens, people will come in droves. There's nothing like celebrity to bring in the crowds.'

Abigail followed Miss Scott up the narrow stone staircase to the first floor and the administrative offices. Scott stopped at a door, knocked and went in. It was a small office. A middle-aged lady sitting at a desk going through some papers looked up as they entered.

'Mrs Smith,' said Scott. 'This is Miss Abigail Fenton. Mr Daniel Wilson is downstairs examining the damage to the iguanodon and he will be joining us when he's finished.' Turning to Abigail, Scott added: 'Mrs Smith is my secretary and knows more about the museum than I do.'

'I think that's an exaggeration, Miss Scott.' The woman smiled, obviously pleased at the compliment.

'Not at all,' said Scott. To Abigail, she explained: 'Mrs Smith was secretary to the previous curator, Mr Danvers Hardwicke.' Turning back to the secretary, she asked: 'Do you have the letter from Petter and Wardle, Mrs Smith?'

'I do,' said Smith, and she lifted it from her desk and handed it to Scott. 'I had it ready because I felt you might require it.'

'Thank you,' said Scott. 'Miss Fenton and I will be in my office.'

As Scott and Abigail walked along the corridor to the curator's own office, Scott said: 'As you see, Mrs Smith is absolutely invaluable. So efficient and always prepared.'

They entered Scott's office. It was a room in which the shelves were laden with books, with more books stacked on the floor in front of the shelves. By contrast, the large desk in the office was cleared of all but a few papers, a decorated inkwell and pens in holders, and a large blotting pad.

'The books are leftovers from my predecessor,' said Scott. 'I haven't had the heart to go through them yet and decide which ones to get rid of, but I shall.' She gestured towards a chair by the desk, and when Abigail had seated herself Scott handed her the letter, before taking her own chair.

Abigail read the missive from Petter and Wardle, who were described in the letterhead as 'Domestic and Commercial Agents', which Abigail felt was a description covering a multitude of activities. The address was in Paddington and the directors were listed as Erskine Petter and Benjamin Wardle; the letter had been signed by the former.

To the Curator of the Natural History Museum,
Cromwell Road, London

Dear Sir,
You are in breach of your exclusive agreement to purchase American fossils of dinosaurs from our client, the Bone Company of America, by the fact that you have purchased similar dinosaur fossils from rival companies in the United

States of America. Unless this situation is rectified and these
renegade fossils are returned to their supplier, and you accept
delivery of those fossils from the Bone Company of America
as agreed, retribution will be taken.

'Retribution,' murmured Abigail. 'That certainly sounds like a threat. So, you believe the damage to the iguanodon is related to the rivalry between competing companies selling dinosaur skeletons found in America.'

'I certainly believe it's a possibility,' Scott said. 'However, the skeleton that was destroyed was found in Sussex here in England, not in America. Unfortunately, when I shared that information with the police constable who arrived to investigate, he said the fact that the destroyed skeleton came from Sussex showed the attack wasn't connected with this letter. I made the point to him that the attackers may not have been aware of where this particular iguanodon was found, to them it was just a dinosaur fossil, and I pressed him to at least look into it. He said he was unable to do that because the firm is in Paddington, which is outside his beat.'

'Not very satisfactory,' said Abigail.

There was a knock at the door to which they both looked. The door opened and Daniel entered, carrying the piece of card and the string by which it had been attached to the skeleton.

'What's your opinion, Mr Wilson?' asked Scott.

'At this moment I'm afraid I've nothing much more to add to your own view, Miss Scott,' said Daniel. He gestured at the piece of card in his hand. 'I'll examine this message that was left and see if that offers anything.' He looked at the letter in Abigail's hand and asked: 'A clue?'

'Possibly,' said Abigail, passing it to him.

Daniel read it, then handed it to Miss Scott.

'The tone is certainly threatening, and the label "Domestic and Commercial Agents" suitably vague,' commented Daniel. 'Addressing the letter with the salutation of "Dear Sir" indicates they are not aware that you as curator are a woman, which suggests their knowledge of the museum is limited. Have you had any correspondence with this Bone Company of America?'

'No. Mrs Smith and I have looked through the files and can find nothing.'

'Do you know if they exist?'

'Yes, they do,' said Scott. 'In fact, I'm sure they were one of the companies the museum considered when the exhibition was being planned. At least according to notes I found in the files left by my predecessor, Mr Hardwicke. But there's no actual correspondence from them, or from Mr Hardwicke to them.'

'Would it be possible for us to talk to Mr Hardwicke?' asked Abigail. 'His information would be first-hand and so very useful.'

'Sadly, he is no longer with us,' said Scott. 'A tragic accident. He died four months ago.'

'I'm sorry,' said Abigail. 'I hadn't realised.'

'Our condolences, Miss Scott,' added Daniel. 'In view of this letter, I think a visit to Petter and Wardle should be our next move. It will be interesting to see how they respond to our enquiries.'

CHAPTER TWO

The offices of Petter and Wardle were quite near to Paddington Station, a relatively short distance from the Natural History Museum in South Kensington, so Daniel and Abigail elected to walk, especially as their journey took them through the greenery of Kensington Gardens, the scent of blooms and shrubs filling the air, a pleasant change from the sulphurous smell of smoky streets. As they walked, Daniel said: 'I was talking to the maintenance manager, Mr Sharp, and he mentioned someone called Bram Stoker. Apparently he visited the exhibition yesterday. The way he said his name suggested I ought to be impressed. Who is he?'

'You've heard of the Lyceum Theatre, I assume. And Henry Irving? And Ellen Terry?'

'There's no need to be sarcastic,' said Daniel. 'Of course I have.

You can hardly open a newspaper without being told that Mr Irving is about to give us his enthralling King Lear, or Hamlet.'

'*Sir* Henry," said Abigail. 'He was recently knighted.'

'An actor knighted?' Daniel sniffed dismissively. 'And as for Ellen Terry, she's still playing Juliet when she's fifty.'

'Almost fifty,' Abigail corrected him. 'And she looks much younger. Especially on stage. Bram Stoker is the business manager of the Lyceum, and is a crucial figure in everything that goes on there. Actors, set designs, publicity, finances. He also arranges the tours the company carry out, such as when they go to America to do a season of plays there. You name it, Bram Stoker is behind it. And he has the ears of most people in London's theatreland, so if he spreads some complimentary words about this exhibition among the people he knows, celebrities will come. And where celebrities go, the general public aren't far behind.'

As they crossed Bayswater Road and began to enter the maze of cramped back streets around Paddington Station, Daniel said: 'By the way, did you know the curator of the museum was a woman?'

'Of course,' replied Abigail. 'Didn't you?'

'Why would I?' asked Daniel.

'There may have been a clue in the name at the bottom of the letter she sent us by messenger.' Abigail smiled. 'Evelyn.'

'Men are called Evelyn as well,' said Daniel. He frowned, puzzled. 'But you didn't say anything to warn me.'

'What was there to warn you about?' asked Abigail. 'Yes, it's rare for a woman to hold a responsible position in such an august establishment as the museum, but she would only

16

have been given the post because she merited it. She's highly qualified. I believe she graduated with a very good degree.'

'So, she's from your old college in Cambridge, Girton?' asked Daniel.

'No,' said Abigail. 'She was at Somerville, Girton's sister college in Oxford.' She looked at him quizzically. 'Does having a woman in charge disturb you?'

'No, absolutely not,' said Daniel firmly. 'It just took me by surprise, that's all. I heartily approve.'

'Good,' said Abigail. 'I'm sure she approves of you as well.' Then she asked: 'What did you make of the message? About betrayal?'

'It was written in block capitals, either to disguise an educated person's handwriting, or because that's how the assailant writes, which suggests someone not so educated.'

'And your guess?'

'The first. Using an unfamiliar phrase from the Bible suggests literacy.'

'I wouldn't have thought it was an unfamiliar phrase,' commented Abigail. 'I recognised it, or at least the fact that it was a misquote, and so did Miss Scott.'

'Both of you are women with university degrees.'

'The Bible is in common use by many levels of society,' countered Abigail.

'Yes, but while most common people are familiar with Old Testament passages, like the Ten Commandments, for example, I doubt if they are with the rather obscure verses. I didn't recognise it, for example.'

Abigail sniffed. 'Heathen.'

They found the offices of Petter and Wardle located above

a butcher's shop within sight, sound and smells of Paddington Station. As with most buildings next to a main railway station, soot from the trains hung in the air, painting the facade of the butcher's and the windows above it. The door to the rooms above the shop was unlocked, and they climbed a flight of grimy, uncarpeted stairs to the first floor and a narrow corridor with four doors, two on either side. The walls of the corridor hadn't seen any fresh paint for some time and the old brown paint was flaking off.

'Not the most prestigious of locations,' grunted Daniel.

A glass-panelled door had the words 'Petter and Wardle' painted on it in gold lettering. Daniel knocked on the glass, then turned the handle, and he and Abigail walked in. It was a small, cramped room, shelves overflowing with bundles of papers tied with ribbons, and four wooden filing cabinets. The desk that took up most of the room was also laden with papers. The dominant smell in the room was a stink of body sweat, combined with decaying paper and cheap gin. The man sitting behind the desk, a red-faced man with a large ginger moustache looked up at them, warily.

'Yes?' he asked.

'Mr Daniel Wilson and Miss Abigail Fenton,' said Daniel. 'We have been engaged by the Natural History Museum to investigate damage done to a dinosaur skeleton, discovered early this morning. It had been smashed.'

'What's that to do with me?' demanded the man.

'Which are you: Mr Petter or Mr Wardle?' asked Daniel.

'I am Mr Erskine Petter,' said the man haughtily. 'Senior partner. And I ask again, what has this smashed dinosaur skeleton to do with me?'

He made no attempt to get up, nor to offer them a seat, although there were two vacant chairs by the window. But the sight of the dust and dirt on the chairs had already made both Abigail and Daniel decide to reject the offer of a seat if it was made.

'We've been shown a letter you sent to the museum as representatives of the Bone Company of America, in which you stated that unless the museum only purchased dinosaur skeletons from your client there would be retribution,' said Abigail. 'You will agree that "retribution" has an ominous, not to mention threatening, tone to it.'

'It was used purely in the context of financial recompense and a loss of reputation of our client. My client has been cheated.'

'By Miss Evelyn Scott?' asked Abigail. 'Who you addressed as "Dear Sir"?'

Petter sniffed. 'I do not know the lady. Our transactions were conducted with her predecessor, Mr Danvers Hardwicke.'

'Yet there seems to be no correspondence in the museum's files from you prior to this recent letter threatening retribution.'

'That is because all previous correspondence was between the Bone Company and Mr Hardwicke directly.'

'But no letters to or from the Bone Company of America have been found in the museum's files,' said Daniel.

'Are you calling me a liar?' demanded Petter angrily.

'No,' said Daniel. 'We're just saying that the museum has no trace of any letters or any sort of correspondence from the Bone Company of America.'

'They must have been deliberately destroyed,' said Petter, flatly.

'Have you any evidence these letters existed?' asked Abigail.

'I have a letter from the Bone Company advising me that the letters of agreement were sent and signed by Mr Hardwicke.'

'Have you seen these letters?' asked Abigail. 'Do you have copies you could show us?'

'Are you questioning my veracity?' demanded Petter, indignantly.

'Not at all,' said Abigail. 'I'm just asking if we might look at them. Then we can advise Miss Scott that we have seen them and suggest she comply with your requests.'

Petter hesitated before saying awkwardly: 'No, I haven't actually seen them. But I have no reason to doubt my client when they say such letters exist.'

'If that's the case and they were in direct correspondence with the museum previously, why did they engage you to take up the issue on their behalf?'

'Because it takes time for letters to cross the Atlantic,' replied Petter. 'That presented no problem while arrangements were being made for the museum to purchase the skeletons because the exhibition was some months away at that time. But now there is an urgency about the situation and the Bone Company felt it was vital that they had a representative here in London who is authorised to act on their behalf to expedite matters.'

Abigail nodded. 'Yes, that makes sense. Could you furnish us with the address and the names of the owners of the Bone Company?'

'Again, you doubt me?' demanded Petter, stiffly.

'Not at all,' repeated Abigail. 'But if we are to persuade our client, the museum, you have a valid case, the more practical information we can provide the better.'

'All correspondence between us and our client is confidential,' said Petter.

'Even just the name of the owner and the address of the company?'

'Especially that information.'

'Perhaps we should arrange a further meeting between ourselves and you, next time with your partner, Mr Wardle,' said Daniel.

'There would be no point.' said Petter.

'At least Mr Wardle should be advised that legal action may result because of this incident.'

'He will be so advised,' said Petter. 'At the moment he is out of the country, but I will inform him by letter. Now, I believe our business is done and I will ask you to leave.'

Daniel looked to Abigail, who nodded, and they left the office, heading back down the grimy stairs and out into the street.

'What a dreadful place,' said Abigail. 'Even this sooty air outside seems fresh after that room. What did you make of it?'

'I'm wondering if there is actually a Mr Wardle.'

'Why? What are you thinking?'

'There's no evidence of any earlier correspondence from them or this alleged Bone Company. The offices are in a shabby back street in Paddington. It suggests to me something dubious.'

'Extortion?' asked Abigail.

'It's been done before. Some disreputable character sees the chance of making money from the Natural History Museum about this exhibition. They lodge a spurious but legal-sounding claim in the hope of being paid off. When that fails, they up the pressure by sending in a thug with a hammer.'

'But why do you doubt the existence of a Mr Wardle?'

'Having two names on the letterhead gives the company greater authenticity, even if one of them is fictitious.'

'You think Mr Petter carried out the attack on the dinosaur fossil?'

Daniel shook his head.

'I can't see him doing the dirty work. It's more likely that he hired some thugs to do the actual damage. Proving it, however, is another matter.'

'Then we look into Mr Petter and his associates,' said Abigail. 'However, first we need to tell Miss Scott about our meeting with Petter and see how far she wants us to go with our investigation, because it could prove expensive. There's a good chance that our turning up at Petter's office may put him off from committing any further damage. Especially if Miss Scott decides to hire a couple of nightwatchmen, which would be the cheaper option.'

CHAPTER THREE

They returned to the museum where they reported on their meeting with Petter to Miss Scott.

'And you think this Mr Petter was behind the attack on the iguanodon?' asked Scott.

'It's possible,' replied Daniel. 'In fact, my policeman's nose tells me there's definitely something suspect about Mr Petter and his whole set-up.'

'Your policeman's nose?' queried Scott.

Daniel grinned and tapped the side of his nose. 'Many years in the Metropolitan Police Detective Division gives you a second sense about these things. However, proving that he was behind it is another matter.'

'I'd like you to try,' said Scott. 'If he did it, but now decides to back off, then someone else might make an attempt. I want to stamp out that prospect.'

'Then we will, but we would also recommend hiring a nightwatchman or two, even just for the duration of the exhibition,' said Daniel. 'We shall come in early tomorrow morning and talk to the cleaners who found the damage.'

'In that case I shall also come in early so that we can have a proper discussion before the museum opens,' said Scott. 'I'll ask Mrs Smith to get out any notes relating to the exhibition so you can examine them, in case there's anything there that may give you evidence backing up your suspicions about these Petter and Wardle people.'

'If we're going to investigate them and the threat contained in their letter, it would help us if you could tell us something about their alleged client, the Bone Company of America,' said Daniel. 'And about any other such companies. From the tone of Petter and Wardle's letter, it suggests that there are a few companies vying for business over dinosaur skeletons.'

'Oh yes. To such an extent that it resulted in what became known as the Bone Wars—'

'One moment,' interrupted Daniel. 'My apologies, but I'm starting from a position of ignorance. Am I right in assuming these Bone Wars took place in America?'

'Yes,' said Scott. 'Between 1877 and 1892. They were called the Bone Wars because that's what they developed into. Men from two rival factions attacking the other side and destroying the fossils they'd found. There were stories that some men were actually killed, but I'm not sure if that's true.'

'How did it reach such a pass?' asked Daniel.

'It was as a result of the expansion of the railroad into the

24

Western states, particularly Colorado, Wyoming and Nebraska. As the ground was dug up and levelled for the railway tracks, so a variety of fossils were uncovered. Some of them very large indeed. News of these finds brought palaeontologists to what became known as the bone beds.'

'Palaeontologists?' queried Daniel at this unfamiliar word.

'Fossil hunters,' translated Abigail.

'Exactly,' said Scott. 'The main protagonists were Othniel Charles Marsh and Edward Drinker Cope. Marsh and Cope were both wealthy men, fanatical fossil hunters and deadly rivals. Each was determined to become more famous than the other in the field, which meant discovering more species than his rival. There is no doubt that they uncovered an astonishing amount of dinosaur skeletons: triceratops, allosaurs, stegosaurus, diplodocus. Skeletons that had never been discovered before, certainly not in Britain.

'As word of their finds and their fame spread, others joined in, and soon the whole of the West was filled with dinosaur hunters battling one another. Marsh and Cope may have been driven by scientific discovery, but these latecomers were there for profit.'

'As a result, I assume the Bone Wars became even more vicious.'

'I'm afraid so. The opportunity for sudden wealth attracts all sorts. To be honest, it became impossible to know who was who: who had a rightful claim to a particular skeleton and who hadn't. We employed an agent in America who arranged the purchase of the skeletons on our behalf, with an assurance that they would guarantee such sales were bona fide.'

'Have you been in contact with your agents in America to ask them about this Bone Company?' asked Daniel.

'I wrote to them as soon as we received the letter from Petter and Wardle, but that was almost a week ago, and correspondence between Britain and America takes some time.

'I must also let you know that I've written to all the trustees of the museum to inform them of the unfortunate incident over the iguanodon. I decided it was preferential that they hear about it from me rather than read about it first in the newspapers. I'm just telling you in case any of them decide to visit tomorrow while you're here.'

That evening at their home in the small terraced house in Camden Town, Daniel tucked enthusiastically into the meal that Abigail laid before him. Usually, Daniel liked to provide the evening meal, but today Abigail had pressured him into letting her take over his much-loved kitchen range. 'I have a special surprise in mind,' she'd told him that morning. She'd barely finished her preparations when the message had arrived from Miss Scott requesting their assistance, just giving her time to pop her surprise dish into the slow cooker before they left for the museum. Now, Daniel was relishing the plate of food before him.

'This stew is delicious,' said Daniel. 'You've excelled yourself.'

'It's not just a stew, it's boeuf bourguignon,' Abigail corrected him.

'French?' queried Daniel.

'*Oui, monsieur*,' said Abigail. 'I found the recipe in a magazine, and I've been looking forward to trying it out. It seemed the ideal dish to cook.'

'It's certainly ideal,' said Daniel. 'When we move, we'll have to make sure our new house has a range in the kitchen if we can produce meals like this.'

Abigail smiled. 'We? I agree you produce lovely food on it, but you've had years of experience using it and you tend to either roast or boil.'

'Techniques that have served me well,' said Daniel. 'But I'm happy to learn new cooking under your tutelage.'

'Excellent,' said Abigail. 'I have recipes I discovered in Greece and Arab countries, interesting ways of cooking goat.'

'Goat?' said Daniel doubtfully.

'Don't dismiss things until you've tried them.'

'If it's as good as this, I look forward to it,' said Daniel, and speared another forkful into his mouth. As he ate, he said: 'I was thinking about what Miss Scott told us about the Bone Wars in America and reflecting how different it is here.'

'Is it?' asked Abigail.

'Well, I've never heard you talk about being attacked by rival archaeologists.'

'No, it happens in a more subtle way here,' said Abigail. 'Reputations are attacked, aspersions cast on another's good name and scientific credentials. It happens in all areas of research. Botany is a hotbed of it. I've often thought it's about trying to achieve immortality by getting your name attached to a new species, whether it's a flower, an insect, a fish or a dinosaur. For example, at the exhibition there's the skeleton on display of an iguanodon that was discovered at Maidstone in Kent. You'll see that it's listed as Iguanodon Mantelli, after Gideon Mantell, who was one of the first people in Britain to discover this creature. But there's some dispute about who really found this particular dinosaur. There were reports that the actual discoverer was Gideon Mantell's wife, Mary Ann.'

'Which would still make it qualify as Iguanodon Mantelli,' said Daniel.

'But there's also a claim that a similar fossil was discovered by a man called William Harding Bensted.'

'Perhaps the best way to get to the truth would be to ask Gideon Mantell.'

'As he died a few decades ago that would be difficult,' said Abigail. 'Also, some people can be quite spurious with the truth. And that includes the man who created the Natural History Museum, Sir Richard Owen. He was awarded the Royal Medal for a paper he'd written on the belemnites, a marine fossil. But he neglected to say that the belemnites had been discovered four years previously by an amateur biologist called Chaning Pearce.'

'So he was a cheat,' said Daniel.

'As a result Owen was voted off the councils of the Royal Society and the Zoological Society. However, he was still knighted some years later.'

'But he was still a cheat.'

'Not completely. Much of the work he published was from his own research. And he was the first person who coined the phrase "dinosaur" to define these creatures. The problem is he was also an opportunist and sometimes took shortcuts.'

'By stealing other people's work?'

'It happens in all areas. Did Shakespeare really write all those plays, or did he borrow some parts from Bacon or Marlowe? It's known he took most of his history plots from Holinshed.'

'Theft is still theft, and that includes plagiarism,' said Daniel.

'It can be a grey area when it involves academic research. Frankly, it's about who gets the credit.'

Daniel laid aside his knife and fork with a smile of pleasure.

'Superb,' he said. 'Which brings me back to where I began, the question of us moving house and making sure it has a range in it. You do still want us to marry, I hope?'

'I do,' said Abigail. 'In fact, it's something I've been weighing up quite seriously recently.'

'Really?' said Daniel warily. 'Why "seriously"?'

'Because if we are going to be married, I'd like to find out more about your family, before I meet them at the wedding.'

'I don't have any family,' said Daniel

'You must have,' said Abigail. 'A cousin many times removed. A distant aunt or uncle.'

'No,' said Daniel. 'None. There's just me.'

'Your parents?' asked Abigail. She hesitated before adding, 'I've often wanted to ask you about them before, but I suppose I was waiting for you to tell me about them yourself.'

'There's not a lot to tell,' said Daniel.

'There is,' insisted Abigail. 'You know about me. You've met my sister, Bella. You know we grew up in a reasonably nice area of Cambridge. When our parents died we were left with some money from my father which enabled me to go to university to study, and for Bella to be able to choose an occupation which suited her. You've met Bella's husband. We have an aunt on our mother's side who lives in Lincolnshire, Aunt Matilda. She's very elderly and I haven't seen her in a long time, but I understand Bella has visited her. Bella is much more aware of family duties than I. Once you know that, you know all there is to know about my family. But about yours, I know nothing. How did you come to be in Camden Town? You said you grew up here. Did your parents live here?'

'I believe they did, at first,' said Daniel. 'My father was an ostler, looking after horses left outside inns. I believe his name was Horace.'

'You believe?'

'I only ever heard people refer to him as Wilson or as Aitch. He died when I was seven.'

'Oh, I'm so sorry,' said Abigail.

Daniel shrugged. 'It happened. I didn't really know him. As an ostler, he spent most of his time outside of inns and much of it inside them. He drank a great deal. That may be one of the reasons he died.'

'And your mother?' asked Abigail.

Daniel paused, before saying: 'She died when I was nine. In the workhouse where we went after my father died because she couldn't support us. The workhouse is still there, in St Pancras Way, not far from where we are now. I left there when I was twelve.' He fell silent, contemplative, then added: 'I had a brother and a sister. My brother was older than me, my sister younger. They both died. Typhus. The scourge of the poor. I sometimes wonder why I survived and they didn't. Luck, I suppose.' He looked at her. 'So, that's it. A workhouse boy. No family of any sort. Except you.'

'Oh, my poor Daniel,' said Abigail, and she left her seat to sit down next to him, then pulled him tightly close to her.

CHAPTER FOUR

Daniel and Abigail arrived at the museum at eight o'clock the next morning to find a woman wearing an apron, her hair tied back in a turban made from a scarf, mopping the front steps.

'It ain't open to the public yet,' she told them. 'Doors open at half past nine.'

'We're here to see Mrs Ada Watson,' Daniel told her. 'Mr Sharp made the arrangement for this morning at this hour.'

The woman stopped mopping and looked at them doubtfully.

'I dunno about that,' she said. 'No one said nuffin to me about no arrangement.'

'Perhaps you'd tell Mrs Watson we're here,' said Abigail. 'Mr Daniel Wilson and Miss Abigail Fenton.'

The woman regarded them suspiciously, then said, 'Wait here. And don't touch my mop.'

She leant the mop against a wall, then disappeared in through the large double doors.

'Do I look like the sort of person who'd steal someone's mop?' asked Daniel.

'Perhaps she was referring to me.' Abigail smiled.

Daniel looked her up and down, then shook his head. 'No,' he said. 'I can't see you with a mop.'

Abigail looked at him, offended.

'I'll have you know that since I moved into your house I have done just as much of the cleaning as you have. More so, in fact. Just because I do it when you're out and can't get in my way . . .'

'Yes, I'm sorry,' said Daniel, apologetically.

Abigail was about to expand her protest, when the door opened and the mop lady reappeared, accompanied by a woman in her forties, similarly attired in an apron and with her hair turbaned.

'Mr Wilson and Miss Fenton?' she asked.

Abigail and Daniel nodded.

'I'm Mrs Watson,' she said. 'Come in.'

'I thought it best to check, Ada,' said the mop lady. 'Especially after what's occurred. You can't trust anyone these days, even the posh-looking ones.'

As Daniel and Abigail followed Ada Watson into the museum, Daniel whispered: 'I've never been described as posh before.'

'What makes you think she was referring to you?' whispered back Abigail.

Ada Watson stopped by the reception desk just inside the body of the museum.

'You'll have to excuse Evie,' she said. 'What's happened has upset everyone. Mr Sharp said Miss Scott has hired you to find out who done it. Smashed the skeleton.'

'That's right,' said Abigail. 'We'd like to talk to the people who first discovered the damage.'

'That was the three of them: Marge Adams, Dolly Tilly and Dolly's daughter, Tess. How it works is the three of them go into the Grand Hall and do a bit, then Dolly and Tess head off and do the smaller room off the Grand Hall, then come back in and help Marge finish off, before they go and do the conveniences.'

'Would it be possible to talk to them now?' asked Abigail.

'I'll go and get 'em,' said Ada.

'Could we talk to them where the skeleton was found?' asked Daniel.

She nodded. 'Wait for us there,' she said, and headed towards a set of steps leading down.

Daniel and Abigail went to where they'd seen the broken iguanodon skeleton the day before. The damage had been cleared away, leaving a vacant space amongst the other exhibits.

'At least there's been no repeat of the attack,' said Abigail.

'Fortunately. If Mr Petter was involved in some way, maybe our visit to him has made him cautious,' added Daniel.

'*If,*' stressed Abigail.

'There's definitely something dubious about him,' said Daniel.

'Your policeman's nose?' asked Abigail.

'Exactly,' said Daniel.

Ada Watson reappeared, accompanied by three women, a short, round woman in her fifties, a thin stick of a woman in her forties and an equally thin young woman in her early twenties. The last two looked similar enough to be Dolly and Tess Tilly, which meant the short one was Marge Adams. All three wore the uniform of patterned aprons and turbans for their hair.

Ada introduced them. 'These are Mr Wilson and Miss Fenton. They're the detectives Miss Scott has hired.'

Tess Tilly regarded Abigail with a look of wonder.

'You're a detective?' she asked in amazement.

'I am,' said Abigail. 'Along with Mr Wilson.'

'But you're a woman,' said Tess.

'Nuff of that, Tess,' rebuked her mother. 'Don't be rude.'

'I wasn't being rude,' defended Tess. 'I was just saying . . .'

'Stick to why they're here,' Ada ordered, her tone firm. 'The skeleton.'

'Yes,' said Marge. 'That was just how it was. We walked in and saw it. At first, we thought it must have just fallen over, but then we saw some of the bones were broken, like they'd been hit with something heavy.'

'Then we saw the piece of cardboard tied to it with words on.'

'"Because of he that betrayeth",' said Ada dramatically.

'Ada can read,' said Marge with admiration.

Abigail let Daniel ask most of the questions of the three women, appreciating his long experience as a police officer conducting investigations, but it soon became obvious that the cleaners couldn't add much to what was already known. They'd discovered the wreckage soon after they'd arrived for work at six o'clock. They'd immediately reported it to Ada Watson, who told them to leave things exactly as they were for the police to examine the damage.

'It was Mr Sharp who arranged for the screens to be put

round it to hide it from the public's eyes,' Ada told them. 'Otherwise they'd have had to close off the whole Grand Hall, and they couldn't do that.'

'Did you notice any particular marks on the floor near the damage?' asked Daniel. 'Boot marks, for example?'

Ada looked at the other three, who shook their heads.

'No,' said Marge. 'Whoever did it had clean shoes, otherwise we'd have noticed it, being cleaners as we are. We spot things like that.'

'Ah, Miss Fenton and Mr Wilson.' They turned to see Miss Scott advancing towards them. 'Here I am, early, as promised. Have Mrs Watson and the others been of assistance?'

'Indeed, Miss Scott, they have,' said Daniel. He turned and smiled at the four cleaners. 'Thank you, ladies. And if we have any other questions we'll talk again.'

CHAPTER FIVE

As Daniel and Abigail followed Scott up the stairs that led to her office, the curator murmured in a low voice: 'I gather they weren't able to help very much.'

'Not really,' admitted Daniel. 'But they were all very conscientious about trying to.'

Once inside Scott's office, the curator handed them a paper folder.

'These are the copies of the letters regarding the exhibition. None of them are from or to the Bone Company, although they are on a list of fossil suppliers that Mr Hardwicke wrote out when the exhibition was being planned. The only letters recorded are those between the Fundamental Fossil Company, based in Boston, who acted as our agents in dealing with American fossil suppliers. You will see that the first letters between the museum and the company are when Mr Hardwicke was still here, and the later ones are addressed to, or signed by, me. There is absolutely nothing in our records from Petter and Wardle except the threatening one I showed you yesterday.'

She gestured towards a smaller desk and some chairs near some filing cabinets.

'Feel free to use that desk while you go through the file. You may find something that I've missed.'

'Thank you,' said Abigail, taking the file from her.

She and Daniel were just walking towards the desk when there was a rapid knocking on the door. It sprang open and Mrs Smith entered, her face flushed with excitement.

'They're here,' she exclaimed.

Daniel, Abigail and Scott looked at her, puzzled.

'Who's here?' asked Scott.

'I was just walking in and as I passed the main reception, I saw them talking to the senior attendant. Sir Henry Irving and Ellen Terry. They're with Mr Stoker. They've come to look at the exhibition,' continued Smith.

Daniel looked at the clock. 'It's not yet nine o'clock,' he said, puzzled.

'They said they wanted to look at it before the public are allowed in,' said Mrs Smith. 'They do get harassed by people, the poor dears. Wanting to shake their hands and so forth.'

'The drawback of celebrity,' said Abigail.

'I trust the senior attendant let them in,' said Scott.

'Indeed,' said Smith. 'He looks so regal, you know. Sir Henry, that is. And Miss Terry is every bit as beautiful as when she's on stage.'

'I shall go and welcome them,' said Scott, determinedly.

And with that, she swept out, followed by the enrapt Mrs Smith.

Abigail looked at Daniel, quizzically.

'Are you coming down?' she asked.

'To gawp at an actor?' asked Daniel, indignantly.

'You are such an inverted snob, Daniel Wilson,' snapped Abigail.

When Daniel and Abigail arrived in the Grand Hall they saw Miss Scott standing beside the reconstructed skeleton of a stegosaurus, obviously explaining about it to the couple who stood there, gazing at the creature and nodding as they listened. Even though it was the first time Daniel had seen them in the flesh, there was no mistaking them: Sir Henry Irving and Ellen Terry, revered actor and actress, stars of the Lyceum Theatre. Irving was the embodiment of the illustrations of him in the newspapers and magazines: tall, thin, with that famous patrician profile, the hawklike nose and the high cheekbones, and, for a man of almost sixty, a full head of luxuriant silvery hair. Terry, by comparison, was a small, elfin figure who looked nearer to her mid-twenties than someone approaching fifty years of age. With her tiny frame, her delicate features, she was the living form of the Pre-Raphaelite image of the romantic heroine. The other thing that struck Daniel about her was that, despite the puritanical censoriousness of the times, when he and Abigail were viewed by many – including Abigail's own sister, Bella – as beyond the pale because they were living together but not married ('in sin' as Bella put it in condemnation), Terry was revered by all society, including the highest in the land, despite her life being littered with broken marriages and former lovers, with at least two children born out of wedlock.

It struck Daniel that most of the museum's attendants seemed to have decided to look after the Grand Hall, because – although they kept a respectful distance – they had all appeared and were gazing in wonder at the illustrious pair.

'I told you Mr Stoker would come through for us,' murmured a happy voice beside Daniel.

He turned and saw Herbert Sharp.

'He brought 'em in, Mr Wilson, like he said he would,' chortled Sharp.

'Where is he?' asked Daniel, searching for a sign of this apparently well-known figure of London's theatreland.

'I saw him going into the small anteroom off the Grand Hall,' said Sharp. 'I've got to go and thank him. This is something very special.'

A man of his word, thought Herbert Sharp delightedly as he made for the anteroom. *That's the kind of friend the museum needs.*

The room was empty except for Bram Stoker, who was kneeling down beside the skeleton of a small dinosaur. He appeared to be examining a roll of cloth lying on the floor next to the fossil.

'Everything all right, Mr Stoker?' called Sharp.

Stoker rose to his feet and turned towards Sharp, a look of distress on his face.

'No,' he said. He pointed at the roll of cloth. 'There's a dead man here.'

Sharp hurried forward in a state of bewilderment. Dead man? Then he stopped, shocked. A corner of the cloth had been peeled back and Sharp could see the face of Raymond Simpson, one of the museum's attendants.

'W-w-what?' burbled Sharp helplessly. 'What? How?' He looked towards Stoker, but the man was already heading in the direction of the Grand Hall.

'Mr Stoker!' called Sharp. 'Wait!'

'How long are we going to stand here watching this?' grumbled Daniel.

Irving and Terry had moved on to another skeleton and were listening to Miss Scott describing it with much waving of arms and pointing of fingers, while the museum staff watched awed from a respectful distance.

'You don't find it interesting, seeing two of the greatest actors in the world in the flesh?' asked Abigail.

'No,' said Daniel. 'During my time with Abberline at Scotland Yard I met many so-called famous people and I found the majority of them to be vain, self-obsessed, and expecting everyone to fawn over them and do their bidding.'

'I think you're being ungracious,' said Abigail.

'Perhaps, but I feel we are wasting precious time which could be spent on the investigation. Instead we are watching people talking to one another, but without being able to hear what they say. It's like watching a mime show without interesting physical actions.' Suddenly he was alert. 'But that may be about to change.'

'In what way?' asked Abigail, puzzled.

As they watched, the figure of Bram Stoker appeared and hurried towards Irving, Terry and Scott. He spoke urgently to them, gesturing towards the main entrance. Immediately, Irving and Terry moved away with him.

'Something's happened,' murmured Daniel, and he moved forward, Abigail following closely behind him. As they did so, a middle-aged man appeared, smiling broadly, and stopped in front of Irving and Terry.

'Sir Henry!' He beamed. 'Miss Terry. Allow me to introduce myself. I am Dawson Turner, one of the trustees of the museum . . .'

'I'm afraid we have to go,' said Stoker, curtly. He took Irving and Terry by the arms and hurried them towards the entrance. Turner stared after them, stunned, then turned to Miss Scott.

'What on earth—?' he began, before he was interrupted by the shocked voice of Herbert Sharp shouting: 'Murder!'

Everyone turned and saw the bulky shape of the maintenance manager standing in the doorway to the smaller anteroom, a look of anguish on his face.

'Murder!' he shouted again. 'Raymond Simpson is dead!'

CHAPTER SIX

Daniel led the charge, followed by Abigail and Miss Scott, with the rest of the staff and Dawson Turner close behind. Sharp had returned to the body concealed in the roll of cloth.

'It's Raymond Simpson,' he said, repeating the words as if he couldn't bring himself to believe it.

He reached down to pull the cloth back more, but Daniel stopped him.

'Don't touch anything, Mr Sharp, until the police have been.'

'Yes.! I must send for the police,' exclaimed Scott. She turned to one of the watching attendants and said: 'Mr Wexford, go out and find a cab while I write a note. Then I want you to take it to Scotland Yard.'

As the attendant hurried off, Daniel said to Miss Scott: 'I would suggest you mark your note for the attention of

Inspector John Feather. He's one of the best detectives there is.'

Daniel stopped Miss Scott as she was about to make for the reception desk, and pen and paper.

'What did Mr Stoker say that made Sir Henry and Miss Terry rush off like that?' he asked.

'He said a man had been found murdered in the anteroom. He said they needed to leave immediately to avoid being caught in a scandal.'

'He should have stayed,' said Daniel. 'The police will need to talk to him.'

'They'll know where to find him,' said Scott. 'At the Lyceum. Now, I must get this note sent.'

She hurried off, and Herbert Sharp intervened. 'It was Mr Stoker who found the body,' he said. 'I came in and found him kneeling by it.'

Dawson Turner peered at the roll of cloth.

'There's something fixed to it,' he said. 'Some kind of label.'

'Careful,' cautioned Daniel. 'We need to leave everything as it is for the police.'

Turner bent down. 'I can see what it says without touching it. "The price of treason".' He looked at Daniel, puzzled. 'What does it mean?' He then looked quizzically both at Daniel and Abigail. 'Also, I'm not sure who you are. The museum isn't officially open yet, and you weren't with Sir Henry's party.'

'Mr Daniel Wilson and Miss Abigail Fenton,' Daniel introduced them.

'Of course,' exclaimed Turner. 'Miss Scott wrote to the trustees yesterday and said she'd engaged you to look into the damaged skeleton.' He looked at Abigail with particular remorse. 'I am especially apologetic in not immediately recognising you, Miss Fenton. I know your work as an archaeologist, of course, and have seen your photograph in magazines. Please forgive me.'

'No apology is necessary,' said Abigail. 'As you say, Mr Turner, the museum isn't officially open yet, so the question is: who left the body, and when? Was it here when the cleaners were still here?'

'Surely they would have remarked to someone if it had been,' said Turner.

'Not necessarily,' said Sharp. 'It was wrapped in cloth. They may have thought it had been left there for some reason, possibly to be displayed later.'

'We need to talk to the cleaners again,' said Abigail. 'Now.'

'Ada Watson lives just a few streets away,' said Sharp. 'I'll go and ask her.'

'Would you mind if one of us accompanied you?' asked Abigail.

'I'd welcome it,' said Sharp. 'You know the questions to ask.'

'You go,' said Daniel to Abigail. 'I'll stay here and wait for Inspector Feather.'

Ada Watson's address was a small terraced house in a narrow street not too far from the museum. Herbert Sharp's knocking at the door was answered by a girl of about nine.

'Is your mother in?' asked Sharp.

The girl looked at Sharp and Abigail with suspicion.

'Why?' she demanded. 'Who wants to know?'

'Who is it, Isobel?' came Ada's voice from inside the house.

'It's Mr Sharp, Mrs Watson,' Sharp called out. 'From the museum.'

Ada appeared at the door, wearing an apron and wiping her hands on a towel.

'I'm just doing a wash,' she explained. She looked down at the girl. 'You can go now, Isobel.'

Isobel gave Sharp and Abigail a sour look, then departed into the house.

'She's a pain, that girl,' she said. 'If she was mine I'd give her the back of my hand, but I'm looking after her for a neighbour who's in hospital.' She cast a glance down the passage to make sure Isobel wasn't within hearing, then lowered her voice and confided: 'They don't reckon she's got long, and Isobel knows it, so I don't like to be too hard on her. But what can I do for you? Is something wrong again at the museum?'

'I'm afraid there is,' said Sharp. 'A man's been found dead in the anteroom off the Grand Hall.'

Ada stared at them, bewildered.

'Dead?' she repeated, shocked.

'Raymond Simpson,' said Sharp. 'One of the attendants. A young man.'

Ada shook her head. 'I didn't know him. We don't really have anything to do with the attendants; we're gone before they get there. How did he die?'

'We won't know until the police have examined the body,' said Abigail. 'But we're sure he was murdered. He was found wrapped in a roll of cloth. There's no other reason the body would have been hidden in that way.'

'It was left beside a dinosaur skeleton,' said Sharp. 'Did you see anything like that this morning?'

'No,' said Ada. 'But I don't do the anteroom. That's Dolly and Tess Tilly. But they didn't say about seeing anything like that. And they'd have said if they'd seen something out of the ordinary.'

'It would be best if we had a word with them,' Abigail said to Sharp.

Sharp nodded and asked Ada, 'Do you have their address?'

'They're over Paddington way,' replied Ada. 'If you hang on, I've got their address written down somewhere. I won't be a minute.'

With that, she hurried indoors, muttering to herself in amazement: 'Murder. Whatever next?'

'I hope Miss Scott will be all right,' Dawson Turner murmured to Daniel. 'I know she's doing her best to hide it, but she's very upset.'

Daniel and the trustee were standing not far from the reception desk, waiting for the arrival of the police, where Evelyn Scott, the subject of their conversation, was giving instructions in an urgent tone to the man on duty, who nodded obediently.

'She seems very organised in a crisis,' commented Daniel.

'Oh yes, she is. There's no doubt about that,' said Turner. 'I've only been on the board of trustees here for just over a month, but already I've been impressed by her efficiency.' Suddenly his attention was caught by the arrival of a well-dressed man in his fifties. 'Mason!' Turner called. To Daniel, he said: 'Mason Radley. Another of the museum's trustees. An excellent man.'

Radley hurried to join them.

'I thought it was you I saw here earlier, Mason,' said Turner, cheerfully.

'What do you mean, earlier?' demanded Radley, puzzled.

'Just before they found poor Raymond's body,' said Turner.

'What are you talking about?' asked Radley. 'I've only just arrived. Who's Raymond? And what's this about his body? I came because I had a letter from Miss Scott about some damage to a dinosaur skeleton, and I find the place in uproar. Areas closed off.'

'One of the attendants has been killed,' said Daniel. 'Murdered, by all accounts.'

Radley stared at him. 'Murdered?' Then he frowned, suspicious. 'Who are you?'

'This is Daniel Wilson,' said Turner. 'It's in Miss Scott's letter. She's hired him and his partner, Abigail Fenton, to find out who was behind the damage to the skeleton, and now they've got a murder to solve.' He frowned, puzzled. 'You sure it wasn't you I saw earlier? I thought I saw you coming up from the conveniences in the basement.'

'Absolutely not,' said Radley, in firm tones. 'As I said, I've only just arrived and found this . . . situation. It must have been someone who looked like me.'

Looking at Mason Radley, Daniel reflected to himself that there would be very few people who looked like him. It wasn't just the suit, made of some shiny fabric, but the thatch of red hair, along with his large red beard, that seemed to stick out in all directions.

'So, what's happening?' asked Radley. 'Have the police been sent for?'

'They have,' said Daniel. 'We're expecting them to arrive at any moment.'

Radley looked uncomfortable. 'In that case, I think I'll make my departure. The last thing someone in my position needs is to be caught up in a police investigation. Especially as I wasn't even here when it happened.' He looked questioningly at Daniel. 'Murdered, you say?'

Daniel nodded.

'How?'

'We won't know until the police arrive and we're able to unwrap the body,' said Daniel.

'Unwrap it?'

'It was left wrapped in some cloth and tied to a dinosaur skeleton,' said Turner.

'The one that was smashed?' asked Radley.

'No, a different one. The smashed one was found yesterday. The dead body was this morning. When Sir Henry Irving and Ellen Terry were here.'

Radley looked at both men, stunned.

'My God. The world's going mad. I must leave. I'm sure Miss Scott will keep me informed of any developments.'

'Yes, I think I'll go with you,' said Turner. He turned to Daniel. 'Or will I be needed to answer questions, do you think? Only, I have an appointment with my solicitor that I need to keep.'

'I'm sure that will be fine,' said Daniel. 'The museum knows where to get in touch with you if the police need to talk to you.'

'Hurry up, Turner, if you're coming,' urged Radley. 'Let's get out of here before the police arrive.'

Daniel watched the two men hurry towards the exit to Cromwell Road, Mason Radley shepherding Dawson Turner in some haste. Miss Scott appeared beside Daniel.

'Was that Mason Radley I saw?' she asked.

'It was,' said Daniel. 'He'd come because of your letter about the damaged skeleton, but as soon as he heard about the murder and learnt that the police were on their way, he expressed a desire to leave.'

'Yes, I've noticed that Mr Radley appears to have a certain antipathy to the forces of authority,' said Scott. 'I don't know why. He's a very successful businessman. He owns a tea company, which imports tea from his own plantation in India.'

'I know of many successful businessmen who prefer to avoid contact with the authorities,' commented Daniel, wryly. 'I think they worry about taxation on their profits.' The arrival of three men caught his eye, and he smiled. 'Inspector Feather is here,' he said. 'And his boss,' he added, as he recognised the bulky and grumpy-looking figure of Superintendent Armstrong. A uniformed constable followed both men.

'You're here, I see, Wilson.' Armstrong sniffed in obvious disapproval. 'Jumping the gun a bit, aren't you? Butting in on a case before the police have even taken a look.'

'We weren't here because of the dead man,' explained Daniel. 'The museum asked us to look into an act of vandalism. A dinosaur skeleton was smashed. Unfortunately, the constable who came said the police were unable to do anything, so the museum asked us to investigate.'

'Us?' queried Armstrong. 'Let me guess, you're still working with Miss Fenton?'

'I am indeed,' said Daniel. He gestured towards the curator, who had been watching this exchange. 'This is Miss Scott, the curator of the museum.'

Armstrong nodded. 'Superintendent Armstrong from Scotland Yard. This is Inspector Feather.'

Feather smiled and reached out to shake Miss Scott's hand.

'I have spent many happy hours in this museum, Miss Scott,' he said. 'It gives me great pleasure to be able to say thank you to you for such a wonderful institution.'

Armstrong scowled. 'Yes, well, I think that's enough of the social pleasantries for the moment. Your note said a murder had been committed.'

'Yes,' said Scott. 'His body was found wrapped in cloth in the anteroom off the Grand Hall. He's one of our attendants; Raymond Simpson.'

'Raymond Simpson?' said Armstrong in surprise. Then he shook his head. 'It can't be the same one.'

Daniel followed Armstrong and Feather as they in turn were led by Miss Scott into the smaller exhibition room. She gestured at the head exposed by the pulled-back cloth. 'Here,' she said.

Daniel looked at Armstrong and saw the superintendent's expression harden.

'It is him,' he announced. He turned to Scott. 'Who found him?'

'Mr Sharp, our maintenance manager,' she said, before correcting herself. 'No, it was Mr Sharp who reported it, but it was a visitor who actually discovered the body. Mr Stoker.'

Armstrong stared at her, a look of almost delight on his face.

'Not Mr Bram Stoker from the Lyceum Theatre?'

'Yes,' said Scott. 'He was here with Sir Henry Irving and Miss Ellen Terry to view the exhibition. They arrived before it was opened to the public.'

'And where are they now?'

'They left,' said Scott. 'Mr Stoker said it was imperative they leave before it was known what had taken place.'

'I bet he did.' Armstrong breathed with a grim expression of satisfaction. He turned to Daniel. 'Were you here when that happened?'

'I was here when Mr Sharp and Mr Stoker came out of this room. Mr Stoker approached Sir Henry and Miss Terry and said they had to leave. At the same time one of the trustees arrived . . .'

'A Mr Turner,' added Scott. 'I'd sent letters to all the trustees to advise them of the malicious damage that had been done yesterday.'

'Malicious damage?' asked Armstrong.

'The skeleton of an iguanodon Mr Wilson referred to. It was smashed.'

'Forget the smashed skeleton,' said Armstrong dismissively. 'Let's get back to why we're here: this dead man. You said your maintenance manager, Mr Sharp, was with Mr Stoker when the body was found. I need to talk to him.'

'He's not here at the moment,' put in Daniel. 'He's gone with Miss Fenton to talk to the cleaners to discover if they were aware of the body.'

Armstrong gave a sniff that suggested disapproval. 'And Stoker? Where did he head for?' he demanded.

'I assume he went to the Lyceum,' said Scott.

'Did he? Right, then that's where I'm headed,' said Armstrong, determinedly. 'Inspector Feather, you carry on with the investigation here. I'll see you back at the Yard.'

With that, the superintendent marched off.

Miss Scott looked in some bewilderment at Daniel and Feather.

'Surely the superintendent doesn't think that Mr Stoker had anything to do with this,' she said. 'He was just a visitor, and a very distinguished one.'

'I'm sure the superintendent just wants to hear first-hand from him what he found,' said Feather, doing his best to reassure her.

'I hope so, because the fact that the body was tied to a dinosaur suggests this is connected once more to the exhibition and the dispute with the Bone Company.'

'The Bone Company?' queried Feather.

'Perhaps if I explain everything about that to the inspector, after we've carried out an examination of the crime scene,' Daniel suggested to Miss Scott.

'I'd be grateful for that, Mr Wilson,' said Miss Scott. 'If you agree, of course, Inspector.'

'That will be fine,' Feather assured her. 'Mr Wilson and I are old colleagues and used to working together.'

'In that case, I'll leave you to do your work while I organise things. I'll also tell Mrs Smith that you will be needing to look at the letter from Petter and Wardle. I assume you'll want to show it to the inspector?'

'That will be perfect,' said Daniel. 'Thank you, Miss Scott.'

As the curator left, Feather turned to Daniel and asked: 'Petter and Wardle?'

'I'll explain after we've taken a look at the remains,' said Daniel. 'Is a doctor on the way?'

Feather shook his head. 'The superintendent said he'd rather the body was taken to the mortuary at the Yard for examination. I'm here just to make notes, look for anything out of the ordinary.'

Daniel smiled. 'I'd think a body wrapped up in cloth and tied to a dinosaur fits that description. I didn't expect the superintendent to put in a personal appearance.'

Feather chuckled. 'It was the words "Natural History Museum" that did it. I think he was worried that they might contact you, and he wanted to get here and stop that. That's why he looked so sour when he saw you.'

'Why? I saved his life. Remember that business at the British Museum?'

'Yes, but he still resents the publicity you and Abigail are getting. All this stuff in the newspapers about the Museum Detectives.'

'That doesn't come from us,' Daniel said, defensively.

'I know that, but the super's very sensitive.'

'I wouldn't have thought of "sensitive" as a word to describe the superintendent,' said Daniel sourly. 'Crass. Bullying, perhaps.'

'Sensitive about his reputation,' explained Feather. 'And the reputation of the Yard. He's not keen on private detectives. Thinks they undermine the reputation of the police.' He chuckled again. 'Especially when they have successes, like Fred Abberline, and you and Abigail.'

'We're lucky because we don't have the same workload as you at the Yard. If we had to look after a dozen cases at once it might be a very different picture. And you know we don't see it as a rivalry between us and the Yard.'

'*I* know that. But the super doesn't.' Feather knelt down beside the roll of cloth. 'Let's take a look at the body.'

He peeled the cloth back further from the head, exposing the neck.

'Strangled,' he said, pointing to the deep indentation in the skin that ran all the way round the neck. 'Thin cord, by the look of it.'

'Possibly the same cord used to tie the label and the body to the skeleton,' suggested Daniel.

Feather looked at the label and frowned. '"The price of treason",' he read. 'Treason about what?'

'Miss Scott thinks it relates to the purchase of skeletons and this business of the Bone Company, but I'm not so sure,' said Daniel.

Feather continued to peel the cloth away from the body, unwrapping it, until the dead body of the young man was revealed in his attendant's uniform. Feather examined the dead man's hands.

'No sign of any blood or skin under his nails,' he commented.

'I expect he was gripping the cord, trying to release it,' said Daniel.

Feather stood looking down at the dead body. 'He's young,' he said. 'Early twenties, I'd say. Who'd want to kill him?' He looked at Daniel. 'Any ideas?'

'None,' said Daniel. 'The question is: was he the target, or is it something to do with the museum itself and the exhibition?'

'It's a bit extreme if it is,' said Feather. He called over the watching uniformed police officer. 'Constable, I want you to get the body back to the Yard. Put it in the mortuary there. I believe that Dr Holden is expecting it. Leave the cloth wrapped round it, just as it is.'

Feather untied the cardboard message and gathered it up, along with the piece of cord, then turned to Daniel. 'Now, let's take a look at this letter of yours and you can fill me in on this Bone Company.'

CHAPTER SEVEN

Dolly and Tess Tilly's home was two rooms in the upper floor of a small house not far from Paddington Station. One was a tiny bedroom, and the other was a cramped kitchen where Abigail and Herbert Sharp now sat with Dolly and her daughter.

'Dead?' said Tess, and she looked in horror at her mother. Dolly shook her head and looked towards Abigail and Sharp.

'There was no roll of cloth there when we finished,' said Dolly, firmly. 'Nothing out of the ordinary at all. We'd have said if there was. Told Ada.'

'And you left at your usual time?' asked Abigail.

Dolly nodded. 'Half past eight as we always do.'

'The attendant's name was Raymond Simpson,' said Abigail 'A young man. How well did you know him?'

'We didn't know him at all,' said Dolly. 'We don't have

anything to do with the day workers, except for Mr Sharp. We're always gone before the attendants come in to work. We finish at half eight and they come in at nine.' Then she gave a thoughtful frown and added: 'Except there have been some occasions when we've had to work over, if there's been a party or something there the night before. There's always more clearing up to do after a party or an event.'

'A party?' asked Abigail.

'Sometimes the museum hosts a special event,' explained Sharp. 'A talk by someone. Or a meeting of the trustees. For example, next week there's going to be a talk on Mary Anning, the famous fossil hunter who lived in Lyme Regis, as part of the exhibition. That's going to be next Wednesday evening.'

'So, we're sure to be working late on the Thursday morning,' said Dolly.

'Not too late, I hope, Dolly,' said Sharp. 'It's a talk, not a dinner.'

'So, you didn't see a roll of cloth by the dinosaur skeleton this morning, and you didn't know Raymond Simpson?' pressed Abigail.

'No,' said Dolly. 'And that's no to both questions.'

Daniel and John Feather sat at the spare desk in Miss Scott's office, Feather studying the letter from Petter and Wardle. Daniel had filled the inspector in on the story of the Bone Wars, the rivalry to sell dinosaur skeletons which Petter and Wardle seemed to have been caught up in.

'Abigail and I paid a call to the offices of Petter and Wardle, and frankly I think there's something dubious about the set-up. Which made me wonder if there even was a Mr Wardle, for example.'

Feather smiled.

'Oh, I think he might be real enough.'

Daniel frowned, curious.

'How can you be sure? Petter said he was out of the country.'

'Did he now? If it's the person I think it is, his being "out of the country" just means being out of circulation. In jail.'

'Jail?'

'The letterhead lists the two partners as Erskine Petter and Benjamin Wardle, and their office as being in Paddington. By coincidence, Benny and Billy Wardle, a pair of thugs who lead a gang in the Paddington area were locked up for assault four months ago. I wonder if they're the same people?'

Daniel frowned.

'I never heard of them when I was at the Yard.'

'After your time, Daniel. I think I'll pop along to Wormwood Scrubs to have a word with Benny and see what he says about his relationship with Mr Erskine Petter.'

'Do you want me to come with you?'

Feather shook his head.

'I've had a couple of run-ins with Benny before. We know one another. He'll talk easier if there's no one else there. Anyway, first I need to find the dead man's address and inform his family. Then I need to catch up with the super and see how he got on with Mr Stoker.'

'I get the impression that the superintendent sees Mr Stoker as more than just a witness,' remarked Daniel, warily.

'And you'd be right,' answered Feather.

'But why?'

'Do you remember the Oscar Wilde case earlier in the year?'

'It was hard to avoid it,' said Daniel. 'The fuss in the newspapers, the lurid stories all over town. Though I feel that Wilde brought things on himself by suing Queensberry, when he must have known he had no chance. Wilde was hardly discreet about his activities, and nor was Queensberry's son, Lord Alfred Douglas.'

'The belief is that Douglas flaunted his relationship with Wilde as openly as he did to deliberately enrage his father.'

'And he certainly succeeded,' said Daniel.

The bitter family row had led to Wilde being tried on charges of sodomy, found guilty, and sentenced to two years' hard labour in prison, where he now languished.

'As you can imagine, Scotland Yard was involved in the case, gathering evidence against Wilde,' continued Feather. 'Armstrong was one of those involved, and he was particularly incensed when people he wanted to bring as prosecution witnesses vanished, with most of them heading to the Continent. He blamed Stoker.'

'Stoker? Why?'

'Stoker has been a life-long friend of Wilde's. They were at university together in Dublin. The superintendent is convinced that Stoker helped some witnesses for the prosecution get to the Continent to stop them testifying.

'The super questioned Stoker at the time but got nowhere. Even though Wilde was found guilty, the super's been upset about it ever since.'

'So, how does that relate to the murder here?'

'The man who was found dead, Raymond Simpson, was a vital prosecution witness in the trial. Simpson hadn't been involved himself in any sexual acts but claimed to have been told by other young men of them engaging with Wilde in such acts, and named places and dates. The stories he told led to these men being brought as witnesses, and it was their evidence that led to Wilde's conviction.

'From what I hear, Wilde is taking his time in prison hard. You know what hard labour's like, Daniel. The treadmill. Picking oakum. And conditions in Pentonville and Wandsworth are harsh as it is. And the food's terrible. It's tough enough for anybody, but for someone like Wilde . . .' He sighed. 'The word is he's dying because of it. His health has completely gone. I can see why the super thinks that Stoker might want revenge on the man who put him there: Raymond Simpson.'

'That's stretching it, John. Simpson was just a witness. What about all the others?'

'It seems that Simpson was a bit more than just a witness. From what we picked up from some of the others, he was a blackmailer who shopped people that didn't pay up.'

'Like Wilde?'

'That's what I heard. So it's not unthinkable that Stoker, someone who's been close to Wilde, goes into the Natural History Museum and sees the villain who a lot of people believe was the one who got him in jail, and pays him back.'

'Hardly, John. Remember the crime scene. The body wrapped in a roll of cloth. The sign saying "The price of treason". That smacks of more than a spur-of-the-moment action. It takes planning. Bringing in the cloth to wrap the body in, for one.'

'According to the maintenance manager, Stoker was in the

building on the Saturday, three days before Simpson's body was found.'

'Yes, he was,' confirmed Daniel.

'So, he sees Simpson, decides to do something about him and does it today.'

Daniel shook his head, doubtful.

'I still don't see it, John. Stoker's too well known to try something like that. He could be spotted.'

'He was, by the maintenance manager. If Sharp hadn't come along when he did, Stoker could have vanished.' Feather picked up the piece of cardboard he'd brought up from the scene. 'Where's the one from yesterday?'

Daniel took the card from a drawer and placed it on the desk alongside the one found with Simpson's dead body. The two men studied them, then Feather announced: 'They're not the same. The cardboard, the string and, more importantly, the writing is different.'

'So, different people did them. I'm guessing the second was done to try and throw us off track. Make us think it's the work of the same person who smashed the skeleton.'

'Which means it would have to be by someone who knew about the first message,' said Feather. 'Which would suggest someone from the museum.'

'Not necessarily,' said Daniel. 'It could be someone with contacts here who may have been told about the earlier message. Everyone here knew about it. We need to look into Raymond Simpson, find out what sort of person he was and who'd have a reason for killing him.'

'The superintendent's already got it into his head that Stoker's involved in some way. Revenge for what he did to Oscar Wilde.'

'I still can't see it,' said Daniel. 'I think he's too high profile.'

'He didn't have to do it himself,' pointed out Feather. 'He could have got someone else to do it.'

'But why draw attention to himself by being found by the body?'

'A double-bluff?' suggested Feather. 'I'm sure we'll have some answers once the super's had a chat with Mr Stoker.'

Superintendent Armstrong sat in the cushioned chair and glowered across the desk at Bram Stoker. They were in Stoker's office at the Lyceum Theatre, a room adorned with playbills from past productions, all of them starring Henry Irving, most of them presentations of Shakespeare's plays. Stoker held the superintendent's malevolent glare, unsmiling and with an expression of grim determination, indeed defiance, on his face. He was a man in his late forties, well-dressed, his red beard neatly trimmed and his hair neatly barbered.

'We have met before, Mr Stoker,' said Armstrong.

'I remember,' responded Stoker coldly. 'During the trial of Oscar Wilde. You accused me of aiding certain witnesses for the prosecution in that case to evade, as you termed it, "justice".'

'Information had been received that suggested as such,' said Armstrong. 'I merely asked you if you had been instrumental, even in part, in their departure to the Continent.'

'And I told you at the time the same as I'm telling you now, Superintendent: no, I had nothing to do with any witnesses avoiding giving evidence at the trial. But I assume that is not why you are here to see me.'

'You assume correctly. You were at the Natural History Museum earlier today, where it is said you discovered the dead body of a man.'

'That is correct.'

'Why did you flee the scene?'

'I did not "flee the scene", as you put it. After I reported the discovery of the body, I left the premises along with Sir Henry Irving and Miss Ellen Terry.'

'Why did you feel the need to depart before the police had arrived?'

'To protect Sir Henry and Miss Terry. They are very public figures, as I'm sure you know, which is why we'd gone to the exhibition early in the morning before it opened to the general public. There was a danger to their reputations if they'd been caught up in the sort of scandal that usually accompanies a murder.'

'You felt it was murder?' asked Armstrong, intently.

'A body wrapped in cloth like that. It hardly appeared to be suicide or a natural death.'

'Did you recognise the young man?'

Stoker shook his head. 'I peeled back the end of the roll of cloth because I was curious as to what it was and why it was there. I thought it might have been part of the exhibit. As soon as I saw it was a human face, I realised it was a person. A dead person.'

'You realised he was dead, not just unconscious?'

'I have seen dead people before, Superintendent. I know the difference.'

'The dead man has been identified as Raymond Simpson. Does that name mean anything to you?'

'No,' said Stoker.

'I'm surprised,' said Armstrong. 'He was a prominent witness at the trial of your friend, Mr Wilde. Your very *good* friend, Mr Wilde.'

'What are you implying, Superintendent?'

'You were one of Mr Wilde's closest friends. You'd been so since your days when you were students together at university in Dublin. During the trial you went to the Old Bailey on many occasions to observe proceedings. I'm surprised you don't recall Raymond Simpson.'

'There were many witnesses, Superintendent. Too many to remember.'

'I spoke to an attendant at the museum who said he saw you there a few days ago looking at the exhibition.'

'That is correct. I found it very impressive, which is why I encouraged Sir Henry to see it.'

'But you didn't view it with Mr Irving . . .'

'Sir Henry,' Stoker corrected him sharply.

'Sir Henry,' conceded Armstrong grudgingly. 'As I understand it, Sir Henry viewed it with Miss Terry while you were separate from them.'

'That is correct,' said Stoker. 'Sir Henry mentioned the exhibition to Miss Terry after I'd spoken to him about it, and she was keen to see it as well, so all three of us went together. But once we were there, Sir Henry intimated that he wished to view it in the company of Miss Terry.' He paused, then added: 'There are times when they prefer to have privacy. I was happy to give them that.'

'On the day you visited on your own, do you recall seeing Raymond Simpson there?'

'No. As I said, I did not recognise him today, nor can I say I recognised him when I was previously at the museum.'

'Despite the fact that this man's evidence has led to one of your closest and longest friends being incarcerated in not very hospitable conditions.'

Stoker gave a sarcastic smile.

'"Not very hospitable" hardly covers the conditions Mr Wilde has been enduring, Superintendent.'

'But you claim that this man, Raymond Simpson, who could be held responsible for Mr Wilde's downfall and imprisonment, was not known to you.'

'That is correct, Superintendent. Now, if you don't mind, I have much work to do. We have a performance of *King Arthur* this evening to prepare for.'

CHAPTER EIGHT

As Daniel and Feather made for the address they'd been given for Raymond Simpson and his parents, Daniel reported the encounter between Turner and Radley he'd observed. 'Turner told Radley he'd seen him at the museum earlier in the morning, coming up from the conveniences in the basement before the body of Raymond Simpson was discovered, but Radley insisted he'd arrived at the museum just a few moments before we saw him, so it must have been someone else.'

'Perhaps it was,' said Feather.

'Indeed,' agreed Daniel. 'But if you saw Mason Radley, I think you'd agree he'd be hard to mistake for someone else. He's got a shock of red hair and a big red beard.'

'Perhaps this Turner chap only saw the outline of someone and he looked a bit like this Mason Radley,' wondered Feather.

'That may be the case, but I thought it worth mentioning. Especially because Radley was very keen indeed to get away from the museum before the police arrived.'

'I'll look into him,' said Feather. 'What do you know about him?'

'Nothing,' said Daniel. 'Except for his distinctive appearance, that he's a trustee of the museum and he owns a company that imports tea from his own plantation in India.'

'So, wealthy,' said Feather.

'Or not,' said Daniel. 'Not every company is profitable.'

They'd arrived at the short, narrow cul-de-sac and made their way to the Simpsons' address. The family obviously took great pleasure in their house: the doorstep shone with red lead and a window box filled with colourful flowers showed their pride in the property.

'This is the part I hate,' said Feather, 'telling a family their loved one's been murdered.'

'Even if that loved one was a blackmailer?' asked Daniel.

'We never actually got proof of that,' admitted Feather. 'If we had, we'd have charged him.'

'So, it was just gossip and rumour?'

'Half-admissions, from people who had a lot to lose if their secrets got out.'

'Shall we raise that with his family?'

'Maybe. We'll see how it goes. They don't know he's dead yet, so we have to tread carefully.' Feather looked at Daniel hopefully. 'Actually, I was going to ask if you'd mind asking the questions. After I've done my official duty, that is, and given them the bad news.'

'Me?' asked Daniel, doubtfully.

'You're good at it, Daniel. You have a knack of getting people to talk without upsetting them. And I want to get to the Scrubs to talk to Benny Wardle, then I need to catch up with the super because he'll want to know what's happening.'

'All right, leave it to me,' said Daniel. 'Shall I come to the Yard later and let you know what I've learnt from the Simpsons, and you can fill me in on Benny Wardle?'

'I'll come to you,' said Feather. 'Just in case the super's in a bad mood if things with Stoker didn't go the way he wanted.'

'All right. The museum in a couple of hours?'

'Make it three,' said Feather. 'Just in case my visit to the Scrubs turns up something I need to look into.' He knocked. 'Let's hope someone's in or I'll have to come back.'

The door was opened by a tall, thin woman who looked out at them warily.

'Mrs Simpson?' asked Feather. When the woman nodded, he took out his warrant card and showed it to her as he continued: 'I'm Inspector Feather from Scotland Yard and this is my colleague, Mr Wilson.'

'Scotland Yard?' said the woman, and her hand went to her mouth in horror.

'Do you mind if we come in?' asked Feather. 'We'd rather talk privately than out here in public.'

Mrs Simpson opened the door wider, and they walked in, wiping their feet on the doormat, then going into the room on their right after she'd indicated for them to do so. It was a sitting room, immaculately clean and smelling of furniture polish. She gestured for them to sit in two of the armchairs and perched nervously on one herself.

'What do Scotland Yard want with us?' she asked, apprehensively. 'We're just ordinary people.'

'Is your husband at home, ma'am?' asked Feather. 'It might be better if we talk to you both.'

'My husband died four years ago,' said Mrs Simpson. 'There's just me and my son, Raymond, and he's at work.'

'I'm afraid it's about Raymond that we've come,' said Feather.

'Has something happened to him?' asked Mrs Simpson, urgently.

'I'm afraid it has. I'm sorry to tell you that Raymond was killed this morning.'

Once more, her hand flew to her mouth. She stared at them, bewilderment on her face.

'No, that can't be right,' she said. 'He's at work.'

'It was at work it happened,' said Feather gently. 'At the museum.'

She continued to stare at them, her mouth open, tears welling up in her eyes.

'No, it can't be,' she said. She swallowed, then asked: 'An accident?'

'I'm afraid not,' said Feather. 'It seems as if he was murdered.'

'No.' Mrs Simpson shot to her feet, now outraged. 'No, that's impossible. No one would want to harm Raymond. You're confusing him with someone else.'

'I'm very sorry, Mrs Simpson. He's been identified by the senior staff at the museum.'

Suddenly, she collapsed back onto the chair, her head in her hands, weeping.

'He was all I had left,' she sobbed. 'His brother and sister died when they were tiny, and then George, my husband.'

Feather shot a questioning glance at Daniel, who nodded in agreement. Feather got to his feet.

'Mrs Simpson, I'm afraid I have to go now, but Mr Wilson here will stay and give you the details, and then we'd be grateful if you'd answer his questions . . .'

'What sort of questions?' she asked, looking up at him, her face stained with tears.

'Questions about Raymond's life, who he knew. We're determined to find out who did this, and the more we know about him, the sooner we'll be able to bring this person to justice.'

She nodded, numbed by the dreadful news.

'You stay here with Mr Wilson, Mrs Simpson. I'll let myself out,' said Feather.

Abigail and Sharp returned to the museum and reported to Miss Scott what they'd been told by Dolly and Tess Tilly.

'They're both certain there was no roll of cloth when they left,' said Abigail. 'So, the body must have been put there after they left at half past eight.'

'They're sure of that?' asked Scott, anxiously.

'They're both very reliable people,' Sharp assured her. 'If they say it wasn't there, it wasn't there.'

'Did the police arrive?' asked Abigail.

'They did,' said Scott. 'Inspector Feather and a Superintendent Armstrong.'

'Ah,' said Abigail, guardedly.

'You know the superintendent?'

'I do,' said Abigail. 'He can be a bit brusque sometimes.'

'That was certainly the case here,' said Scott, obviously annoyed. 'He went rushing off to question Mr Stoker at the Lyceum.'

'Why?' asked Abigail.

'He seemed to have formed an idea that Mr Stoker may have been involved in some way.'

'Well, he found the body,' said Abigail.

'In addition to that,' said Scott.

'You mean as a suspect?' asked Abigail, in astonishment.

'He didn't say so, but that was the impression he gave.'

'But that's ridiculous,' exclaimed Abigail.

'Absolutely,' agreed Sharp, with equal vehemence. 'Mr Stoker is a gentleman. And I was with him when he discovered Raymond's body.'

'Did Inspector Feather go with the superintendent?' asked Abigail.

'No. He and Mr Wilson have gone to inform Raymond's family about the tragedy. I imagine they'll be back shortly.'

'If you'll excuse me, Miss Scott, I'll get back to my duties,' said Sharp. 'I see the body's been removed, but there will be things to organise.'

Scott nodded. 'Of course.'

The maintenance manager left, and Abigail said: 'We need to find out more about Mr Simpson. Who might have had a grudge against him, that sort of thing. Do you know who he was closest to at the museum?'

'To be honest, I didn't really know him,' answered Scott. 'The best person to speak to is the senior attendant, Brandon Walpole. Mr Walpole engages the attendants. He'll be better informed about him than I.'

'Thank you. I will.'

Abigail was about to leave to go in search of Mr Walpole when Miss Scott stopped her.

'I was thinking: now the investigation looks as if it's going to be more complicated and could take more time, I was wondering if it wouldn't be better for you and Mr Wilson if you made use of the spare desk in Mrs Smith's office as the base of your operations. I foresee all manner of people coming in and out of my office over the next few days.'

'I understand completely,' said Abigail. 'Thank you, that will be excellent. So long as Mrs Smith doesn't mind.'

'I'm sure she won't. She's out at the moment taking some papers to the British Museum, but I'll tell her when she returns.'

They were interrupted by the door bursting open and the arrival of a short, round, pugnacious woman wearing a fur coat, with a string of expensive-looking pearls around her neck.

'Miss Scott!' she boomed, obviously enraged at something.

'Lady Fortescue.' Scott gestured towards Abigail. 'This is Miss Abigail Fenton, who's looking into the tragic events that have happened here along with her partner, Mr Daniel Wilson.'

'There wouldn't have been any such events if you'd done your job properly.'

'Lady Fortescue—' began Scott in gentle protest, but she was overridden by the bombastic woman.

'This is your responsibility. I said we should have given the post to Mr Watling. He wouldn't have allowed this to happen! Well, on your head be it. I'm here to inform you that I shall make my views known to the other trustees at the next board meeting. You have failed, Miss Scott. Failed! And I shall see to it that you are removed.'

With that, she headed for the door and made her exit.

Abigail looked after her, stunned, then turned back to Miss Scott.

'I'm sorry you had to witness that,' apologised Scott. 'Lady Fortescue is one of the trustees of the museum, and as you know I asked Mrs Smith to write to all the trustees to inform them about the damaged iguanodon skeleton. I imagine when she arrived she learnt about the unfortunate death of Mr Simpson, which would have given more fuel to her anger. As you heard, she doesn't approve of me. She wanted the post of curator to be awarded to William Watling.'

'The anthropologist?'

Scott nodded. 'The same. Fortunately for me, she was in a minority, which has made her even more resentful.' She gave a rueful sigh. 'But I have become used to her anger and her way of expressing her views. And the other trustees seem to be supportive of me.'

'If there's anything I can do to help, anyone I can speak to on your behalf,' offered Abigail. 'I know Sir Jasper Stone over at the British Museum quite well.'

'Thank you, but I'm sure there's no need,' said Scott. 'Sir Jasper has been supportive of me as well. But I do appreciate the sentiment. Now, I'd better get back to preparing some correspondence for Mrs Smith's return. And when she does, I'll make arrangements with her for you and Mr Wilson to take occupation of her spare desk.'

* * *

73

Daniel watched sympathetically as Mrs Simpson wiped her eyes.

'He was all I had left,' she said, miserably. It was the third time she'd said it.

'Which is why we need to bring the person who did it to justice,' said Daniel. 'And to do that, we need to know all we can about Raymond. Did he have any enemies?'

She shook her head. 'None. He was a popular person, and he enjoyed being at the museum.'

'How long had he been there?'

'Two months,' said Mrs Simpson.

'Where did he work before that?'

'Before that he was a waiter and then an usher at a theatre, which meant working late evenings.'

'At which theatre?' asked Daniel.

'The Lyceum. That Sir Henry Irving's place. Very posh. But he didn't like the late evenings, that's why he left. He preferred the museum because it was regular hours during the day and regular pay, not like being a waiter when it's about tips.'

'I can imagine,' said Daniel, sympathetically. 'A waiter's wages can be very unreliable. Where did he work?'

She hesitated, then said, apologetically, 'I can't remember. He didn't talk about it much.'

'Did he ever talk to you about the trial?'

She looked at him, bewildered.

'Trial? What trial?'

'The one he was a witness at earlier this year.'

She shook her head.

'Raymond was never a witness at any trial.'

'Inspector Feather, along with Superintendent Armstrong, of Scotland Yard told me he was.'

'No, they're wrong. Raymond would never have got mixed up in anything like a trial.'

'It was in the spring,' said Daniel. 'The trial of Oscar Wilde, the playwright.'

She looked at him now, angry.

'No,' she said, sharply. 'Raymond would never have had anything to do with that. He's decent.'

'It was at the Old Bailey . . .'

'No,' she repeated, firmer this time. 'He wasn't even in London at that time. He was on the south coast. Brighton. They must have meant another Raymond Simpson.'

'Superintendent Armstrong recognised Raymond,' pressed Daniel. 'I was with him when he did.'

'No!' This time it was an angry shout. She stood up and glared at Daniel. 'I'll trouble you to go. I won't have lies about Raymond said in this house.' She pointed towards the passage and the front door. 'Out!'

Resignedly, Daniel got to his feet.

'I'm sorry to have troubled you,' he said, apologetically. 'And I am sorry for your dreadful loss.'

With that, he left, aware the whole time of Mrs Simpson's look of venom directed at him.

CHAPTER NINE

Inspector John Feather sat in the small interview room at Wormwood Scrubs prison. Across the table sat Benny Wardle, wearing the distinctive prison uniform printed with broad black arrows. A warder stood guard, grim-faced, his eyes on Wardle. Feather had told the warder there was no need for his presence there, as a Scotland Yard detective with many years' experience he was perfectly capable of being left on his own with the prisoner.

'Rules,' said the warder, sourly. 'A warder has to be present if the prisoner's out of his cell, whoever he's with. He could attack you, and then where would be we? Me, I'd be out of a job.'

So, Feather resigned himself to the fact that his conversation with Wardle would have an audience, which he hoped wouldn't hamper the man answering his questions.

'Tell me about the Bone Company, Benny,' said Feather.

'What Bone Company?' he asked, looking baffled.

'The Bone Company of America,' said Feather. 'According to your partner, Erskine Petter, you and he have a contract with them to sell dinosaur skeletons.'

Wardle looked at him with even more bewilderment. Then he laughed.

'Dinosaur skeletons?'

'That's what your partner said when he wrote to the Natural History Museum. I've seen the letter, and it's got your name at the top as a partner. Petter and Wardle.'

'I'm a partner all right. I look after the debt collection side of the business.' He looked ruefully about him and at the grim-faced warder. 'At least, I used to. There's not much chance to do that from inside here.'

'So, you don't know anything about selling dinosaur skeletons?'

'Inspector, I've been in here for almost three months. I've had nothing to do with anything that Erskine's been up to in that time.'

'He said this dinosaur skeleton business was started months ago.'

'Well, it may have been, but he never said anything to me about it.' He scowled. 'In fact, I haven't heard anything from Erskine for a month now, and he said he'd look after me and Billy while we was in here.'

'Maybe you ought to write him a letter and ask what's happening,' said Feather.

Wardle grinned, then chuckled.

'Come on, Inspector. You know I don't write. Look, if you see Erskine again, can you put in a word for me? Ask him to call in and see me. That's all I ask. That ain't much, is it?'

'I'll see what I can do,' said Feather. 'But what exactly does Petter and Wardle do?'

Wardle looked puzzled.

'You said you've seen Erskine,' he said. 'What did he say?'

'He said you're agents representing people.'

Wardle nodded. 'Well, that's what we are, then.'

'What sort of people do you represent?'

'That's Erskine's side of the business,' said Wardle. 'I don't have anything to do with that.'

'You just collect debts.'

Wardle nodded.

'And you know nothing about dinosaur skeletons.'

'Mr Feather, I don't even know what a dinosaur is,' said Wardle. 'What is it?'

'They were animals that lived hundreds of thousands of years ago,' Feather told him. 'Possibly millions of years ago. They're extinct.'

'They stink?' frowned Wardle. 'What of?'

'Extinct,' repeated Feather, speaking slowly and stressing the word. 'There are none left now. So, their skeletons are very rare and worth money.'

'And Erskine's got one?' asked Wardle.

'He claims to represent a company who's got some.'

'So, he must be worth a bit now,' said Wardle. He frowned again. 'I hope he's making sure I'll get some of it when I come out.'

'That's between you and him,' said Feather.

'Well, when you see him, tell him I'll be expecting he'll look after me.'

'I will,' said Feather. He stood up. 'But if you want my advice, when you come out I'd look for something else other than being Erskine Petter's strong-arm man. Remember, that's what got you in here in the first place.'

'It wasn't his fault,' defended Wardle. 'Me and Billy went to the wrong shop.'

'Then that's another piece of advice for you,' said Feather. 'Learn to read.' He walked to the door and banged on it for it to be opened.

'Remember what I said, Mr Feather. About Erskine looking after me. I'd like to see him. They do visiting days here.'

'I'm sure Erskine knows that,' said Feather. 'But when I see him, I'll pass on your message.'

Abigail found Brandon Walpole in the Grand Hall, inspecting the dinosaur skeletons and fossils on display to make sure they were clean. He smiled in greeting when he saw her.

'Can I help you, Miss Fenton?'

'Yes. I'm trying to find out as much as I can about Raymond Simpson.'

'A tragedy,' murmured Walpole. 'A very promising young man.'

'How did he get on with the rest of the staff?'

'He appeared very sociable. He was a nice enough young chap. Polite. Keen to engage in conversation with visitors, which we encourage. If people are made to feel welcome they'll return again and again, and encourage their friends to do the same.'

'How long had he been here?'

'Two months.'

'How did he come to be engaged? Was he recommended by anyone?'

Walpole shook his head.

'No. He arrived and asked to see the senior attendant. I saw him, and he said he wondered if there were any vacancies for attendants here. He told me he lived near to the museum and had often come here as a visitor.'

'Was that unusual as a way of taking on staff?'

'Yes. Usually it's done by personal recommendation, but I thought his approaching us in that way showed initiative.'

'Did he say where he'd worked before?'

'He'd done various jobs: he'd been a waiter in a restaurant and had also worked as an usher at the Lyceum Theatre.'

'Did he bring any references from his previous employers?'

'No. He told me he hadn't asked for references from them because he didn't want to carry on with the kind of work he'd been doing before. He said the unsocial hours didn't suit him as he had a widowed mother to look after and he wanted to be at home with her in the evenings. As I say, I found him personable and felt he was genuine, so I decided to give him a week's trial. I was not disappointed by him. He seemed the ideal person to be an attendant here, and so I made his engagement permanent.'

'You say he was an usher at the Lyceum Theatre. Do you also know which restaurant he worked at as a waiter?'

'Actually, I do,' said Walpole. 'Not because he told me, but because it's a local place and earlier this year I went there for a meal with my sister. It was her birthday. And young Raymond was a waiter there. The Rigatoni on Cromwell Road.' He gave a smile of nostalgia. 'You know, I'd quite forgotten that until this moment.'

'But he never had a reference from them?'

'No. As I said, he hadn't asked for references from them because he didn't want to carry on with the kind of work he'd been doing before. And because I'd seen him at work at the Rigatoni and was impressed by his manner and efficiency, I didn't think any were needed in this case.' He looked distressed as he added: 'I can't think of any reason why anyone would want to harm him.'

Feather mounted the narrow, grimy staircase, then walked along the passageway to the door marked 'Petter and Wardle', where he knocked on the glass before opening it and entering.

Erskine Petter looked up from his desk suspiciously at his caller.

'Let me guess,' he grunted. 'Police. You've got it written all over you. Well, there's nothing wrong here. I run a legitimate business.'

'Interesting that you should have a sixth sense about police officers when they're in plain clothes,' observed Feather.

'It's the look,' growled Petter. 'That and the flat feet.'

'Inspector Feather from Scotland Yard,' Feather introduced himself.

'Scotland Yard?' echoed Petter, warily. 'What's your business here?'

'I've been at the Scrubs today, talking to your partner, Benny Wardle.'

'Mr Wardle's incarceration is nothing to do with me,' said Petter.

'So, he and his brother weren't acting as your strong-arm men in collecting money?' asked Feather.

'Certainly not,' snapped Petter. 'And if that's what he told you—'

'What he told me about your business will keep for the moment. I'm here because I understand you have a letter from the Bone Company of America authorising you to act as their agents over the sale of dinosaur skeletons.'

'Who says I have?' blustered Petter.

'The Natural History Museum. So, have you, or haven't you?'

'As you ask, yes, we have,' said Petter, stiffly.

'I'd like to see it,' said Feather.

'I regret that will not be possible,' said Petter. 'Client confidentiality takes precedence.'

'Not when a murder's involved,' said Feather. He held out his hand. 'The letter.'

Petter stared at him, shocked.

'Murder?' he gasped. Then he began to bluster. 'This is nonsense. A skeleton was damaged at the Natural History Museum, so I'm informed. How can that be classed as murder?'

'I'm talking about the murder of a young man at the museum. Strangled and left tied to a dinosaur. Now, let me see that letter and any others you have from this Bone Company.'

Petter looked at him, apparently lost for words, before blurting out: 'I haven't got them here in the office.'

'No?' said Feather, in disbelief. 'Then you won't mind if I look.'

'Yes, I do mind,' said Petter, moving to stand in front of the filing cabinet. 'You can't start searching here without a warrant.'

'Then I'll be back with a warrant. And if you try to stop the search, I'll arrest you for obstructing the police.'

Feather headed for the door, then stopped and turned back to Petter.

'Oh, by the way, Benny asked me to give you a message. He'd like you to visit him.' He gave a smile as he added: 'I got the idea he thinks you've been ignoring him. Not a nice way to treat a partner.'

CHAPTER TEN

When Daniel returned to the museum, he found Abigail organising space on the spare desk in Miss Scott's secretary's office.

'We're going to be in here from now,' she told him. 'Miss Scott thinks we could be at the museum for a while and she wants her own office back.'

'That's understandable,' said Daniel. 'Is Mrs Smith all right with that?'

'I'm sure she will be,' replied Abigail. 'She's out at the moment, but Miss Scott said she'd talk to her about it when she gets back. How did you get on with the Simpsons?'

'Only Mrs Simpson. She's a widow, and Raymond was her only living child. She'd had two others, but they died young, she told me.'

'The poor woman,' said Abigail. 'She must have been upset.'

'She was,' said Daniel. 'But she became much more upset when I asked her about Raymond being a witness at Oscar Wilde's trial. She denied it absolutely. According to her he wasn't even in London when the trial was on. She said he was in Brighton.'

'But Superintendent Armstrong recognised him,' exclaimed Abigail.

'Exactly. So, either she's lying, or he lied to her. Whichever it was, she became very angry when I brought the subject up and ordered me out of the house. So, I never got the chance to ask her about the accusation of him being a blackmailer.' He gave a rueful smile. 'I expect if I had she'd have hit me with something.'

'The senior attendant at the museum, Mr Walpole, describes him as sociable, a nice enough young chap, polite, keen to engage in conversation with visitors,' said Abigail. 'That doesn't fit with Armstrong's view of him as some villainous blackmailer.'

'Perhaps he changed his ways?' suggested Daniel. 'It does happen.'

'So completely and in such a very short space of time?' queried Abigail.

'Plenty of blackmailers appear to be nice people on the surface,' pointed out Daniel. 'It's how they worm their way into getting people's confidence and finding out their dark secrets. We definitely need to look into young Raymond's life and find out just what sort of person he really was. The problem is I think that information might be hard to get hold of. The only thing I learnt from Mrs Simpson was that he'd worked as an usher at the Lyceum.'

'Yes, and also as a waiter, according to Mr Walpole.'

'Mrs Simpson mentioned that as well, but she said she didn't know which restaurant it was.'

'Mr Walpole did,' said Abigail, with a smile. 'The Rigatoni on Cromwell Road.'

'Very local,' commented Daniel. 'Which makes it seem strange that Mrs Simpson didn't know it.'

'I'd say suspicious rather than strange,' said Abigail.

'Yes, I agree. So that's two places we can check him out at.'

'Which one first? The Lyceum or the restaurant?'

'I think the restaurant,' said Daniel. 'John Feather said he'd report back to us on how Superintendent Armstrong got on with talking to Mr Stoker at the Lyceum, so I don't think we should go blundering in there until we know that outcome.' He looked quizzically at Abigail. 'No word from John yet, I assume?'

'No. But then one never knows if the superintendent may have held him up for some reason.'

'Knowing Armstrong, that's very likely,' said Daniel. 'So, shall we go to the Rigatoni?'

'He's slippery, this Stoker,' growled Armstrong. 'I feel it in my bones.'

John Feather had come to the superintendent's office to report on his interviews with both Benny Wardle and Erskine Petter, but found Armstrong seething with anger about the Lyceum's business manager.

'He's involved in some way with this dead man at the Natural History Museum. It's obvious. He turns up there and within minutes the man who's given evidence against his best friend is found trussed up and murdered. It can't be a coincidence.'

'We'll certainly be looking into it,' Feather assured him.

'But with caution,' warned Armstrong. 'We're going to have to tread very carefully here, Inspector. Stoker is a man with powerful friends. If we put a foot wrong, we'll feel the weight of the commissioner on our backs. How did you get on at the museum?'

Feather told the superintendent about the letter from Petter and Wardle, and what he'd learnt about the Bone Wars. 'There's definitely something wrong about Petter and Wardle. They may or may not be involved with the dead body, but as it followed so soon after the smashed dinosaur skeleton, and especially because this Erskine Petter denied me access to his records—'

'Did he, by God,' exclaimed Armstrong.

'—I told him I'd come back with a warrant, and I've just got one.'

'And I'm coming with you.' Armstrong grinned as he got to his feet, a gleam of triumph in his eye. 'That's what I like: real villains.'

The Rigatoni was a small, intimate restaurant that appeared to cater to patrons at the upper end of the market. The seven tables were covered with pristine white tablecloths; the cutlery was silver, as were the cruet sets on each table. The walls were decorated with paintings by Italian masters. The face of the owner, Ginetta Morell, a rather rotund woman in her fifties, darkened as Abigail mentioned Raymond Simpson.

'Who are you again?' she asked, suspiciously.

'Private investigators hired by the Natural History Museum to look into the death of Raymond Simpson, who we understand once worked for you as a waiter.'

'How did he die?'

'He was murdered.'

She scowled and muttered something in Italian that sounded like an oath.

'You didn't like him?' asked Daniel.

'I did not,' she said. 'But that doesn't mean he deserved to die.'

'What was he like? How did he strike you?' asked Abigail.

'When he first came to me to ask for a job, he seemed a very nice boy. Well-mannered. Eager to please. I tested him out for one day in the restaurant, and he showed that he knew how to deal with customers, polite and efficient. And with a smile. Good manner. So, I hired him.' She scowled. 'More fool me. I thought I could smell trouble, but he was too clever for me. He touched nothing for the first month he was here. In fact, he even handed in some money that a customer had dropped.' Her face darkened again. 'At least, that's what he told me. But, thinking about it, perhaps he did that to show me he was honest.' She gave a short sarcastic laugh. 'Honest? Ha!'

'I assume he stole from you?' asked Daniel.

'The second month he was here. At first, small sums. Someone would have a little meal, and I believe he pocketed the money instead of paying it in. As I say, small sums so they wouldn't be noticed. But then bigger. And then money began to disappear from the cash register.

'I knew it had to be him because all the rest of my staff have been with me for years, so I set a trap. I marked a ten-shilling note and put it in the part of the cash register used as a reserve, so it wouldn't go out with the change. When I checked, it had gone. I demanded he turn out his pockets. He refused. He got angry. When I insisted he threatened violence.' She gave a caustic laugh. 'Violence against me, who grew up with seven brothers, all of them hard fighting men.'

'What did you do?' asked Abigail.

'I called my two best waiters over, and they took hold of him and made him turn out his pockets. There it was, the ten-shilling note, as I suspected it would be.

'At first he claimed it must be a mistake, that he got it confused with change for a customer, but when I told him I was going to call the police he began to cry and beg. Said he had a widowed mother who was an invalid and he'd only done it this once because she needed medicines.'

'You believed him?'

She shook her head.

'But you didn't call the police?'

'No restaurant wants the bad publicity that goes with that kind of thing. Accusations of cheating by the staff. So, I took the money from him and kicked him out.' She gave a satisfied smirk. 'Literally. My boot up his backside.' She looked pensive. 'And now he's dead. Murdered. I guess he cheated someone less forgiving than me.'

'Do you remember when it was he actually worked for you?' asked Daniel.

She nodded. 'Earlier this year, April time.'

* * *

The door to the office of Petter and Wardle was locked. A note had been tied to the door handle: *Away. Letters to Jones the Butcher downstairs.*

'Away,' grunted Armstrong. 'Let's find out where he's gone to.'

Ordering the constable they'd brought with them to wait beside the door, the superintendent and the inspector went downstairs and into the butcher's shop, where a man in a striped apron was working on a sheep's carcase with a knife, carving the ribs from the animal.

'Mr Jones?' asked Armstrong.

'That's me,' said the man.

'We're looking for Erskine Petter,' said Armstrong.

'Are you now?' said Jones, and he returned to butchering the sheep. 'Well, he ain't here.'

'Where is he?'

Jones shrugged. 'How would I know? He don't work for me.'

'He's said for letters for him to be left with you,' said Armstrong. 'So where do you send 'em?'

'Nowhere,' said Jones. 'I keep 'em till he comes back.'

'And when will he be back?'

Again, the butcher shrugged. 'No idea.'

Armstrong moved nearer to the butcher, his face a mask of anger as his last bit of patience vanished.

'Now, listen you,' he snarled, 'we're police—'

'I didn't think you were from the local chapel,' snorted Jones, sarcastically.

'—from Scotland Yard,' snapped Armstrong, 'and we're investigating a murder. So, you can stop butchering that animal and pay attention, or I'll take you down the Yard for questioning.'

This had the desired effect. Jones stopped working on the carcase and stared at the two policemen, worried. 'Murder? Erskine never said anything about no murder.'

'No, he wouldn't,' growled Armstrong. 'Now, when do you expect him back?'

The butcher gulped nervously. 'I don't know. He never said. All he said was he had to go away and he didn't know how long for.'

'When did he go?'

'About an hour or so ago.'

'Just after I left him,' said Feather.

'Have you got a key to his office?' demanded Armstrong.

'No. I just take his letters in. That's all.'

'Where does he live?'

'I don't know,' said Jones. As Armstrong moved menacingly towards him, the butcher held up his hands in desperate appeal. 'I don't! Honest!'

'Did he take much with him?' asked Armstrong.

Jones shook his head.

'Just a big bag. One of them travelling bags.'

'Right,' said Armstrong. 'My name's Superintendent Armstrong. From now on you keep any sort of correspondence that comes for him, just like he told you. But I'll be the one collecting it. Or an officer collecting it in my name. Have you got that?'

The butcher gave another nervous gulp and nodded. Armstrong turned to Feather.

'Right, Inspector. Let's get back upstairs.'

They left the butcher's shop and returned up the stairs to where the constable was waiting for them.

'Right, Constable, kick the glass in,' ordered Armstrong.

The constable looked at the superintendent apprehensively.

'I might cut my leg and bleed to death,' he said.

'All right, then, just kick the door in.'

The constable looked at the door warily.

'Oh, for God's sake!' exploded Armstrong.

He pushed the constable aside, took up a position a pace back from the door, then smashed one of his heavy boots against it as hard as he could. The wood splintered, and a second kick took the broken door off its hinges.

Armstrong glared angrily at the constable.

'That's how you do it. Don't you know anything?'

He stormed into the office. Feather looked at the unhappy constable and gave him a sympathetic shrug, then followed the superintendent.

CHAPTER ELEVEN

When Daniel and Abigail returned to the museum, Mrs Smith still wasn't back. Nor had there been any word from Inspector Feather.

'While we wait for them to arrive, I'd quite like to look at the exhibition,' said Abigail. 'With everything that's been going on we haven't had a chance to take a proper look.'

'Yes, I'm quite intrigued by it myself,' replied Daniel.

They made their way down from Mrs Smith's office and into the Grand Hall.

'There's a good crowd today,' said Daniel, noting that the number of visitors to the exhibition seemed to have increased substantially from the previous day.

'It appears that Mr Stoker has succeeded in spreading word about the exhibition amongst his circle, as he promised Mr Sharp,' said Abigail. She gestured towards a stout man wearing an expensive-looking suit and a florid, flowered waistcoat, his face adorned with a large bushy moustache that flowed into equally exuberant side whiskers. 'William Schwenck Gilbert.'

Daniel scanned the rest of the crowd.

'No sign of his partner, Arthur Sullivan,' he commented.

'If the stories about them are true, you'd be unlikely to see them together, except at a performance or when preparing a new production. It's said they don't get on. Sullivan resents the fact that he's known for working with a comedy lyricist rather than his serious music, and Gilbert resents the fact that Sullivan has received a knighthood and he hasn't. And their relationship has never recovered from a dispute Gilbert had with D'Oyly Carte. Gilbert claimed D'Oyly Carte was spending excessive amounts of their money on an opera composed by Sullivan, to the detriment of their joint work.'

Daniel sighed. 'Money. The rift between so many friends and partnerships.'

It took some time for them to make their way around the exhibition, not just because of the crowds but because Daniel found each item fascinating enough to want to spend time examining it.

'The archaeopteryx,' he murmured as he studied the skeleton of the bird-like creature, and the reconstruction next to it with the display of feathers of different colours. 'Fascinating. Here we have an identifiable bird, albeit with teeth. I'd always thought of dinosaurs in terms of the large carnivorous creatures, rearing up with those terrifying teeth and claws.'

Abigail nodded. 'Tyrannosaurus rex. But that is what is so good about this exhibition, it covers the range from those massive carnivores, and the even larger herbivores, the diplodocus and the stegosaurus, to the marine creatures and the flying pterodactyl.'

'The triceratops is particularly intriguing,' commented Daniel, gesturing at the huge four-legged skeleton with its massive frill of bone in several savage points around its neck. 'It looks terrifying, very dangerous. And yet it turns out it was a herbivore. A vegetarian.'

'The bony frill with its sharp points was for protection against carnivores,' said Abigail. 'Similar to a modern bull or bison, herbivores with horns to protect themselves against predators like wolves.'

'Ah, there you are.'

They turned and saw that John Feather had arrived.

'I'm sorry I'm later than planned,' he apologised. 'Armstrong insisted we go and serve a search warrant on Erskine Petter immediately.'

'A search warrant?' asked Daniel.

'It came about after I went to see Benny Wardle in the Scrubs. I then went to see Petter at his office, and it was obvious that he was hiding something. He refused to let me look at his correspondence, so I went to get a search warrant. When Armstrong found out about it, he insisted on accompanying me. I got the impression it hadn't gone well for him at the Lyceum with Stoker, so he wanted to do something to vent his anger.'

'And did he? On Petter?'

Feather grinned. 'On the door of Petter's office. When we got there, Petter had vanished leaving everything locked. The superintendent kicked the door in.'

Daniel chuckled. 'That must have cheered him up.'

'It did, as did the haul of letters we found, proving that the letter he sent to the Natural History Museum was just one of a whole load he'd sent trying to extort money using legal jargon to intimidate people, but with no real basis for his claims.'

'So, he wasn't representing the Bone Company?'

'If he was there was no correspondence from them to back up his claim of being authorised to act on their behalf. And, judging by some of the other letters he'd sent, it was a dodge he used more than once. The letters have all been taken to the Yard, if you want to see them. How did you get on with Mrs Simpson?'

Daniel filled him in on his encounter with her and her denial that her son was in any way involved in the trial of Oscar Wilde.

'I can assure you he was,' said Feather. 'I was with the super when he talked to him.'

'Yes, well, it's pretty obvious that Mrs Simpson was lying, and we got confirmation when we went to the restaurant where Raymond worked. A restaurant from which he was sacked for theft. Incidentally, he also worked at the Lyceum Theatre, as an usher.'

'Did he?' said Feather. 'It must have been after the trial or we'd have picked that up.'

'The point is, Stoker must have known him from the Lyceum. Which gives more credence to the superintendent's suspicions about him over Raymond being killed when he was here. Is it worth talking to Stoker about Simpson, see what he says about him at the Lyceum?'

Feather looked doubtful.

'I'm not sure,' he said. 'To be honest, I doubt if Armstrong would get much joy from seeing him again. Stoker doesn't like him. And the super's warned me off from talking to Stoker. I think he's worried that Stoker might register a complaint about him with his "powerful friends", as Armstrong calls them.'

'Perhaps if we went to see Mr Stoker?' suggested Abigail. 'We're representing the museum, not the police. He might be more receptive to us.'

'Yes,' said Feather, thoughtfully. 'That's a good idea. But first I wonder if we shouldn't go and talk to Mrs Simpson again, in view of the latest you've picked up.'

'She refused to talk to me,' said Daniel.

'But she'll talk to me,' said Feather. 'She knows I'm from Scotland Yard, and I could take her in for questioning if she gets obstructive. I don't think she'd like that.' He looked at Daniel. 'It might be a good idea if you came along, after the way she acted with you. That way she won't be able to lie about her denials to you.'

'Yes, good idea,' agreed Daniel. He looked at Abigail. 'Would you like to come with us?'

She shook her head. 'I think I'd rather wait here and see Mrs Smith when she gets back. A bit of courtesy and politeness always pays off.'

'Yes, good thinking,' said Daniel. He turned to Feather. 'Right, let's go and challenge Mrs Simpson.'

As Daniel and John Feather walked to the Simpson house, Feather gave Daniel more details about the letters they'd uncovered at the office.

'He seemed to target public organisations and large companies rather than small firms,' said Feather.

'More chance of getting money out of them,' said Daniel. 'Small traders have to watch every penny; it's their money. But people working for big outfits are more worried about their job being under threat if they've done something wrong, like not paying a bill that's due.'

'The tone of the letters was always the same: the threat of retribution if payment wasn't forthcoming. And some of the people Petter claimed to be writing on behalf of The Houses of Parliament. The Courts of Justice. Major newspapers like *The Times*. And he seemed to specialise in firms based in America. The Bone Company was just one. He also quoted the Chicago Stockyard Corporation, claiming non-payment for a consignment of beef. Then there's the San Francisco Steamship.'

'All companies it would take time to contact for verification,' said Daniel. 'I assume he used strong-arm tactics to enforce these claims.'

'I'm sure he did. But with Benny and Billy Wardle under lock and key these last few months, I guess he hired replacements . . .'

'. . . who broke up the dinosaur skeleton,' finished Daniel. He stopped as they entered the cul-de-sac where the Simpsons' house lay. 'Looks like Mrs Simpson has a visitor,' he said.

A man had just come out of the Simpson house and was locking the door. As he began to walk away, John Feather gave a shout at him: 'One moment!'

The man, a middle-aged character wearing a brown suit of large checked material, stopped and regarded the approaching Daniel and Feather guardedly.

'Was that Mrs Simpson's house we saw you coming out of?' asked Feather.

'Who wants to know?' demanded the man, belligerently.

In response, Feather produced his warrant card and showed it to the man.

'Police,' he said.

The man stared at them, his eyes bulging in shock.

'Police?' he repeated, worried. 'But I ain't done nothin'.'

'Is Mrs Simpson in the house?' demanded Feather.

The man gulped, then shook his head. 'No,' he said.

'How come you have a key?' asked the inspector.

'Because it's my house,' said the man. 'I'm her landlord.'

'Name?' asked Feather.

'Dobbs. Alf Dobbs. I own most of the houses along here. You can ask anyone. Knock on any door.'

Feather and Daniel exchanged glances, then Feather asked: 'What were you doing in the house?'

'Making sure everything's safe. Mrs Simpson just called on me and told me she's got to go away urgent, so she's giving up the house. Some family business. She paid me the rent due and for another week. She said she'd write to tell me where to send her things. She's got quite a bit of furniture. She's paid me for the hire of a van to move her stuff once she knows where to send it.'

'So, the house wasn't let furnished?' asked Daniel.

Dobbs shook his head.

'No. That's all hers in there. Good stuff, as well. And all paid for. Nothing on tick.'

'Has she always paid her rent on time?' asked Daniel.

'Always,' said Dobbs. He gave a sad sigh. 'She was a good tenant. Reliable. Clean. Kept the place spotless. I wish I had more like her.' He frowned and looked at them quizzically. 'What are you doing here, anyway? The police?'

'We wanted to talk to her about her son.'

'Raymond? Why, what's he been up to?'

'Tragically, he was killed earlier today.'

Dobbs stared at them, his eyes bulging once more.

'Killed? How?'

'Murdered,' said Feather, 'at the place he worked: the Natural History Museum. I'm sure it'll be in the papers tomorrow. Didn't Mrs Simpson mention that to you?'

'No. Poor her. She depended on Raymond. What's she going to do now?'

'That's what we'd like to know,' said Feather. 'When she gets in touch with you with the address to send her things, let me know at once. Inspector Feather at Scotland Yard.'

'Scotland Yard?' echoed Dobbs, impressed.

Feather nodded. 'It's important you do that. As soon as you hear from her.'

'I will,' Dobbs assured him.

'I'll need your address, in case we need to get in touch with you,' added Feather.

'12 Albert Crescent,' said Dobbs. 'It's just two streets away. If I'm out, my daughter Gladys will be there. She looks after things for me.'

'Then make sure you tell her the same, she's to contact Inspector John Feather—'

'At Scotland Yard.' Dobbs nodded. 'I got that.'

Daniel and Feather walked off, leaving the stunned Dobbs standing on the pavement looking after them.

'Another one done a runner,' said Feather. 'First Petter, now her.'

'And for a similar reason, I suspect,' said Daniel. 'To avoid being caught for criminal activities.'

'Criminal?' queried Feather.

'Absolutely. Her son was a thief and possibly a blackmailer. Her house is full of good quality furniture and possessions, all paid for. Her aggressive and defensive attitude when I asked questions about Raymond makes a lot of sense now.'

'She was in it with him?' He looked thoughtful. 'She could have just been taking the money and not known where it came from.' Then he shook his head. 'No. She was part of it.' He looked at the street, with its terrace of neatly kept houses. 'Very clever. Outward appearance of respectability. A widow raising her son in a respectable area. Very different from Erskine Petter and Benny Wardle. Crooks certainly come in all sorts of guises.'

CHAPTER TWELVE

Abigail stood before the part of the dinosaur exhibition devoted to the work of Mary Anning and remarked to herself on the amazing work this woman had carried out during her short life. The daughter of a carpenter who'd died when she was eleven and one of ten children, Mary had spent her childhood in poverty and therefore had to forego any idea of a classical education. And yet when still a child she'd taken to exploring the cliffs and beaches around her home in Lyme Regis in Dorset with her brother, Joseph, where she'd excavated and identified the skeletons of marine animals from the Jurassic period. It had been Mary Anning who'd discovered the first ichthyosaur in 1811 when she was just twelve years old, and later the first two plesiosaur skeletons.

I am so in awe of her, thought Abigail. With no advantages in her childhood and receiving only a basic education at her church where she learnt to read and write, Mary's work as a palaeontologist had broken new ground in the field, her discoveries creating the platform for others to follow.

'Miss Abigail Fenton?'

Abigail turned and beheld a small, dumpy man in his late twenties, a beaming smile of greeting beneath his moustache. 'Herbert George Wells. I'm such an admirer of your work, Miss Fenton. I have followed your career as an archaeologist, your work with Petrie in Egypt, as well as your digs in Greece, Mesopotamia and Palestine.'

'Thank you.' Abigail smiled, taking the fleshy hand he offered and shaking it.

Wells returned her smile. 'I am a writer. I don't know if you've read my creation, *The Time Machine*?'

'Alas, no,' said Abigail. She tried to remove her hand from his but was surprised to find he still kept a firm hold of it.

'It was serialised in instalments in *The New Review* and then published as a novel. Some great names have remarked on its ingenuity and invention.'

'How fortunate,' said Abigail, and she pulled her hand from his grasp with a sudden jerk. Wells did not appear to notice.

'I would very much like to send you a copy,' he continued in his rather high-pitched, squeaky voice. 'Inscribed by me personally. I would be most grateful for your opinion.'

'That's very kind of you,' said Abigail, politely, 'but I could not possibly take advantage of your generosity.'

'I would not consider it taking advantage,' insisted Wells. 'It would be a privilege to have the opinion of someone like yourself, who I admire so much. And to find that such a highly intelligent woman, a great brain, also has beauty.' He leant in towards her and murmured, 'My close friends call me George. Would you consider joining that happy band?'

'Mr Wells.' Wells spun round to see Miss Scott approaching. 'What a pleasure it is to see you again.'

'Miss Scott,' said Wells, bowing to her. 'I was just saying to Miss Fenton—'

'Indeed, and I am so very sorry to interrupt, but it is Miss Fenton I need to see as a matter of urgency.' She looked towards Abigail and said: 'My apologies, Miss Fenton, but there is something in my office that needs your attention.'

'Of course,' said Abigail.

'Perhaps we could continue our conversation after you've finished with Miss Scott?' suggested Wells, a smile of hope and expectation on his chubby face.

'That would be lovely,' said Abigail, with a smile of apology, 'but I am due to meet my partner here. He will be arriving at any moment.'

'Your partner?' asked Wells, his smile fading.

'Daniel Wilson, the detective,' said Abigail.

'The museum has engaged Mr Wilson and Miss Fenton to investigate certain things that have happened here at the museum,' added Miss Scott.

'What sort of things?' asked Wells, eagerly. 'Supernatural? Criminal?'

'This morning one of the attendants was found murdered,' said Scott.

'Murdered? How wonderful,' exclaimed Wells, an expression of delight on his face. Then he looked serious. 'Not for the poor victim, of course. But as an incident that sparks so many questions.'

'Indeed,' said Scott. 'But I must steal Miss Fenton from you.'

'Of course,' said Wells.

He bowed as the two women headed towards the stairs to the first floor and the offices. Abigail was curious as to what might have happened for Miss Scott to hurry her away with such urgency, but Scott didn't speak until they were in her office.

'My apologies, Miss Fenton, but I felt the need to intercede.'

'To intercede?' repeated Abigail, puzzled.

'When I saw Mr Wells talking to you . . .' She hesitated, then said: 'I wanted to warn you about him before he made his advances. He seems to have made lechery his major pastime. He is not to be trusted.'

Abigail smiled as she said, 'I had rather formed that impression of him myself.'

'Then you are not offended by my action?'

'Not at all. I am grateful. It gave me the chance to escape without any rancour. He said he is a writer.'

'Yes, and rather a good one.'

'You've read his work?'

'I have, and he has talent. But he also has roving hands and is not easily put off.'

'You speak as if you had personal experience of it.'

'Not just I, but almost any woman who comes within his vicinity.'

'How did you deal with it?'

'I told him that I was not attracted to men in that way.'

'And how did he respond?'

Scott looked uncomfortable. 'It only seemed to encourage

him more. In the end I – er – accidentally trod on his toes with the heel of my shoe. It seems he suffers from corns. I apologised, of course, but it seemed to do the trick.'

There was a knock at the door.

'Perhaps that's Mr Wells with some excuse to continue his pursuit,' said Abigail, with an amused smile.

'Come in,' called Scott. The door opened, and Mrs Smith entered.

'I'm so sorry it took me longer than I thought,' she apologised. 'The people at the British Museum wanted to discuss some of the figures in detail.'

'That's perfectly all right, Mrs Smith,' said Scott.

Mrs Smith looked at Abigail, then back at Scott and said: 'I'm sorry if I've interrupted a conversation.'

'Not at all.' Scott smiled. 'In fact, your arrival is very opportune. I've suggested to Miss Fenton that she and Mr Wilson use the spare desk in your office as the base for their investigations, if you have no objections.'

'Not at all,' Mrs Smith assured them, enthusiastically. 'It will be my pleasure.'

'In that case, I'll leave you to arrange things,' said Scott.

'Are you free now, Miss Fenton?' asked Smith.

'I am indeed,' said Abigail.

She thanked Miss Scott, then followed the secretary along the corridor to her office.

'I'm so glad Miss Scott suggested it, and that you agreed,' said Smith. 'It will be a nice change to have company.' Then quickly she added: 'Not that I will interrupt or interfere with your work.'

'You can interrupt as much as you like,' said Abigail. 'I'm sure both Mr Wilson and I will be in need of your assistance, just as Miss Scott is.'

Mrs Smith took some papers from the top of the spare desk to clear it for Abigail, and asked: 'Have you reached any conclusions as to who may have been responsible?'

'Not yet,' said Abigail, seating herself at the desk. 'We are still examining different possibilities. Actually, one of the trustees, Lady Fortescue, was here earlier.'

'Yes. Miss Scott asked me to send letters to all the trustees advising them what happened to the skeleton.'

'So Miss Scott told me. Lady Fortescue seemed to blame Miss Scott for what had happened, both to the skeleton and to Mr Simpson.'

'I'm not surprised,' said Smith, sadly.

'She said these incidents wouldn't have happened if Mr Watling had taken the post of curator.'

'Yes, she would say that,' said Smith, bitterly. 'I believe she and Mr William Watling are . . . very close.' She scowled and added: 'An odious man, in my opinion.' Suddenly she stopped, alarmed at what she'd just said, and hastily added, 'I didn't mean that. I didn't mean to speak out of turn.'

'Rest assured, you're not speaking out of turn,' Abigail assured her. 'I only saw the man once, at a distance, but I, too, felt he had an odious personality.' Pressing on, she said: 'I would be interested to know the background of the situation. Why Lady Fortescue seems so bitterly opposed to Miss Scott, for example. The more we know, the sooner we'll be able to uncover what happened, and why.'

'I doubt if Mr Watling and Lady Fortescue are involved in any way with the dreadful things that have happened here, but you can be sure they'll use them to attack Miss Scott.'

'Why?'

Smith hesitated, obviously weighing up how much to reveal. Then she made up her mind.

'I was here before Miss Scott came. I was secretary to her predecessor, Mr Danvers Hardwicke.' She gave a sad sigh. 'Such a dreadful tragedy.'

'What happened?'

'He drowned. He fell into Regent's Canal. Everyone was shocked. He was such a nice man. Fortunately for me, Miss Scott was chosen to succeed him.'

'You knew Miss Scott already?'

'No, but I was familiar with William Watling. After Mr Hardwicke died, he made no secret of the fact that when – not if – he was appointed he'd get rid of me and employ a secretary of his own. A man. Mr Watling has no time for women at places of work, except in menial roles. Cleaners, that sort of thing.'

'He must have been furious when Miss Scott was appointed.'

'Furious doesn't even begin to describe it. I heard him ranting and raging at one of the trustees, poor Mr Desmond, vowing vengeance.'

'Vengeance?'

Mrs Smith nodded. 'His very words. That's the kind of man Mr Watling is: a man given to rages. To be honest, if he'd been appointed I'd have left of my own accord before he could dismiss me.' She looked thoughtful as she added. 'In fact, I often thought it was strange.'

'What was strange?' asked Abigail.

'That poor Mr Hardwicke should have been walking along the canal towpath with Mr Watling when he fell in and drowned. They were such very different characters: Mr Hardwicke was gentle and kind while Mr Watling is such a brutal and rude person. I find it odd that they should have kept company.'

'Didn't anyone else find it odd?' asked Abigail.

'No. Mr Watling said they were both going to London Zoo and had decided to walk to it along the canal together.'

'And Mr Watling made no attempt to save Mr Hardwicke when he fell in?'

'He may have tried, but I recall the police telling me that they'd asked about that, and Mr Watling had told them he couldn't swim.'

'Interesting,' mused Abigail. 'Do you know why Miss Scott was given the position over Mr Watling? After all, Mr Watling does have a great reputation as an anthropologist. Was it just because his aggressive manner put the trustees off?'

Smith hesitated, then said: 'Far be it for me to speak out of turn, Miss Fenton, but I heard two of the trustees discussing the situation, and one said he had concerns about Mr Watling's gambling debts. He was concerned they might adversely affect the museum's reputation if they became a scandal.'

That evening at home, as they tucked into the remainder of the boeuf bourguignon, which Daniel insisted tasted even better the second time as it had had 'time for the juices to mature', they discussed the latest events they'd uncovered in the case: the abrupt disappearance of Mrs Simpson – a sure sign of guilt, they both agreed – and especially what Abigail had learnt from Mrs Smith about William Watling and the death of the previous curator.

'It makes me wonder if it could be the museum that was the target, rather than Raymond Simpson. Or, more exactly, Miss Scott. We have a man full of rage who is desperate to get the job of curator because of the eminence of the position, and the handsome salary will help recover his financial difficulties. Fortunately for him, the then curator falls into the canal . . .' She paused, then added: 'Or is pushed.'

'Or is pushed.' Daniel repeated, then nodded thoughtfully. 'But instead of waltzing into the job he craves, he is cast aside for a woman. So, you're asking: is he capable of committing murder to discredit Miss Scott and her running of the museum in order to get her dismissed so that he can take her place?'

'Absolutely he is,' said Abigail. 'Especially when you bear in mind the organisational structure.'

'What do you mean?' asked Daniel.

'The Natural History Museum isn't an independent body. Its official title is The British Museum: Natural History.'

'So, it's governed by the British Museum?'

'Yes.'

'But it has its own board of trustees.'

'But they, in turn, are subordinate to the board of trustees of the British Museum. We know that Lady Fortescue is on Watling's side, if she and Watling have been able to persuade some of the trustees on the board of the British Museum . . .'

'I see what you mean. But surely that's unlikely. After all, it must have been these same trustees who appointed Miss Scott to the position of curator.'

'Unless the main board at the British Museum has recently appointed some new trustees.'

'Have they?'

'I don't know,' admitted Abigail. 'But if they have . . .'

'And if the new appointees are associates of William Watling and Lady Fortescue,' added Daniel, grimly.

'Exactly,' said Abigail. 'I think it might be worth having a word with Sir Jasper Stone at the British Museum. He was very grateful after the case we solved there, and I'm sure he'd be approachable.'

'But we'd have to be careful not to mention why we want to know,' said Daniel. 'We don't want our suspicions getting back to Watling.'

'Perhaps if I made a call on him on some unrelated matter,' suggested Abigail. 'To do with the museum's Egyptian collection, perhaps. That way it would look less like us investigating as detectives. And I could ask about recent appointees to the board, say I'm interested if any of the new members are Egyptologists.'

'Yes, good idea,' said Daniel. 'But our first visit tomorrow should be to the Lyceum to talk to Mr Bram Stoker and ask him about Raymond Simpson. Remember, that's what we agreed.'

CHAPTER THIRTEEN

Next morning Daniel and Abigail decided to take a bus to the Lyceum rather than walk. 'It will give us a chance to see if the newspapers have anything about the murder, and the victim, before we meet Bram Stoker,' Abigail had suggested.

'We don't even know if he'll be at the theatre yet,' said Daniel.

'I'm sure he will be,' replied Abigail. 'As far as I can gather, he virtually lives there. He is at the heart of everything that happens at the Lyceum. And if he isn't there, we'll leave a message asking for an appointment, and then I'll go on to see Sir Jasper at the British Museum, so the morning won't be wasted.'

They caught the bus at Mornington Crescent and managed to find two seats together on the upper open deck, where they scanned the newspapers they'd bought.

'*The Times* and *The Telegraph* both have reports,' said Daniel, as he passed her *The Times*.

'The popular press doesn't appear to have anything,' said Abigail. 'But then, I've noticed that unless it's some sensational scandal, they're a day behind the quality papers. I assume they take their stories from them and then add their own ghoulish touches.'

'*The Telegraph* mentions us,' commented Daniel. '"The Museum Detectives, Daniel Wilson, of Ripper notoriety, and Abigail Fenton, the famed Egyptologist".'

'What nonsense,' groaned Abigail.

'Why notoriety?' asked Daniel. 'You're described as famed, but me, I'm notorious.'

'I think they mean the case was notorious,' replied Abigail. 'And I'm much more than an Egyptologist. I've worked in Greece, Italy, Palestine, along Hadrian's Wall—'

'Yes, but the press talks to the public in brief images,' said Daniel.

The journey was slow because of the amount of other traffic, first along Eversholt Street and then in Southampton Row. All traffic finally came to an unplanned halt at the junction where Southampton Row crossed High Holborn before becoming Kingsway, because a horse lay dead in the middle of the road, still harnessed between the shafts of a removal van. The distraught van driver sat in the road beside the dead horse, stroking its head and crying.

'None of this traffic is going anywhere for a while,' said Daniel. 'Not until they bring a cart to remove the dead horse and a spare horse to move the removal van.'

'The Lyceum isn't far from here,' said Abigail. 'We'll walk.'

Most of the other passengers had reached the same decision, but whereas they hurried past the fallen horse, Daniel made for the grieving driver, Abigail following.

'Is there anything we can do?' Daniel asked.

The driver, a man in his late fifties, looked up at them, his grimy face streaked with tears.

'I told the boss Joshua wasn't well,' he said, between sobs. 'He was past the age when he could haul a heavy van like this. He should never have been pulling that van.'

A uniformed police constable regarded Daniel and Abigail quizzically, 'Are you the owners of this vehicle?' he asked.

Daniel shook his head. 'No,' he said. 'We were just passengers on that bus. We thought we'd offer our assistance, if there is anything we can do.'

'Everything's being organised,' said the constable. 'I've sent for another van to take the carcase away.'

'He's not a carcase!' shouted the upset driver, angrily. 'He's a horse! My horse!'

Daniel nodded at the policeman. 'We'll leave you to it, then, Constable.'

They left the grieving driver still sitting in the road, his arms around the dead horse's neck, and headed down Kingsway. It wasn't too long before they arrived at the ornate exterior of the Lyceum Theatre. Outside, the walls were decorated with large posters publicising the current production of *King Arthur*, starring Sir Henry Irving and Miss Ellen Terry. They pushed open the double doors and entered the plush reception area, thickly carpeted and adorned with posters from previous productions. A man wearing a striped waistcoat and with his shirtsleeves rolled up appeared.

'Box office ain't open yet,' he informed them.

'We're not here to purchase tickets,' said Abigail. 'We're here to see if Mr Stoker is available.'

'Why?' asked the man, warily.

'We'd like to see him.'

'And who are you?'

'Abigail Fenton and Daniel Wilson, on behalf of the Natural History Museum.'

The man hesitated, studying them, then grunted: 'Wait here.'

He disappeared through a heavy red curtain. Daniel stood studying the decor of the reception area: a mixture of red and gold painted areas on the walls in between the posters. A ticket booth was at one side, with the words BOX OFFICE above the shuttered window.

'Have you ever been here to see a production?' asked Abigail.

Daniel shook his head.

'It's very impressive,' she added.

The man returned. 'Mr Stoker will see you,' he said, his manner still suspicious but now slightly less grumpy.

They followed him down a corridor to an office and found themselves in a small room. The man they recognised from the previous day as Bram Stoker was sitting behind a desk. He stood up as they came in and gestured towards two plush-looking cushioned chairs, again decorated in red and gold, opposite him.

'Please join me,' he said.

They took the seats, and Stoker sat. He lifted a copy of that day's *Telegraph* to show them.

'I was just reading about you both and what happened yesterday,' he said. 'They call you "The Museum Detectives".'

Daniel sighed. 'That's not a title we came up with.'

'It's an invention of the press,' added Abigail.

'You don't need to tell me about the vagaries of the newspapers,' said Stoker vengefully. 'We suffer the distorted views of their critics more often than I care to think. It's vanity, of course. And jealousy. People of inferior talent trying to tear down the reputations of those who are truly gifted and successful.' He scowled. 'That oaf, George Bernard Shaw, for example.' He forced a smile that did not extend to his eyes. 'Forgive me, but Sir Henry works so hard and has been so successful that when I see his name traduced in print by an inferior talent, I lose my sense of good humour.'

Inwardly, Daniel reflected that what he'd seen so far of Bram Stoker gave little indication of the man having a sense of humour.

'I know both of you by your reputations, of course. Your individual reputations, that is. I have often felt in awe of your work as an archaeologist, Miss Fenton. In fact, if I'd known you were there when that unfortunate incident occurred, I would have been tempted to remain instead of rushing off as I did.'

Abigail smiled. 'We quite understand,' she said. 'You were protecting Sir Henry and Miss Terry.'

'Quite so,' said Stoker. He turned to Daniel. 'And my knowledge of your work with Inspector Abberline has suggested to me that you are of a different stamp of policeman to some of those I have met.' He regarded Daniel warily. 'Are you acquainted with Superintendent Armstrong of Scotland Yard?'

'I am,' said Daniel.

'Mr Wilson saved his life not very long ago,' said Abigail.

Stoker gave a sniff of disapproval. 'We all make mistakes.'

'I know the superintendent on a professional level,' said Daniel, carefully. 'We have different views on policing.'

'Yes, that's what I'd heard,' said Stoker. 'Which is why I'm happy to talk to you. Both of you. You have questions?'

'About Raymond Simpson,' said Abigail. 'He worked here as an usher.'

'He did,' said Stoker.

'Why did he leave?'

'I sacked him,' said Stoker.

'May we ask why?'

'You may. I sacked him when I discovered he was the villain who'd sold out my friend, Oscar Wilde.'

'Sold him out? For money?'

'Of course. What else. That was all Simpson was interested in. I'm sure he was paid to dig up the evidence that was used against Oscar.'

'Paid by whom?'

'I have no proof, but my guess is it was by agents of the Marquess of Queensbury.'

'If you knew what he was like, why did you hire him in the first place?'

'I did not hire him. The hiring of front of house staff such as ushers and programme sellers is done by our house manager, Derek Warner. I have enough on my hands with arranging casting and set designers.'

'So, you recognised him.'

'No. Mr Warner mentioned to me that he'd overheard Simpson bragging to one of the other ushers of his involvement in the trial. I asked him to look into it, and when he confirmed that this was the same Raymond Simpson, I dismissed him at once.'

'Were you surprised when you saw him at the Natural History Museum?'

'To be honest, I didn't recognise him. I peeled the cloth back and saw a man's face, obviously dead. I didn't study him. And the maintenance manager was there at once, so I had no time to look at him properly.'

'You didn't notice him when you visited the museum on Saturday?'

Stoker shook his head.

'No. At least, I wasn't aware of him. I didn't really take in the attendants; they were just men in uniforms. And some women, I recall.'

'We're trying to find out all we can about the man in order to try and discover who might have killed him.'

'I believe Superintendent Armstrong thinks it was me,' said Stoker. 'It wasn't.'

'Can you think of anyone who might have wanted him dead?'

'Many, I imagine. But no particular person springs to mind. The man was untrustworthy, villainous, and I assume he must have tried to blackmail others as he did Mr Wilde. That would have made him enemies.'

'Can you think of any friends of Mr Wilde's who would have felt strongly enough over what happened to want that sort of revenge?' asked Daniel. 'I believe Mr Wilde is suffering in prison.'

Stoker gave a harsh and bitter laugh. 'Suffering barely covers it.' Then he shook his head. 'No, I can't think of anyone in his circle who would kill anyone, let alone be so careful in the planning.'

'You know it was planned?' asked Daniel.

'What else could it be? Sir Henry, Miss Terry and I arrived before the museum opened and before the general public was admitted. That leaves a very narrow window indeed for the crime to have been committed, and for the culprit to have escaped. Which makes me think the person who did it was an employee of the museum.'

'That's certainly a possibility,' said Abigail, thoughtfully. Then she asked: 'By the way, Mr Stoker, do you happen to have a copy of *Who's Who* here? There's someone I'd like to look up.'

'If it's someone in the theatrical world, perhaps I can help.'

'No, it's no one theatrical,' said Abigail. 'I was interested to find out about William Watling, the anthropologist.'

Stoker shook his head. 'Never heard of him.'

He got up, went to his bookshelves and took down a thick tome, which he handed to Abigail.

'Here you are. It's the latest edition. I like to be sure of facts before I meet people.' He smiled again as he added: 'Even though some of those so-called facts often need to be taken with a pinch of salt. People often lie about their achievements to try to boost their reputations.'

Abigail flicked through the pages and located the entry for William Watling, which she studied briefly before handing the book back to Stoker.

'Thank you, Mr Stoker.'

'Was it useful?'

'It was indeed.'

'What prompted you to look up William Watling?' asked Daniel as they left the theatre.

'I wanted to find out a bit more about him before I meet Sir Jasper. I thought it might be useful to see what Sir Jasper knows of him and I wanted to have something to introduce him into the conversation.'

'And what did you discover?'

'He was born in '55, so that makes him forty. He was educated at Ampleforth College before going to Oxford.'

'Married?'

'Widowed.'

'I wonder what his wife died of.'

'Hopefully Sir Jasper will be able to enlighten me. I once worked with a very good archaeologist called Jeremy Swanton who's now at University College. Jeremy was also at Ampleforth and he'd be about the same age as Watling. While I'm in the area I thought I'd also go and see him, after I've been to the British Museum. For one thing, Jeremy should be able to let us know whether Watling could swim or not when they were at school.'

Daniel looked back at the theatre's ornate facade. 'This is a different world to the one I'm used to,' he said. 'Names keep popping up that you are familiar with but I'm not. This George Bernard Shaw, for example. Who is he and why does Stoker hate him so?'

'He's a drama critic,' said Abigail. 'He's also a writer. Not very successful so far, I believe, although he's recently turned to drama and his stage play, *Arms and the Man*, has had some success. Rumour has it that George Bernard Shaw is secretly in love with Ellen Terry and hates the fact that Miss Terry and Sir Henry are . . . well . . . close. That's possibly why his reviews of some of the productions at the Lyceum invariably praise Ellen Terry, while at the same time being severely critical of Sir Henry, calling his performances overblown and artificial.'

'How do you know all of this?' asked Daniel.

'How do you know that if a diamond robbery is carried out it's likely the work of a particular nefarious underworld character with a name like Jimmy Jeweller?'

'There's no such person,' said Daniel.

'You know what I mean.'

'It's the world I live in and have experience of,' said Daniel.

'Then the same applies to me,' said Abigail.

'But you and I both live in the same world,' said Daniel.

'As far as detecting goes,' agreed Abigail. 'But I have other interests. Archaeology, obviously. Theatre. Music. The arts. And I satisfy that interest by reading about them in magazines.'

'We could go to the theatre if you'd like,' suggested Daniel.

'You would hate it,' said Abigail.

'That depends on what it was,' said Daniel. 'A Shakespeare might be all right, so long as it wasn't too wordy.'

'The whole point of Shakespeare is his wordiness,' said Abigail with a smile. 'How about opera?'

'If it was in English,' said Daniel. 'And funny.'

'I think you're talking about Gilbert and Sullivan,' said Abigail. 'They're more "comic operetta". Most opera is in Italian.'

'So you can't understand the jokes.'

'There are very few jokes in classic opera,' said Abigail.

'So, it's Gilbert and Sullivan, or possibly a less-wordy Shakespeare,' said Daniel.

'It's a start,' said Abigail. 'And now, I shall head for the British Museum and see if Sir Jasper's available, and then I'll make for University College to see Jeremy. Shall we meet at home?'

'Yes,' said Daniel. 'I was going to suggest going to Scotland Yard and catching up with John Feather to see what he's been up to. But in view of your very crowded afternoon, I think it might be better to leave that till the morning.'

'You could always go and see him while I'm at the museum and University College,' suggested Abigail.

'True, but it'll be better if we both see him after you've gathered your information about William Watling.' He leant forward and kissed her. 'I'll see you at home.'

Once again, John Feather was in the interrogation room facing Benny Wardle across the table, with the same grim-faced guard in attendance.

'Two visits in two days, Inspector?' Wardle grinned. 'Someone must be on your back big time.'

'Superintendent Armstrong and I paid a visit to your partner after I saw you yesterday.'

Wardle scowled at the mention of Armstrong's name. 'Don't talk about that man to me. He was the one who put me in here.'

'Not personally, he didn't,' Feather pointed out. 'I rather thought that was the result of you and Billy beating up the Maxwell brothers.'

'He was having me watched. That's persecution, that is.'

'You were being watched because of the things you'd been getting up to.'

Wardle shrugged. 'Yes, well, that may be. Anyway, did you give Erskine my message?'

'I didn't have the opportunity,' said Feather. 'He'd done a runner.'

Wardle frowned.

'A runner?'

'Scarpered. Locked up the office and vanished, telling the butcher downstairs he didn't know when he'd be back. We recovered most of the correspondence we were after, but there was no sign of any money, which definitely makes us think he's gone for good.'

Wardle looked at Feather uncomfortably.

'So, that's why I'm here today, Benny, to ask: where's the money kept?'

'What money?' muttered Wardle.

'The income for Petter and Wardle. I assume some money came into the company.'

'Erskine looked after that.'

'So, where did he put it? In a bank? Under his mattress?'

'Like I say, that was his side of the business.'

'So long as you got paid, you didn't bother. Is that right?'

Wardle nodded in agreement.

'But I'm guessing no money's come your way while you've been in here. And as your brother is here as well, I doubt if Erskine popped in and paid him either. And you haven't got a wife and family he'd have given it to. So, what's happened to your share, Benny?'

Wardle glowered at the detective.

'Erskine will see me right,' he growled.

'Well, he hasn't done so far, not since you've been in the Scrubs,' said Feather. 'And now it looks like he's done a runner. Any bets he's taken your money with him and left you high and dry?' When Wardle didn't say anything, just sat and scowled at him, Feather added: 'Where's his hidey hole, Benny? He's gone to ground somewhere, with the money he owes you and Billy. Don't you think you ought to try and lay your hands on it? We can do that for you if you tell me where he's hiding.'

Wardle glared at him.

'I've never been a snitch,' he said, curtly.

'I'm not asking you to inform on him,' said Feather. 'All we want to do is ask him some questions about those dinosaur skeletons.'

Wardle shook his head. 'Don't you worry, he'll see me right. Me and Billy both.'

CHAPTER FOURTEEN

Sir Jasper Stone, Executive Curator-in-Charge at the British Museum, greeted Abigail with a hearty handshake and a warm smile of welcome as she entered his office.

'Miss Fenton. What a pleasure to see you again.' His face clouded as he added: 'Although I wish it were in better circumstances. Miss Scott wrote to me and told me she had hired you and Mr Wilson to look into the recent tragedies there.'

'Yes. Fortunately, Miss Scott is very supportive, as you were when we were here, which makes our work a little easier. But, alas, the murder is still a mystery.'

'Dreadful.' Stone sighed. 'And it seems inexplicable. For someone to have killed this poor attendant in the short space of time between the cleaning staff leaving and the guests arriving – a matter of minutes.'

'Indeed,' said Abigail. 'But we are following some interesting lines of enquiry. However, that's not the reason I've come to see you today.'

'It's not?'

'No. I've been considering writing an article for a magazine about our work excavating the pyramids at Giza, and I'd very much like to mention the importance the British Museum had on our work.'

Sir Jasper smiled in obvious delight.

'Why, that is so flattering.'

'Flattery has nothing to do with it,' said Abigail. 'Without the support and expertise of the British Museum so many archaeological discoveries would never have happened. But first I wanted to check that such a piece would have the *approval* of the British Museum. I'm aware that the trustees would need to give their consent.'

'I don't see that as being a problem,' said Stone, confidently. 'They, too, will always be eternally grateful for your work here, not just as an archaeologist but as a detective. And you know most of them already.'

'True,' said Abigail. 'But it's possible that some trustees may be recent appointments who are unfamiliar with me, and I with them.'

Stone gave a friendly laugh.

'You do yourself a disservice, Miss Fenton. None of the trustees will be unfamiliar with you and your work.'

'Out of curiosity, who are the recent additions to the board? Just in case I may know them.'

'Let me see,' mused Stone, thoughtfully. 'There have been two new appointees in the last six months, both replacing previous trustees who sadly passed away.'

'Yes, Sir Gerald Tubb and Mr Mitchum Wells,' said Abigail. 'I saw their obituaries in the newspapers. Both very good men and absolutely dedicated to the work of the museum.'

'Their replacements are Lord Carlisle of Derby and Professor Challenger from the University College of London.'

'I know Professor Challenger.' Abigail smiled. 'I worked with him at some excavations in Palestine.'

'Then I'm sure you'll have his full approval. And I have no doubt the same will be true of Lord Carlisle. Although his interest is mainly in the cultures of South America, the Maya, Inca and Aztec, which has led to some interesting acquisitions for us. In particular, some crystal skulls.'

'I would be most interested in seeing them.'

'At the moment they are in storage while we determine how best to display them,' said Stone. 'But once they are on show I will make sure I send a message to inform you.'

'Thank you, Sir Jasper. I look forward to that.' Then a pensive look crossed her face and she said: 'Actually, and forgive me if I'm speaking out of turn, I met one of the Natural History Museum's trustees recently. A Lady Fortescue.'

'Ah,' said Stone, warily. 'Lady Fortescue. Yes. A very . . . energetic lady.'

Abigail smiled. 'Energetic indeed, Sir Jasper. To be honest, I found her a little too energetic. She is a woman of very strong opinions.'

'She is,' agreed Stone, his tone still wary.

'She talked at some length and with some passion, in support of William Watling.'

'Ah,' said Stone, ruefully. 'He was . . . ah . . . a candidate to be the curator at the Natural History Museum after Mr Hardwicke's tragic accident.'

'Yes, so I understand. But, although I can't say that I know him, and it's therefore difficult for me to judge, I have been very impressed by Miss Scott. I believe she is an ideal choice as curator.'

'I'm glad you think so.'

'As I say, I don't really know Mr Watling. All I know of him is that he is an eminent anthropologist and that he was widowed a few months ago.'

Stone nodded. 'Correct on both fronts.'

'His wife must have died young,' mused Abigail.

'Yes. She was only thirty,' said Stone. He looked sad. 'She drowned.'

'Drowned?'

'In the bath at home. She must have had a seizure of some sort and slipped down beneath the water. A dreadful tragedy. Made worse for Mr Watling by the fact that it was he who found her.'

Daniel's route home took him along St Pancras Way, past St Pancras railway station and heading for the junction with Crowndale Road and Royal College Street. Often, he took unfamiliar routes home just to observe different areas, but today he'd taken a deliberate detour to take him past the workhouse where he'd spent much of his childhood. He'd often walked along this road over the years, and usually he'd ignored the large red-brick building with its two rows of high, narrow, barred windows. But his conversation about his past with Abigail had brought up memories that he'd done his best to forget. Looking at the workhouse again, the memory of walking into it with his mother, brother and sister all those years ago, when he was seven years old, came back to him as clear as the day it had happened. Then this road had been called Kings Road. He couldn't remember when the name had been changed to St Pancras Way. Had that happened while he was imprisoned here? No, 'imprisoned' was possibly being unfair, but that's what it had felt like to him.

He hadn't known why they had come to this place, all he knew was that his mother was carrying his baby sister, Lou – for Louisa – and his brother, Harry, nine years old, was holding Daniel's hand as they walked into the entrance where they were met by a tall, strict-looking man.

They were taken to a room where they were all examined by a nurse. Then their clothes were taken from them, and he and Harry had each been issued with a striped shirt made of a rough material, a grey jacket with matching short trousers and heavy boots. He and Harry had been taken to a large room with lots of beds in it and allocated a bed each. This was the ward for boys under fourteen.

His mother was sent to the women's ward. Lou was allowed to stay with their mother because she was still a baby, under two years old.

Daniel had no memories of life in the workhouse, except for picking oakum – a dirty task which consisted of tearing apart old ropes and collecting the fibres of hemp. The work made his fingers and thumbs bleed at first, but gradually the skin hardened up.

He barely saw his mother and Lou, and then only at a distance. The women ate separately from the men and boys. They walked around the outside exercise yards at a separate time to them too.

When Daniel was nine, after two years at the workhouse, he and Harry were summoned to the superintendent's office where they were told their mother and sister were dead. Sickness, they were told. There was a lot of sickness at the workhouse. Typhus, Daniel discovered later, caused by foul air, the lack of proper ventilation and poor sanitation. The next year, Harry got sick, as did many of the boys in their ward, including Daniel. Ten boys died. Among them was Harry. Daniel survived. Why? It was a question that had haunted him ever since.

He'd stayed a further two years at the workhouse, and then signed himself out. Now twelve years old, he could do that. The board of the workhouse didn't object; on the contrary, they encouraged people to leave because it was less of a drain on the public purse. And so, Daniel had gone out into the world vowing two things: he would survive and never again would he pick oakum.

He looked again at the huge red-brick building where he'd spent those miserable years, a time and memories he'd blotted out of his mind until now, then turned and walked away. That was the past. It was dead and gone. Now there was the future. With Abigail.

Abigail was relieved to find that Jeremy Swanton was in and available, when she called at the large white building that housed University College London. She remembered Jeremy as someone who was always busy, always occupied, so she'd half expected him to be lecturing or tutoring students, or out at one of the many committees he seemed to be on. The man on duty at the reception desk sent a note to Swanton to inform him that Miss Abigail Fenton was here, if he was able to see her, and within minutes the short, rather plump but very energetic figure of Jeremy Swanton appeared.

'Abigail. This is a surprise. And a very welcome one. It must be – what? – a year since I last saw you?'

'Indeed, at that reception at the British Museum,' said Abigail. 'I was last here six months ago to see Charles Winter and I checked to see if you were in, but you were out doing good works somewhere.'

Swanton chuckled. 'An exaggeration,' he said. 'I just did a couple of days helping Thomas Barnardo at one of the ragged schools he's set up for street urchins. Orphans mostly. Wonderful chap, Barnardo. Do you know him?'

'No, although I know of him and his work. He seems an exceptional man.'

'He is. Do you know he's been helping these orphans for nearly thirty years? Thirty years!' Then he smiled. 'Anyway, you didn't come here to listen to me wax lyrical about Barnardo. What can I do for you? And would it be nicer to chat in my room, where we can have a cup of coffee?'

'That would be lovely,' said Abigail.

A short while later they were ensconced in Swanton's room, a study where the shelves and every available space seemed to be piled with essays and papers from students.

'How are your students?' asked Abigail. She gestured at the shelves. 'They certainly seem to keep you busy.'

'They're not all current,' said Swanton. 'Some of the really good pieces of work I keep for reference. Fortunately, the students seem happy to make a copy for me.' He chuckled again and added: 'They think it puts them in my good books and will get them a better mark.' He sipped at his coffee, then asked: 'So, how can I help you?'

'I've come to delve into your memory,' said Abigail, 'concerning Ampleforth.'

'Ampleforth?' Swanton frowned. 'What's my old school got to do with it?'

'Were you there at the same time as William Watling?'

'The anthropologist? Yes, I was, as a matter of fact.'

'What was he like?'

'Not a very nice boy, as I recall. A bit of a bully.' He looked at her quizzically. 'What's this to do with? Has he been up to something bad? Is he being *investigated*?' He gave her a conspiratorial smile. 'You can't deny that you and your erstwhile partner, former Scotland Yard Detective Inspector Daniel Wilson, have started to feature prominently in the newspapers of late. The Museum Detectives?'

Abigail sighed. 'The press often exaggerates.'

'But I did read a report this morning about a body being found at the Natural History Museum. Murdered, by all accounts. And it's well known on the academic gossip mill that Watling was very keen to be appointed curator at the Natural History Museum after poor Hardwicke died. So, do you suspect Watling of being involved in some way?'

Abigail smiled. 'You should have been a detective yourself. The answer is . . . perhaps. But then, it's pure guesswork at the moment, and I'm sure he's perfectly innocent of any wrongdoing, so please don't pass this on to anyone else. As you say, there is a gossip mill that can get very active.'

'My lips are sealed, I promise you,' Swanton assured her. 'So, how can I help you with Watling? I doubt if I can be of much use. I didn't like him at school so took pains to avoid him, and I like him even less as an adult so he and I rarely meet socially and then only at a distance.'

'Do you know if he can swim?' asked Abigail.

'Swim?' Swanton laughed. 'My God, like a fish. Swimming champion of the school, in fact. He was always top at all sorts of sports. He was good at anything physical and he knew it. Why?'

'Nothing,' said Abigail. 'It's just a line of enquiry we're following up.'

Swanton gave a laugh. 'Oh, for heaven's sake, Abigail, with platitudes like that, you're sounding like a Scotland Yard plod. And how does whether or not he can swim connect to this dead body at the Natural History Museum?'

'To be honest, Jeremy, we're not sure that it does. We're groping in the dark at the moment. But I promise you, when we know more, I'll let you know.'

'Please do. Especially if it's bad news about Watling. I'd love to see him arrested for something, even if it's using bad language in a place of worship.'

'He was that bad at Ampleforth?'

'Awful. He put my head down a toilet. That's the sort of bully he was.'

CHAPTER FIFTEEN

When Inspector Feather walked into his office at Scotland Yard the next morning he found a note on his desk in Superintendent Armstrong's familiar handwriting: *See me*. He picked it up and cast a quizzical look at Jeremiah Cribbens, his detective sergeant.

'He just walked in and put it there about five minutes ago,' said Cribbens, puffing at his pipe and sending clouds from the evil-smelling shag tobacco he smoked around the office. 'Didn't even say good morning to me.'

'Possibly he was afraid to open his mouth and breathe in that awful muck you pollute the place with,' grunted Feather. He went to a window and opened it.

'It's my only pleasure,' defended Cribbens. 'It's the only one I can afford on my pay.'

'I'll go and see what he wants,' said Feather.

The superintendent was sitting at his desk leafing through a report and looking decidedly sour. But then, that seemed to be Armstrong's standard demeanour, thought Feather.

'You wanted to see me, sir?'

Armstrong gestured for Feather to sit.

'This Simpson case,' he snapped. 'What's the latest?' He picked up a letter and showed it to Feather. 'I had this from the commissioner demanding to know what we're doing. That's always the way when the top nobs are involved: we get interference.'

'I'd hardly describe Raymond Simpson as a "top nob", sir,' said Feather.

'I'm referring to the trustees of the museum. They want their reputation protected. Anything more on Erskine Petter? Have you laid hands on him yet?'

'No, sir. And I went to see his business partner, Benny Wardle, in Wormwood Scrubs again yesterday, but he claims he doesn't know what Petter's been up to. He also refused to say if Petter had a hideaway.'

'Refused,' barked Armstrong, outraged. 'I'll give him refused. Put him on the treadmill and keep him there until he talks.'

'I doubt if that will have much effect on Benny, sir. He's an old lag. He's more at home in prison than outside. He won't talk. Also, it's quite likely he may not know anything.'

'But Petter's his business partner.'

'In name only, sir. Benny's just Petter's muscle.'

'So, we're nowhere.' Armstrong scowled.

'Not necessarily. I got a list of the staff of the Natural History Museum, to see if any of them had form of any sort.'

'And had they?'

'No, but two names struck me. Two of the cleaners, Dolly and Tess Tilly, mother and daughter. They were the ones who cleaned the small anteroom where the body of Simpson was found.'

'And?' asked Armstrong, intrigued.

'It jogged something in my memory and yesterday I went back to our notes when we talked to Simpson about Oscar Wilde. He named three boys who he claimed had sexual relations with Wilde and his friends, and one of them was a Tom Tilly.'

'Yes, he did, by Jove,' exclaimed Armstrong. 'I remember now. He killed himself, didn't he?'

'He did, sir. Hanged himself. I remember it because I was the one who had to go and tell his mother and sister the bad news. Dolly and Tess Tilly.'

The superintendent slammed his fist down on his desk excitedly.

'That's it, Inspector. It has to be them. Everything fits. Opportunity? They were there, in the room.' He gave a triumphant laugh. 'I knew it was connected to the Wilde case. I felt it in my bones. I admit I thought it was Stoker, but it's still the same case with the same motive: revenge.' He beamed happily. 'Bring 'em in, Inspector.'

As Daniel and Abigail entered Scotland Yard they met John Feather and his sergeant walking across the marble floor of the reception area, heading for the exit.

'John.' Daniel smiled. He also smiled at Cribbens. 'And good morning to you as well, Sergeant.'

'Morning, Mr Wilson. And you too, Miss Fenton.'

'You look like you're off on important business.'

'We are,' said Feather. He turned to Cribbens and said: 'Go to the stables and arrange a van for us.'

Cribbens nodded and headed off.

'A van?' said Daniel. 'You're making an arrest?'

'Bringing in suspects for questioning in the Raymond Simpson case,' said Feather.

'Oh? Who?'

'Dolly and Tess Tilly.'

'No,' burst out Abigail, shocked. 'Not them, surely. Why?'

Feather told them of the connection with the case to Tom Tilly.

'I remember them because I was the one who went to deliver the bad news about Tom killing himself.'

'Because he'd been exposed by Raymond Simpson?' asked Daniel.

Feather nodded.

'Did you tell them that it was Simpson who'd told the police about Tom?'

'No,' said Feather. 'I didn't tell them why he'd killed himself, just that he had. But they could easily have found out the reason and blamed Simpson for his death. As the superintendent says, they had motive and they certainly had the opportunity. They were working in the room where his body was found. What did you make of them?'

'I only spoke to them about the skeleton being smashed,' said Daniel. 'It was Abigail who saw them after Simpson's body was found.' He turned to her. 'What do you think?'

She frowned. 'They didn't strike me as murderers,' she

said. Then she gave a sigh. 'I hope it's not them. I'm hoping it'll be someone like that Petter man.'

'Because he's awful.' Feather smiled. 'But sadly, some of the nicest people turn out to be murderers.'

'Talking of other suspects,' said Daniel, 'what did you feel about the death of Mr Hardwicke, the previous curator at the museum?'

'The one who fell in the canal?' said Feather. 'What was there to feel about it? He fell in and drowned. It happens a lot, sadly.'

'Nothing strike you as suspicious?'

Feather shook his head.

'We had a witness who saw him fall in,' he said.

'Yes, William Watling,' said Abigail. 'Was there any suspicion that he may have pushed Hardwicke in?'

Feather stared at her. 'William Watling? He's an eminent scientist. A pillar of society, not some hooligan.'

'What did Watling say?'

'Hardwicke suddenly tripped and fell. He struck his head on the edge of the towpath and tumbled into the canal.'

'Watling didn't go in and try to save him?'

'He can't swim. At least, that's what he told us. Also, Hardwicke disappeared completely beneath the surface, and you know what the water is like in the canal, it's more like thick soup than water.' He looked at them suspiciously. 'What's brought this on? And what's this got to do with the murder of Raymond Simpson?'

Daniel turned to Abigail. 'You tell him,' he said. 'You're the one who unearthed it.'

Abigail told Feather what she'd learnt from Mrs Smith: Watling's determination to become the curator at the museum, his anger at Miss Scott's appointment, his gambling debts, his rages.

'And I've also learnt that he was a champion swimmer when he was at school. Which gives the lie to his reason for not trying to rescue Hardwicke.'

'So, you think he pushed Hardwicke into the canal?'

'After first hitting him on the head,' added Daniel.

Feather shook his head in disbelief. 'I can't believe it,' he said. 'No one would go that far just to get a job.'

'People have done it before, John,' Daniel pointed out. 'One job going and two men after it. We've seen it. Remember Bert Brown and Colly Wethers.'

'Yes, but that was about getting a stoker's job at a factory.'

'For a few pounds a week. The curator's job at the Natural History Museum is worth much more, especially to someone desperate for money and social prestige.'

Again, Feather shook his head. 'The coroner's decision has already been made: Hardwicke died an accidental death. I can't see the superintendent agreeing to open an investigation, especially with the class of people we're talking about. And right now, everything's about solving the Simpson murder. And I can't see that being connected to William Watling.'

They were joined by Sergeant Cribbens. 'The van's ready, Inspector. The driver's pulling it round to the front for us.'

'Thank you, Sergeant,' said Feather. He nodded at Daniel and Abigail. 'I'll let you know what happens.'

'By the way, John,' said Daniel, 'did you look into Mason Radley?'

'Who?' asked Feather.

'The museum trustee. The one with the red hair and big beard.'

'Oh yes,' said Feather, suddenly remembering. 'That other trustee told you he thought he'd seen him earlier at the museum than he'd claimed.' He gave an apologetic shrug. 'No, I haven't had a chance. And now I've got to bring in Dolly and Tess Tilly, who look more likely suspects.'

'Do you mind if we look into him?' asked Daniel. 'Have a word with him?'

'Not at all,' said Feather. 'In fact, I'd be grateful. I've got enough on my hands already.'

CHAPTER SIXTEEN

Daniel and Abigail made their way back to the museum, where they sought out Mrs Smith. The secretary smiled brightly when she saw them enter her office, then asked, apprehensively: 'Is there any news?'

'We're still looking at various lines of enquiry,' Daniel told her. 'One thing that would be useful is if you could let us have a list of the trustees, so we can check we've talked to everyone we need to.'

'Of course,' said Mrs Smith. 'Would you also like their addresses?'

'Just Mr Radley's and Mr Turner's for the moment,' said Daniel. 'We thought we'd start with the trustees who were here on the morning the body was found.'

'And also Lady Fortescue's, if you have it,' added Abigail. 'After my encounter with her the other day, I'd be interested to know more about her. Is she married?'

'A widow,' said Smith as she opened a drawer in her desk and took out some papers with the information they were after. 'Her husband died in a tragic accident six months ago. He was cleaning his gun, and it went off and killed him.'

'His gun?'

'Lord Fortescue was a well-known sporting gentleman. Hunting, shooting and fishing. He was very much a mainstay of the establishment. So much so that his funeral was held at Westminster Cathedral.'

As Daniel and Abigail made their way to the address in Marylebone they'd been given for Mason Radley, their main topic of discussion was the facts they'd learnt about William Watling and Lady Elizabeth Fortescue.

'We have two people who – if the rumour Mrs Smith alluded to is to be believed – are romantically entwined. And both their spouses died in tragic accidents within the last year,' said Daniel.

'And both Mr Watling and Lady Fortescue are Catholics, which means they would have been unable to divorce their spouses.'

'How do you know they're both Catholics?' asked Daniel.

'Watling went to Ampleforth college, which is a Catholic public school. Lord Fortescue's funeral was held at Westminster Cathedral, which is Catholic. It's Westminster Abbey which is Anglican.'

'But some Catholics do divorce,' pointed out Daniel.

'Rarely at that level of society,' countered Abigail.

'So, what are we thinking? That they murdered their spouses so they could be together. If that's the case, why aren't they married already?'

'Because they have to let a decent interval elapse.'

'And what's a decent interval?'

'At that level, a year,' said Abigail.

Daniel thought this over. 'I must admit, I find the idea of an experienced sportsman like Lord Fortescue accidentally shooting himself while cleaning his gun to be unlikely.'

'Murder?'

'Or suicide,' said Daniel. 'Covered up as an accident because it is a mortal sin in the Catholic religion. But why would he commit suicide?'

'Because he found out his wife was having an affair with Watling?'

'It's more likely he'd have shot Watling. Or his wife.'

'So, it's murder, then?' said Abigail.

'Not necessarily,' said Daniel. He shook his head. 'It's all conjecture. We have no proof of anything. And, as John Feather pointed out, none of this is connected with the murder of Raymond Simpson.'

'It is if it means that Watling and Lady Fortescue are capable of murder and killed Simpson as part of a plan to disgrace Miss Scott and have her dismissed.'

'But no one mentioned seeing either of them at the museum around the time the body was discovered,' said Daniel.

'That doesn't mean they couldn't have hired someone else to carry out the killing,' said Abigail. 'From what Jeremy Swanton told me about Watling, he sounds just the sort of person to hire someone else to do his dirty work.'

Mason Radley's house in Marylebone was large and expensive-looking, with Doric columns either side of a black oak front door, embellished with gleamingly polished brass door furniture. Their tug at the bell-pull was answered by a middle-aged woman dressed in a long apron.

'Yes?' she asked.

'Good day,' said Daniel. 'My name is Mr Daniel Wilson, and this is Miss Abigail Fenton. We've been retained by the Natural History Museum to look into some events that have happened there recently and we'd like to talk about them with Mr Radley. Is he available?'

'I'm afraid Mr Radley's not here,' said the woman.

'Oh? Do you know when he'll be back?'

'I don't think he'll be back for a while,' said the woman. 'He's gone to India. He has plantations there. He said he had to go there at once. Something urgent.'

Daniel and Abigail exchanged puzzled looks, then Abigail asked: 'When did he go?'

'The day before yesterday,' said the woman. 'I'm his housekeeper, Mrs Walton.'

'What time of day was it when he departed for India?' asked Daniel.

Mrs Walton hesitated, and they could both see something was worrying her very deeply, then she said: 'It must have been just before lunchtime, because I was preparing his meal for him, when he suddenly came home unexpectedly. "I've got to go, Mrs Walton," he said. "Urgent business in India. If anyone asks for me, tell them that's where I've gone."

'Then he packed a suitcase and went. Didn't even attempt to have a taste of the meal I'd made for him. But then, he did look all of a dither, so whatever it was that had happened must have upset him.'

'Did he take a large suitcase with him or a small one?' asked Abigail. 'We're trying to get an idea of how long he expected to be away.'

'A small one,' said Mrs Walton. 'But then, he has his own things out in India already, so he doesn't need to take much.'

'Does this happen often?' asked Daniel. 'Him having to go off to India all of a sudden like this?'

'No, sir,' said the housekeeper. 'In fact, I've never known it before. So, whatever it is, I can only think it's serious. I just hope everything's all right out there when he arrives.'

'Do you know where his plantations are in India?' asked Daniel.

'I'm afraid not, but his office will know.'

'And do you have the address of his office?'

'Yes, sir. Portland Place. Number 30. Which isn't far away. Easy walking distance, as Mr Radley says.'

'And the name of the company?'

'Anglo-India Tea.'

'Thank you, Mrs Walton,' said Daniel, doffing his hat.

As they walked away, Daniel remarked: 'She seemed very worried. Much more than her words. Did you notice how she kept twisting her hands together?'

'Yes,' agreed Abigail. 'She's frightened. Do you think she knows something?'

'I'm not sure,' said Daniel. 'I feel she was deeply worried about Radley.'

'I think you're right,' agreed Abigail, adding: 'India? All of a sudden? Within a few hours of Raymond Simpson's body being found dead at the museum and Dawson Turner saying in front of you that he was sure he saw Radley early that morning at the museum.'

'Do you think it's that simple?' asked Daniel. 'That Radley killed Simpson, and once he realised that Turner had spotted him, he decided to make a run for it? But why would he want to kill Simpson?'

'Perhaps we'll find the answer at his office.'

In the interrogation room at Scotland Yard, Inspector Feather sat beside the bulky figure of Superintendent Armstrong. Across the bare wooden table on the opposite side sat Dolly and Tess Tilly, mother and daughter pressed arm and arm against one another for comfort, their hands clasped together. Behind them stood a uniformed police constable. They both looked terrified, although the fear showed more openly on the face of Tess. How old was she? Feather struggled to remember. Twenty? Twenty-one? She didn't look much older than that.

'The prisoners will separate from one another,' growled Armstrong. 'I don't want any hand signals between you while I'm asking questions. So, come on, move those chairs apart.'

Dolly Tilly, protective of her daughter, although fearful, gave a hateful look at Armstrong, then slowly disentangled her hand from Tess's and shuffled her chair a few feet away.

'Don't worry, Tess,' she muttered. 'I'm still here. I won't let them hurt you.' And she added, with a challenging look at Armstrong and Feather, 'And we haven't done anything wrong.'

'No?' said Armstrong. 'We know you killed Raymond Simpson because of what he did to Tom.'

Both Tess and Dolly stared at him in astonishment.

'Tom?' said Dolly. She looked at Tess, who sat with her mouth open in a state of bewilderment, before turning back to Armstrong. 'We were told he killed himself. Are you saying now that Simpson killed him? That he killed our Tom?'

'No, Tom killed himself, but you know that it was because of Raymond Simpson,' said Armstrong, firmly.

They looked back at him, even more bewildered than ever.

'We don't know what you're talking about. What had Tom got to do with Raymond Simpson?'

'The trial,' said Armstrong.

'What trial?' asked Tess.

'The trial of Oscar Wilde? For gross indecency?'

They stared at him, horrified.

'Are you trying to say that Tom—?' began Dolly, angrily.

'He killed himself because of what came out at the trial about him. And that only came out because Raymond Simpson told on him, and you know that.'

'We didn't know that,' cried out Tess, and then she burst into tears.

'Of course you did,' snapped Armstrong. 'It was in all the papers.'

'We don't read the papers,' said Dolly. 'We can't read.'

'That's irrelevant,' barked the superintendent. 'It was public knowledge. Someone must have said something to you about it.'

Feather gave a discreet cough, then said quietly: 'Could I see you outside for a moment, Superintendent?'

'Now?' demanded Armstrong, impatiently.

'Just for a moment, sir. It is important.'

Armstrong scowled. He stood up and snapped at the constable: 'Keep an eye on 'em.'

Feather followed Armstrong out of the room into the corridor.

'What do you mean by interrupting an interrogation like that?' demanded Armstrong, angrily.

'Tom Tilly never made the papers, sir. He was going to be called to give evidence, but he killed himself before he was due to appear. Simpson named him, but only to us. We passed his name to the prosecutor, but it never got to the public.'

'So? He was their family. They must have known what was going on – he lived with them.'

'If you remember, sir, he didn't live with them. He hadn't done for six months before he died. He was in lodgings.'

Armstrong stared at Feather. 'But you said it was them. You said they were the ones who most likely did it.'

'No, sir, I said their names came up when I was looking through the evidence. Like you, when I saw their names on the list, I thought it was likely that someone had told them about why he killed himself and about Raymond Simpson. But now I've seen them . . . I'm not so sure, sir.'

'Don't start going soft, Inspector. It *is* them. It's got to be.'

'I think, sir, we have to find out if they knew about Simpson and Tom. We need to talk to their neighbours and the other cleaners at the museum, find out if anything was said that connected the two men. Otherwise, it could be just a coincidence. Maybe they're telling the truth. Maybe they didn't know about the connection.'

Armstrong stood, his mind in a state of ferment, the side of his face twitching in agitation.

'It's got to be them,' he hissed. 'It all fits.'

'But not if they didn't know about Simpson naming Tom.'

Armstrong looked so furious that for a moment Feather thought the superintendent was going to strike him. Finally, Armstrong appeared to bring his rage under control.

'Go and talk to the neighbours, Inspector,' he grated between his clenched teeth. 'Find the evidence that says they knew. Until then they're remaining in custody. Once we've got the word of someone who says they *did* know about Simpson and Tom, then I'll force confessions out of them.'

Number 30 Portland Place was a smart four-storey building in a plush terrace, every one of which seemed to house offices. The offices of Anglo-India Tea were on the second floor, a neat and tidy suite of rooms with smartly dressed staff, both men and women, at desks working on papers of various sorts, mostly orders and invoices, from what Daniel and Abigail could make out as they entered the first and largest room. A severe-looking man dressed in a suit of clerical black and a stiff white starched shirt approached them.

'May I help you?' he asked.

Daniel introduced themselves, adding: 'We're here to ask some questions about Mr Radley. We understand he's out of the country at the moment, in India.'

The man gave a puzzled frown.

'Really?' he said. 'I am Septimus Sprigg, I'm Mr Radley's office manager, and he never said anything to me about going to India.'

'That's what his housekeeper, Mrs Walton, told us,' said Daniel. 'That Mr Radley has gone to India as a matter of urgency, that he left the day before yesterday.'

Mr Sprigg remained unconvinced.

'Mr Radley called here the day before yesterday and informed me that he would have to be away for a few days, possibly a week, but he never mentioned anything about going to India. Is it possible that Mrs Walton misheard him?'

'She seemed very sure,' said Abigail. 'We need to get in touch with him, so we've come to ask for the addresses of his plantations in India.'

'I can certainly give you them, and by all means you're welcome to write to him there. But your letter will take some time to arrive, and – as I said – I'm not even sure he is in India.'

'Do you know where else he might have gone?' asked Daniel.

'No,' said Sprigg. 'When he last came here all he said was he would be away for a few days, just as I told you. I didn't ask him where he was going, it wasn't my place to enquire, and if he'd thought I needed to know he would have told me.'

As Sprigg talked, Daniel's attention was caught by a tall, very thin young man who seemed very uncomfortable. He had left his desk and moved to a set of filing cabinets nearer to where Daniel and Abigail stood with Sprigg, and although he had opened one of the filing cabinet's drawers, Daniel was fairly sure he wasn't involved in looking at any of the papers inside; it was merely in order to eavesdrop.

'I see,' said Daniel. 'Would you excuse us one moment? I need to discuss something with my colleague.'

Sprigg nodded, and Daniel led Abigail outside into the common passageway.

'What's going on?' asked Abigail, curious.

'Did you see the tall young man by the filing cabinets?' asked Daniel.

'No,' said Abigail. 'I was concentrating on Mr Sprigg.' She gave him a quizzical smile and asked: 'Your policeman's nose?'

'Yes, and it's definitely twitching.' said Daniel. 'Keep an eye on him this time.'

They returned to the office. The young man had returned to his desk, and Daniel noticed that now he kept his head firmly down, eyes fixed on the papers.

'Him,' whispered Daniel to Abigail, gesturing to the young man. Then he turned to Sprigg. 'I wonder if it would be possible for us to have a word with your staff?' he asked. 'In case some of them may have any information that may help us.'

'I don't see—' began Sprigg, stiffly.

'As I explained, we are here on behalf of the Natural History Museum where Mr Radley is a trustee, and we're fairly sure that Mr Radley would expect us to leave no stone unturned in order to get an urgent message to him. It will be important to *him*.'

'Very well,' said Sprigg, with reluctance. 'But I would appreciate it if you could carry it out with the least possible disturbance.'

'Thank you,' said Daniel. He pointed at the young man whose head was bowed over his desk. 'I just wish to talk to that young man. What is his name?'

Sprigg looked surprised. 'That's Simon Purcell,' he said. 'Why do you think he can help?'

'Simon Purcell. Thank you.'

At the mention of his name the young man looked up, and now Daniel saw fear in his face as he approached him.

'Mr Purcell—' he began.

'I haven't done anything,' said Purcell, defensively.

'An interesting response, as I haven't asked you anything yet,' said Daniel.

'What's this about?' demanded Purcell, aggressively. 'I don't have to answer your questions.' He suddenly shot a look at the clock. 'Anyway, I have to go. I have an appointment.'

He stood up, and Daniel could now see he was agitated, his movements nervous and jerky. Sprigg stared at him 'What appointment?' he demanded. 'You never said anything to me about an appointment.'

'I was going to,' said Purcell. He tried to push past Daniel. 'I have to leave.'

Daniel blocked his path.

'Mr Purcell, we've been engaged by the Natural History Museum to look into the murder of Raymond Simpson,' he said. 'To that end we're working with the police, who've asked us to bring things we'd like investigated to their attention. We'd very much appreciate it if you'd come with us to Scotland Yard . . .'

'No!' shouted the young man. 'You've got no authority. You're not police. You can't stop me from leaving.'

'I can,' said Daniel. 'If necessary—'

The young man didn't give Daniel time to finish. He lashed out with his foot, kicking Daniel in the shin. As Daniel fell back in pain the young man rushed for the door, but before he could get there, Abigail had grabbed him by one arm, then swung him sharply so that he crashed face first into a wall. He kicked out at her, but she nimbly dodged his flying foot and pulled his arm up behind his back, twisting it. He gave a cry of pain.

'Try any more kicks and I'll break your arm,' Abigail hissed at him.

Sprigg, along with the rest of the staff, stared at Abigail and Purcell, open-mouthed, shocked.

Daniel got to his feet and limped across the office.

'Thank you, Mr Sprigg,' he said, politely. 'And we are very sorry for the interruption.'

He opened the door, and Abigail forced Purcell out with further pressure on his twisted arm.

'Well done,' Daniel complimented her. 'And now to find a hansom cab.'

CHAPTER SEVENTEEN

John Feather sat at his desk and wrote the address of Dolly and Tess Tilly on a piece of paper, watched by Sergeant Cribbens.

'Go to the nick by Paddington Station and see the station sergeant,' Feather instructed his sergeant. 'Tell him you need a word with the beat copper who does the area around where the Tillys live.' He slid the piece of paper across the desk to Cribbens. 'He's to ask around amongst their neighbours and people who know them and find out if the two women knew why Tom Tilly killed himself. Any gossip, any information at all. And if there was ever any mention of Raymond Simpson, either from them or from Tom Tilly when he was living with them.'

'Right, sir,' said Cribbens. 'In fact, there's a mate of mine, Jim Bunn, who works out of Paddington nick. I'll have a word with him as well. Sometimes the local coppers will mention something to one of their own they won't say to Scotland Yard.'

'Very true. Good thinking, Sergeant.'

After the sergeant left on his mission, Feather studied the list of museum employees again, especially the names of the cleaners. Maybe, if the Tillys hadn't talked to their neighbours, they might have said something to one of the other cleaners. He'd need to talk to them.

There was a knock at the door which opened, and Daniel and Abigail appeared, ushering in a tall, thin young man with a sullen expression on his face and a bruise around his right eye. Feather noticed that Abigail and Daniel were each holding the man by one of his wrists.

'Good morning, Inspector,' said Abigail. 'We have someone we think it might be worth your talking to.'

'I don't know anything!' shouted the young man. 'These people attacked me!'

'His name's Simon Purcell, and he works at the offices of Mason Radley's tea company,' continued Abigail. 'Unfortunately, he tried to run away when we began to talk to him, so we were forced to restrain him.'

Hence the black eye. Feather smiled silently to himself.

'Mason Radley. That's the trustee you mentioned,' said Feather. 'The tea plantation owner.'

'That's him,' said Daniel. 'It seems that Mr Radley has disappeared.'

'Disappeared?'

'Run away to India, according to his housekeeper. And we have a feeling that Mr Purcell here has information about why.'

Feather got up from his desk, went to his door and summoned a nearby constable.

'Constable, take this young man down to the cells.'

'You can't lock me up!' shouted Purcell. 'I haven't done anything wrong!'

'Then you've got nothing to worry about,' said Feather.

The constable took the frightened Purcell away, holding one of his arms in a firm grip, and Feather gestured to Daniel and Abigail to sit.

'Letting him stew to soften him up?' asked Daniel.

Feather grinned. 'There's nothing like sitting in a prison cell for a short while, listening to the sound of boots in the corridor, keys being turned in the locks, to loosen someone's tongue. Especially if they're new to it, and this character Purcell looks to me like he's just that.'

'Not an old lag, I agree,' said Daniel.

'So, tell me what prompted you to bring him in?'

'You remember I told you that another trustee, Mr Turner, said he thought he saw Mason Radley at the museum around the time that Raymond Simpson's body was discovered?'

Feather nodded. 'And I asked you to have a word with him.'

'We also intend to talk to Turner, but first we went to Radley's house, where his housekeeper told us that he'd suddenly left for India the day before yesterday, just before lunchtime. In other words, soon after the discovery of the body.'

'Suspicious,' said Feather.

'We went to his offices to see if they could give us the address of his tea plantations in India, in case there was a way of contacting him through the authorities there. But while we

156

were there, I felt there was something suspicious about one of the clerks. He was edgy, and I felt it was to do with Radley.'

'Daniel's policeman's nose.' Abigail smiled.

'I went to talk to him, but he turned nasty. Kicked me in the leg and tried to flee.'

'So, you blacked his eye,' said Feather.

'No, that was me,' said Abigail. 'Not deliberate, I assure you. It happened as I stopped him trying to escape.'

'From what you've said, he certainly needs looking into. And this Mason Radley.'

'How did you get on with Dolly and Tess Tilly?' asked Abigail.

Feather gave an unhappy sigh. 'Not well,' he admitted. 'They say they didn't know anything about why Tom Tilly killed himself, or Raymond Simpson having anything to do with him. I'm convinced they're innocent, but I can't persuade the superintendent. He insists they're lying, that they must have known. But Tom Tilly hadn't been living with them for six months before he killed himself, so it strikes me as quite likely they didn't know what he was up to or who he was mixing with. I've sent Sergeant Cribbens to Paddington nick to check out their story among their neighbours and acquaintances, then I thought I'd have a word with the other cleaners at the museum to see if they can back up their story.'

'How did they take being arrested?' asked Abigail.

'They were terrified,' replied Feather. 'They've never been in this kind of situation before.'

'Do you mind if I have a word with them?' asked Abigail. 'I'd be a friendly and sympathetic ear. They sound like they need one.'

'That would be good,' said Feather. 'Thanks.' He stood up. 'In fact, I'll arrange for someone to bring Dolly and Tess up to my office for you to talk to them. Nicer surroundings.'

'Where will you go?' asked Abigail. 'I don't want to force you out of your own office.'

'While you talk to them, Daniel and I can go to the cells and have a word with Mr Purcell. Much less comfortable surroundings there. More intimidating. What do you say, Daniel?'

'Yes, but be careful of him; he kicks.'

'Not here, he won't,' said Feather. 'Not with a burly constable standing guard over him.'

The door to Feather's office opened, and the two Tilly women were ushered into Abigail's presence by a uniformed constable. Tess looked scared, Dolly wary and suspicious. Dolly was holding Tess firmly by the hand.

'Thank you, Constable,' said Abigail. 'You may go now.'

The constable frowned, unhappy with this instruction. 'Are you sure, miss?' he asked. 'These are prisoners. They could be dangerous.'

'I am certain,' said Abigail. 'If I need any assistance, I shall call.'

The constable hesitated, still uncertain, then left, pulling the door shut behind him.

'Please, sit down,' said Abigail, gesturing at the two chairs she'd placed near her own so that they were close to one another, rather than facing across the desk. Gingerly, the two women sat, Dolly's suspicious look firmly on Abigail.

'You may remember I came to see you with Mr Sharp,' said Abigail.

Dolly nodded.

'I am here to try and get you released,' said Abigail, and at these words Tess suddenly burst into tears. Dolly put her arm around her daughter and pulled her close.

'Wait, Tess,' she said. 'We ain't out yet.' She looked at Abigail challengingly and said: 'There's a "but", ain't there?'

'Yes,' answered Abigail. 'The inspector you were with before, Inspector Feather, I feel he believes you and that you had nothing to do with the death of Raymond Simpson.'

'We didn't,' said Dolly, firmly.

'And I believe that also,' said Abigail. 'But the person to convince is Superintendent Armstrong.'

'He don't like us,' said Tess, wiping her tear-stained cheek with her hand. 'He thinks we did it.'

'That's why I wanted to talk to you,' said Abigail. 'If I ask you some questions – no trick questions, I promise you – and we're able to establish that you didn't know about any connection between Raymond Simpson and your Tom, we'll talk to the superintendent and put your case to him.'

'We didn't know about any connection between Simpson and our Tom,' said Dolly. 'We already told him that.'

'Tell me about Tom,' said Abigail. 'What was he like?'

At this question, Dolly looked uncomfortable, and there was hesitancy in Tess's eyes.

'What do you mean?' asked Dolly.

'As a boy. What was he like?'

Dolly shrugged. 'He was just an ordinary boy.'

'How old was he when he left home?'

'He was fifteen,' said Dolly. 'Coming up to sixteen.'

'And he thought it was time to leave?'

'Yes,' said Dolly, shortly.

'How did you feel about that?'

Dolly hesitated. Then she said: 'It was for the best.'

'For whom?' asked Abigail.

'All of us,' said Dolly. She looked at Abigail, studying her, aware that Abigail wanted to know more. Finally, reluctantly, she said: 'He'd been difficult.' Again, Abigail waited, saying nothing. 'He started going out and not saying where,' said Dolly. 'He'd come home smelling of drink and perfume. We guessed it was women, but we didn't know who he was seeing. Sometimes he had money to spare and sometimes he didn't have any, and when he didn't he'd get all sullen.'

'Was he working?' asked Abigail.

'He was supposed to be, but some days he just stayed at home in bed. We didn't know what was going on with him. In the end I lost my temper with him. "I can't afford to support you," I told him. "You're old enough to pay your own way. Me and Tess are working hard to pay the rent and put food on the table and we never see a penny from you."'

'How did he take it?'

'He said if he wasn't wanted at home he knew people who would want him. And one day me and Tess come home from our cleaning at the museum, and he was gone. His clothes weren't in the cupboard.'

'Were you upset?'

'Of course I was upset. But he'd been leading me and Tess a merry dance with the way he was living. We couldn't be doing with it. I was glad to see the back of him, to be honest. But

I thought it'd only be for a day or two, then he'd come home with his tail between his legs, like he always used to when he'd run out of money. But he didn't. Days went by, then weeks. I kept expecting him to be there when we came home from work, but he never was.'

'He didn't write?'

'Waste of time,' said Dolly. 'Neither me nor Tess can read. But even if we could, I don't think he'd have written. Out of sight, out of mind. And then the day come when that police inspector who was here turned up to tell us Tom had been found dead. Killed himself, he said. Hung himself from a lamp post. Somewhere in Whitechapel, it was. He wanted to know if we knew anything about it. What he'd been up to. I told him we didn't know what sort of life he'd been living, that we didn't know he was in Whitechapel. We hadn't seen him in six months.'

'Did the inspector mention Raymond Simpson?'

Dolly shook her head. 'No. Not till this morning when that big policeman, the superintendent, told us that Simpson had done something to Tom and that's why we killed him.' Her face tightened in indignation. 'I told him, we didn't know anything about Raymond Simpson, except he worked at the museum as an attendant. We didn't know that he knew Tom.' She frowned as she said to Abigail: 'He said that Tom was involved in some trial.'

'That's the allegation,' said Abigail.

'So, it wasn't a woman,' said Dolly. 'That perfume.'

'I don't know the details,' said Abigail. 'I've been told that Simpson was a witness at the trial of Oscar Wilde earlier this year when he was charged with—'

161

'Yes, all right,' interrupted Dolly sharply. She gestured at her daughter. 'No need for Tess to hear all this. He was her brother.'

'It's all right, Ma,' said Tess.

'No, it ain't,' said Dolly. She looked again at Abigail. 'Is that why he did it? Tom? Because he was being blackmailed by Simpson?' She shook her head. 'I can't see it. Tom never had any money to pay blackmail.'

'The inspector told us that Simpson had named Tom as one of the people who'd . . . been with Oscar Wilde and his friends, and that he was going to be called as a witness at Wilde's trial,' said Abigail. 'They think he killed himself rather than be exposed in public court.'

Dolly fell silent, and Abigail now saw tears glistening in her eyes. Suddenly, she wiped them away. 'Poor Tom,' she whispered. 'He should have come home. We'd have looked after him.'

CHAPTER EIGHTEEN

Feather and Daniel stood by the barred door of the cell in the basement of Scotland Yard looking down at the miserable figure of Simon Purcell, who sat on the concrete bench that doubled as a bed.

'This is all so unfair,' moaned Purcell. 'I haven't done anything wrong. I shouldn't be here.'

'What do you know about Mason Radley?' asked Feather.

'Nothing. Just that he came to the office and said he had to go away for a few days, just as Mr Sprigg told you.'

'What about Raymond Simpson?' asked Feather.

At the name, they saw fear in Purcell's eyes.

'Who?' He gulped, the quaver in his voice showing his distress.

'Did you kill him?' asked Feather. 'Did you kill Raymond Simpson?'

'No,' squealed Purcell.

Feather fixed the young man with a threatening stare. 'A man has been murdered and your employer has vanished. Everything about your attitude, your voice, your manner, tells me that you know what's going on. In which case, you are an accomplice. An accomplice to murder. That's a hanging offence.'

'No,' repeated Purcell, and he broke down, his face dropping into his hands, his body racked with great sobs. Feather watched him, calmly, impassionate, waiting for the burst of crying to subside. When at last it did, Purcell raised his head and looked beggingly at the inspector, his face grimy with the streaks of his tears.

'I didn't do anything wrong,' he whispered, desperately.

'Let me be the judge of that,' said Feather. 'What did you do? Something with Raymond Simpson?'

Purcell nodded.

Feather shot a look at Daniel, then both men moved to sit on either side of Purcell on the bench.

'What did you do with him?' asked Feather.

'I gave him some information he wanted,' said Purcell, sniffing back his tears.

'About what?'

'About the company.'

'Anglo-India Tea?'

Purcell nodded, all the fight gone out of him now.

'What sort of information?' prodded Daniel.

'There was a letter,' said Purcell.

'A letter?'

'From the regional governor in the part of India where the company has a plantation. There'd been some killings.'

'What sort of killings?'

'Some of the workers, the tea-pickers. They'd been protesting they hadn't been paid and were talking about striking. The local manager had said he wasn't going to give into threats and he was going to make an example of them. According to the letter, he hired some thugs to beat the tea-pickers. But the beatings got out of hand. Some died.'

'How many?'

'Fifteen. The thugs who did it weren't caught. They just disappeared. But some of the tea-pickers who survived told their story to the regional governor. The letter from him was to demand compensation be paid to the families of those who died, to avoid a scandal.'

'And this letter was sent to the company?'

'Yes.'

'To Mr Mason Radley directly?'

'Yes. He's the managing director of the company.'

'And how did you come to see this letter?'

'I do the filing. The letter was with other letters to be filed.' He hesitated, then admitted: 'I think it got into the pile by mistake, because Mr Radley got very worried and asked if anyone had seen a letter from the regional governor.'

'And what did you say?'

Again, Purcell hesitated, then he hung his head before admitting: 'I said I hadn't seen it and asked what it was about in case it turned up.'

'And what did Mr Radley say to that?'

'He didn't answer at first. Then he said it wasn't important, but I could tell by the way he acted that it was.'

'What did you do with the letter?'

Purcell fell silent and looked so agonised that Feather thought he was going to burst into tears again.

'Did you give it to Raymond Simpson?'

'Yes,' whispered Purcell, miserably.

'Why?'

'Because he said if anything ever came my way that suggested a scandal, we could make money out of it. He said I wouldn't have to do anything; he'd do everything and we'd share the money we made.'

'You knew he was talking about blackmail?'

'He never used that word.'

'But you knew that was what he meant.'

'Yes,' admitted Purcell, lowering his head, averting his face from Feather's probing eyes.

'How did you know Simpson?'

'I worked for a time as an usher at the Lyceum Theatre. Raymond was there, and he used to talk about how easy it was to make money from people who had secrets they wanted to hide.'

'When I came to the office you were nervous,' said Daniel. 'Afraid. Why?'

'I knew Mr Radley was a trustee at the Natural History Museum and when I read in the papers about Raymond being murdered there I remembered how Mr Radley was when he came into the office that day – all in a hurry and looking a bit panicky – and I thought he might have done it. Killed Raymond, that

166

is. And if he did it could be because of the letter I'd passed to Raymond, and I was worried I'd be involved.'

'You are involved,' said Feather.

He got up, as did Daniel.

'What's going to happen to me?' begged Purcell. 'I didn't do anything. I didn't kill anyone.'

'You gave someone a letter they could use to blackmail someone,' said Feather. 'You did it for money. That's a criminal offence.'

As the two men walked to the barred door, Purcell shouted out, his voice rising in with panic: 'I don't want to hang!'

Daniel and Feather walked back upstairs to the inspector's office, where Abigail was waiting.

'Where are the two women?' asked Feather.

'They've gone back down to the cells,' she said, her tight-lipped look showing her disapproval. 'They shouldn't be here. They didn't do it.'

'No,' agreed Daniel. 'It looks like Mason Radley is the person we're looking for.'

'You got that from Purcell?'

Daniel nodded. 'Purcell was blackmailing Radley, along with Simpson,' he said. He told her about the contents of the letter and the killings at the tea plantation.

'So, all things considered, Radley has to be our main suspect,' said Feather. 'He was spotted at the museum around the time Simpson was killed and he was being blackmailed over these killings at his plantation.'

'He couldn't be prosecuted for them,' pointed out Abigail. 'One, they were in India, which is a separate jurisdiction. Two, the decision to employ these thugs was made by his manager, not by him.'

'Yes, but if word about the killings leaked out it would affect his company's reputation and its share price,' said Feather. 'The fact that immediately after Simpson's body was found and Radley realised he'd been seen he ran for it, is the clincher.'

'In view of this, we ought to tell the superintendent that Radley is now our main suspect, and he should let the two Tilly women go,' said Abigail. 'There's no reason to keep them in custody.'

Superintendent Armstrong stared at them, stunned, as they told him what they'd learnt from Purcell.

'A trustee of the museum?' he said, shocked.

'Who was being blackmailed by Simpson,' repeated Feather.

'Which means the two Tilly women are innocent,' said Abigail. 'They should be released. With an apology.'

'We were just following procedure,' snapped Armstrong, defensively. Then he nodded and grunted reluctantly to Feather: 'Send 'em home, Inspector.'

'Yes, sir,' said Feather.

As he headed for the door, Armstrong asked him: 'So, where's this Radley gone?'

'According to what his housekeeper said, to India, sir. But then we hear his office manager said he had no knowledge of that.'

'So, he could still be in this country, hiding out somewhere.'

'He could,' said Feather, and Daniel and Abigail both nodded in agreement.

'Right, Inspector, once you've released the Tillys, get a search going for him,' said Armstrong. 'The usual stuff. Check passenger manifests in case he really has left the country. And talk to people who know him and see if they can think where he might hole up.'

'We'll talk to Miss Scott at the museum,' Daniel offered. 'As he's a trustee there she might be able to offer some insight.'

'Good,' said Armstrong. 'Good work. At least I've got something to tell the commissioner.'

CHAPTER NINETEEN

Sergeant Cribbens strode alongside his uniformed colleague, Sergeant Jim Bunn, as they made their way through the back streets of Paddington towards the house where Dolly and Tess Tilly lived.

When Cribbens had met his old pal at Paddington police station and told him he was after information about whether Dolly and Tess Tilly had known Raymond Simpson, Bunn had given a big smile and told him: 'You've come to the right man.'

'You know 'em?'

'Of course I know 'em,' said Bunn, slightly offended. 'This is my patch. Even better, I know someone who'll be only too pleased to dish any dirt on them, if there is any. A sharp-tongued woman called Mrs Henrietta Chapman.'

With that, they'd set off from the station, Bunn leading the way at a brisk pace.

'You think this Mrs Chapman will be able to help us?'

'If she can't, there's no one else I can think of who can,' said Bunn. 'Mrs Chapman can't stand the Tillys, and there's nothing like someone who can't abide people to get another side of the story from everyone who'll tell you what lovely people Dolly and Tess are.'

'And they aren't?' asked Cribbens.

'Well, I've never found anything against them,' said Bunn. 'As far as I'm concerned they're decent people, but Tom was a different kettle of fish, and it was Tom that used to get Mrs Chapman upset. She'd come and see me at the station to make complaint after complaint.'

'About what?'

'Tom and his cronies hanging around outside her door. See, she lives on the floor below the Tillys, and she said there was disgusting things happening outside her door that shouldn't be allowed and she wanted 'em charged.'

'What did you do?'

'I told her there wasn't a lot I could do. The stairs was private property. I said if they were doing it out in the street I might be able to charge them with causing a nuisance, but even then it would be their word against hers if it came to court.'

'What were they doing?'

'Messing about with one another, according to her. You know, in ways that men shouldn't.'

'How did she know? Did she open the door and see them?'

'She looked through her letterbox at them.'

'And Raymond Simpson was one of them?'

'I never got all their names. They used to scarper when a

copper turned up. We grabbed two of them, both sixteen: Harry Bentham and Walter Harris, but they denied they'd been doing anything. They said they were just hanging about on the stairs because their pal Tom's ma didn't like them going to his place.'

'And you never arrested any of 'em?'

'Like I say, on what charge? We had no proof; it was their word against Mrs Chapman's. So, I had to be content with warning them, threatening them with jail for causing a nuisance. It seemed to work because, shortly after, Tom left home.'

'Where did he go?'

'I didn't ask. I was just relieved he'd gone, because the other lads stopped going to the house, so there was no more of that playing about on the stairs. The next thing I knew was when Tom topped himself.' He shook his head sadly. 'What a mess, eh?'

They stopped in front of the house where just a few hours earlier Sergeant Cribbens and Inspector Feather had called to take Dolly and Tess Tilly into custody.

'Right,' said Bunn. 'Let's go and call on Mrs Chapman.'

Daniel and Abigail were also on foot, in their case heading back to the Natural History Museum after their encounter with John Feather and Superintendent Armstrong.

'It was very fortunate that we took Purcell to Scotland Yard, otherwise who knows how long Dolly and her daughter would have been kept locked up. It wouldn't have happened to them if they were middle-class women,' observed Abigail.

'Sadly, I have to agree,' said Daniel. 'It's an unfortunate truth that the wealthy and better connected are more likely to escape punishment for their crimes than the poor. Which is why this business of William Watling irks me. We need to call on him and confront him.'

'But he's nothing to do with the case,' pointed out Abigail.

'Perhaps not, but he and Lady Fortescue have got it in for Miss Scott and are trying to get rid of her so that Watling can replace her. That strikes me as wrong. So, a visit to him letting him know – in the most subtle way possible – that we have suspicions about the death of Mr Hardwicke might make him back off.'

'It might have the opposite effect,' cautioned Abigail. 'It might make him even more determined in his efforts to get her job.'

'In which case we'll be watching and we'll snaffle him.'

'It's not what we're being paid for,' Abigail said.

'No, but it's about doing the right thing,' Daniel replied. 'Say he did murder Hardwicke, is it right that he gets away with it?'

'No, but proving that is going to be difficult, and we don't have the resources the police have, and they found there was no case.'

'Maybe,' said Daniel. 'But it rankles with me when there's injustice done to good people and the perpetrators get away with it.'

'You remind me of those old time Knights Errant, the figures of chivalry,' Abigail mused fondly.

'Knight Irritant might be a better description,' said Daniel. 'I certainly want to irritate Watling enough to make him stop his persecution of Miss Scott.'

'You have a soft spot for her?' asked Abigail.

'I admire her, but not in any romantic fashion,' said Daniel. 'It's just that she seems defenceless in the face of attacks from Watling and Lady Fortescue.'

'I think you're misjudging her,' said Abigail. 'I believe she's much tougher than you think.' She smiled. 'Still, I agree with you about confronting Mr Watling. However, as he doesn't approve of women, do you think it's a good idea for me to be there?'

'I think it's an excellent idea,' said Daniel. 'I'm counting on your presence unsettling him, rattling him in some way.'

Their journey had now brought them back to the Natural History Museum, and they made their way in and through the large Grand Hall, then up the stairs to Miss Scott's office. The curator was at her desk, going through papers, when Daniel and Abigail knocked and entered.

'Mr Wilson, Miss Fenton. Do you have news?'

'We do,' said Abigail.

Scott gestured them to two chairs.

'Two pieces of news,' added Abigail. 'First, Dolly and Tess Tilly were taken into Scotland Yard for questioning early this morning.'

'Dolly and Tess Tilly,' exclaimed Scott. 'Why?'

'Superintendent Armstrong believes they were the ones who murdered Raymond Simpson.'

'Absolute nonsense,' said Scott.

'We agree, and fortunately we were able to prove they were not the culprits, so they've just been released,' said Abigail. 'However, we were only able to do that by identifying someone else as a more likely suspect.'

'Oh? Who?'

'One of your trustees, Mason Radley.'

Scott stared at them, bewildered.

'Mason?' She shook her head. 'No, that's impossible. I know him. He's incapable of that kind of violence.'

'We're afraid the evidence points to it being him,' said Daniel. 'It appears he was being blackmailed by Simpson about the deaths of some of his plantation workers at the hands of hired thugs. Simpson got hold of the letter naming Radley's managers in India as being responsible for the deaths. And on the morning when Simpson was killed, we now know that Radley was here at the museum at that time, from what Mr Turner said about seeing him.'

'But . . . h-have you spoken to him?' stammered Scott. 'There could be some explanation.'

'We tried to see him, but we discovered that he's vanished. Possibly fled the country, according to his housekeeper, and gone to India. But the police are checking that. There is a possibility that he's still in the country and this claim of him going to India is a smokescreen intended to put us off looking for him. So, we wondered if you could suggest any places where he might hide out. Other properties he may have in addition to his house in Marylebone. Friends in London or the country he might be staying with.'

Scott stared at them, obviously shocked.

'I can't believe it,' she said. 'Mason Radley is the last person I would have thought of. He's such a gentle man.' She gave a deep and unhappy sigh. 'But, from the evidence, it must be true.' She looked at them and shook her head. 'As for knowing where he might be, I'm afraid I can't help. I don't spend time with him socially, we just meet at museum events: trustee meetings and exhibition launches.'

'Is he married?' asked Abigail. 'Does he have family?'

'He's a widower,' said Scott. 'His wife died two years ago, I believe. As far as I know, he has no family living. His parents are dead, and I understand he was an only child, so there are no siblings.'

'Aunts and uncles? Cousins?' hazarded Abigail.

Again, Scott shook her head. 'If there are, I've never heard mention of them. But then, his business takes up all of his time and what little there is left he devotes to the museum.' She looked at them, quizzically. 'How much of this is common knowledge? About Mr Radley being a suspect?'

'So far only we and the police are aware of it,' said Daniel. 'Although, as there's a search on for him, I don't know how long it will be before the news becomes public.'

'I'd prefer it if, for the moment, we keep this to ourselves,' said Scott. 'For the reputation of the museum. Mr Radley is a highly respected member of the trustees.'

Abigail nodded. 'We understand.'

'However, be aware that some newspaper reporter might pick up the story and want to write about it,' advised Daniel. 'Most reporters make a point of paying serving police officers for snippets of information on their rivals.'

'If they do, I'll make sure all enquiries are referred to me, and I'll deal with them.'

'What will you say?' asked Daniel.

'I'll tell them that at the moment everything is speculation and we don't respond to gossip.'

'It won't stop them publishing the story,' warned Daniel. 'I'd advise offering them a sop. Tell them that at the moment it's all speculation, but promise them that, as long as they respect the museum and refrain from writing their story, as soon as anything is confirmed, you'll give them an exclusive interview with the full story.'

'I can't give them *all* an exclusive interview,' pointed out Scott.

'You give them separate interviews,' said Daniel. 'They'll put their own individual touch to what you say to them.'

Scott nodded. 'I'd better alert Mrs Smith,' she said. 'She'll be the first one who gets asked any questions.'

Inspector Feather looked up as the door of his office opened and Sergeant Cribbens walked in.

'How did you get on at Paddington nick?' asked Feather. 'You were longer than I expected, so I'm guessing you turned something up.'

'I did,' said Cribbens. 'It turns out the Tilly women did know about their Tom and Raymond Simpson.'

Feather frowned, his brow darkening showing his concern as he asked: 'Are you sure?'

Cribbens nodded. 'My mate, Jim Bunn, he's a sergeant there, remembered the case and he told me about how a neighbour of the Tillys, a Mrs Henrietta Chapman who lives on the floor below them, had reported Tom and this bunch of lads for what they did on the stairs of the house outside her door.'

'And what did they do?'

'According to Mrs Chapman they were getting up to homosexual acts.'

'On the stairs?' said Feather, incredulous. 'Anyone could have seen them.'

'They did. This Mrs Chapman.'

Cribbens then related Jim Bunn's story about warning the lads and threatening them. 'But as he had no proof except what Mrs Chapman said she saw, and it would be her word against theirs, he said there wasn't a lot he could do. But his warning led to Tom Tilly leaving the house, and then all the messing about stopped.'

'And you're sure Raymond Simpson was involved?'

Cribbens nodded. 'Yes, sir. Me and Jim Bunn went to see Mrs Chapman, and when I mentioned Raymond Simpson she got furious. It seems she knew him by sight because she'd seen him taking an apple from a display at the local grocer's and she gave the alarm, but he got away before the grocer could lay a hand on him. The grocer said to her, "That's that Raymond Simpson. He's a bad lot. I had cause to find out his name when he stole an apple from me before. If I knew where he lived I'd send the police round. He should be in jail." She recognised Simpson as one of the lads who used to hang around on the stairs with Tom Tilly and the others.'

Feather looked thoughtful. 'Did you see Dolly and Tess Tilly while you were at the house?'

Cribbens looked at him, puzzled. 'How could I? They're locked up here.'

Feather shook his head. 'The super ordered them released.'

'Why? I thought he was dead sure they were the ones.'

'He was, until some new evidence turned up.'

'About the Tilly women?'

'About a new suspect who turns out to be a more likely candidate. A man called Mason Radley, a trustee of the Natural History Museum who was being blackmailed by Simpson. Radley was at the museum at the time when Simpson's body was found, and now he's vanished. Gone abroad, so his housekeeper says.'

'Done a runner.'

'It certainly looks like it.' He gave a sigh. 'But now, thanks to this latest from Mrs Chapman, it looks like we may have let the Tilly women go too soon.' He got up and reached for his overcoat. 'So, let's go and have another word with them.'

'Are you going to tell the super?' asked Cribbens.

'Not yet,' said Feather. 'His day's been upset once already. If it turns out it was them after all and we let them go, he's not going to be in a good mood.'

CHAPTER TWENTY

Alf Dobbs returned home from his weekly inspection of his properties to find a letter on his doormat in handwriting he didn't immediately recognise. Curious, he opened it. It was from Mrs Simpson.

> *Dear Mr Dobbs,*
>
> *I am now able to have my furniture and possessions. Please have them delivered to the address below on Saturday, when I shall be here to receive them. The money I paid you should be enough to cover it, but if the cost is extra, please advise and I will pay the carter.*
>
> > *Yours sincerely,*
> > *Mrs Nora Simpson*

It was short notice. Today was Thursday, and it was already

late in the afternoon. However, the address she gave was in Brompton Road, not too far away from her old house, so he was sure he could find a carter to handle the removal.

Dobbs weighed up his options. He could do as she instructed him and possibly add a couple of pounds to the carter's charge for his trouble, or he could do as that Scotland Yard detective had ordered him and pass the information on to the police. He was well aware what his civic duty told him his decision should be, but civic duty didn't pay bills and put food on his table. But then again, disobeying instructions from the police could be dangerous. Especially because the instructions came from Scotland Yard, not just the local cop shop.

He needed to think about it. In the meantime, he put the letter back in its envelope and slipped it into the inside pocket of his jacket. The first thing he needed to do was make an arrangement with a reliable carter. It was short notice, but Nora Simpson was paying for it.

Miss Scott knocked at the door of her secretary's office and entered to find Mrs Smith putting on her coat.

'Ah, good, I caught you before you went home,' she said.

'I was coming in to tell you I was off,' said Mrs Smith. 'As I always do.'

Scott caught the tone of defensiveness and slight reproof, and gave her a reassuring smile.

'I know, and for that I'm very grateful,' she said. Inwardly, she thought, *But you weren't here when I called in an hour ago. Nor when I called again twenty minutes later*. For the first time, Scott began to wonder about her secretary's absences. There had been that recent occasion when she'd gone to the British Museum to deliver some papers and had been gone for most of the day. And there were other occasions when Mrs Smith seemed to have disappeared for a length of time, only to reappear later and be found at her desk. *I need to keep an eye on her*, she decided. *Something is going on.*

Aloud, she said: 'Mrs Smith, I have some news that is quite shocking. It seems that one of the trustees is suspected of being the person who killed Raymond Simpson.'

Smith stared at her, as horror-struck as Miss Scott had been when she was first told.

'One of the trustees? Who?'

'I'm afraid I'm not at liberty to say at the moment. I'm telling you in case you're approached by anyone, particularly anyone from the newspapers, asking about it. If that happens, please refer them to me.'

'But . . . why would one of the trustees want to kill Raymond Simpson?'

Scott hesitated, weighing up how much to tell her. Then she decided she owed her secretary at least that much. 'It seems that Simpson may have been blackmailing them. I'm afraid I can't tell you any more than that, and even that must remain between us.'

'I understand,' Smith assured her. 'Is there anything I can do?'

'Not at the moment, but I just thought you ought to know.'

Mrs Smith nodded, but Scott noticed that this latest news had rattled her secretary very much indeed by the way she stood quivering, her face white.

There is definitely something going on, thought Scott, as she headed back to her own office.

Feather and Cribbens knocked again at the door of the Tillys' home, but there was still no answer.

'I'd have thought they'd have been back by now,' said Feather.

'Maybe they've done a runner,' suggested Cribbens. 'Everyone else connected with this case seems to have: Erskine Petter, Mrs Simpson, that trustee bloke.'

'I hope not,' grunted Feather. 'We'll have a word with your Mrs Chapman downstairs, see if she's seen them.'

Mrs Chapman opened her door at their knock and looked out at them through the narrow gap, before opening it wider when she saw who it was.

'Mrs Chapman, I'm Inspector Feather from Scotland Yard. You'll remember Detective Sergeant Cribbens.'

'Yes, he was here earlier,' said Mrs Chapman. 'With Sergeant Bunn. They was asking me about Tom Tilly and Raymond Simpson.' She leant expectantly towards the two policemen and asked eagerly: 'I know you arrested them two upstairs. Have they confessed? Did they do it? Kill the Simpson boy?'

'The murder of Raymond Simpson is still being investigated,' said Feather. 'Mrs and Miss Tilly weren't arrested; they came voluntarily to answer some questions about the case. In fact, they were released not long ago.'

The expression on Mrs Chapman's face showed her extreme disappointment.

'Released?' she echoed, bitterly.

'Yes, and we'd like to talk to them some more, but there's

no answer at their door. Did you see them return?'

She glared at him. 'What do you think I am, a snoop who has nothing better to do than watch what my neighbours are up to?' she demanded.

'No—' began Feather, but he was cut off by the angry woman.

'I'm a busy, law-abiding woman, I am. Someone who's always done her best to help the police, but did I get any thanks for that? No. If you've let 'em go it means you've been taken in by them, like everyone else seems to be. Well, I'm washing my hands of it. As far as I'm concerned you can sling your hook.'

With that, she closed the door firmly, but not before giving them a final glare.

'Well, that's told us,' said Feather, ruefully.

'What are we going to do, sir? Wait and see if they turn up?'

'No,' said Feather. 'With luck, they've maybe just gone to get some shopping. If so, we know where they'll be tomorrow morning first thing. It'll be an early start for us, Sergeant. Six o'clock at the Natural History Museum.'

William Watling's house was one of an expensive-looking terrace of grand houses in Bayswater, with a classical portico in Portland stone framing the dark oak front door. Daniel pulled the bell-pull, and the door was opened by a maid wearing a cotton cap and a white apron over her dark dress.

'Yes?' she enquired.

'Is Mr William Watling at home?' asked Daniel. 'My name is Mr Daniel Wilson, and this is Miss Abigail Fenton. We'd like to talk to him about the Natural History Museum.'

'Who is it, Millie?' boomed a loud voice from inside the house.

'It's a Mr Wilson and a Miss Fenton, sir,' called Millie.

The figure of William Watling appeared behind the maid. He was tall, neatly and expensively dressed in formal wear, even though he was in his own home. His dark hair was pulled back from his slightly flushed face and kept in place with pomade. The same, or something similar, had also been applied to his large bushy moustache, which curled back from his mouth and across his cheeks to merge with his hair.

'I'm Watling,' he snapped, his tone and posture aggressive and challenging. 'What do you want?'

'We're sorry to disturb you at home, Mr Watling, but we've been asked by the Natural History Museum to look into recent disturbing events that have taken place there,' said Daniel, calmly. 'A dinosaur skeleton being smashed, and a murder.'

'So?' growled Watling. 'I don't see what that's got to do with me.'

'We're investigating the possibility that it may be part of a wider vendetta against the museum,' continued Daniel. 'Following as these events do on the recent tragic demise of Mr Danvers Hardwicke, the late curator of the museum.'

Watling stared at them, and there was no mistaking his anger and indignation.

'What on earth are you talking about?' he demanded. 'There was nothing deliberate about that. It was an accident. I know because I was with him when it happened.'

'Yes, sir, that's what we've been told. Do you mind if we come in and discuss it?'

'There's nothing to discuss,' barked Watling. 'Please leave.'

'Indeed, we will, Mr Watling. But we just want to ascertain

the facts from the one person who was there: yourself. He fell into the canal, we understand.'

'Yes. The towpath on that stretch of canal is notoriously unstable.'

'But you didn't jump in to try and save him?'

They could tell that Watling was having difficulty controlling his temper at their continued questions, but he forced himself to maintain his decorum. 'No,' he told them curtly through gritted teeth. 'The canal water is very thick. He disappeared from sight straight away, and there was no way of knowing where he was.'

'The police said you told them you didn't go into the water because you can't swim,' said Abigail. 'But someone who knew you at Ampleforth told us you were a very keen swimmer. In fact, a champion.'

Watling's mouth fell open in outrage, before snapping shut. 'How dare you?' he thundered. 'You've been talking to my friends about me? And the police.'

'As we said, the museum has asked us to investigate the death of one of their attendants and damage to a fossil,' said Daniel, calmly.

'And how is the death of Danvers Hardwicke anything to do with that?' demanded Watling.

'Perhaps it isn't,' said Daniel. 'Or perhaps his death may not have been an accident.'

Watling's face began to turn purple with rage and he pointed an angry finger at them.

'Are you daring to suggest—?' he began.

'That it may have been deliberate,' said Daniel, smoothly. 'Suicide?'

Watling swallowed, then forced his reply through gritted teeth: 'It was an accident. Just as I told the police.'

'Of course,' said Daniel. 'But we do owe it to the museum to make a full investigation.'

He looked towards Abigail, and they gave polite smiles at Watling.

'Thank you for your time, Mr Watling,' said Abigail.

They waited until they heard the door shut firmly behind them before Daniel said: 'Well, that was interesting. A man with a very short fuse. And I think we upset him.'

'I think we did,' agreed Abigail. 'The question is: did we upset him because he's naturally like that, very aggressive, or because he's worried about us asking questions?'

Daniel smiled. 'For that, we shall have to wait and see.' He pulled out his watch and looked at it. 'My stomach is right. It feels like suppertime is upon us, and my watch confirms that. So, I suggest we head home, and on the way collect a bowl of pie and mash. What do you say?'

'If that's the best you can come up with, I suggest we consider employing a cook part-time on days when neither of us has time to prepare a meal,' said Abigail, tersely.

'When I was in the workhouse I used to dream about pie and mash. With parsley sauce,' said Daniel.

'You are not in the workhouse now, and you left it behind you more than twenty years ago,' said Abigail, shortly. Then she relented. 'However, far be it from me to decry a hard-working man his childhood dreams. Pie and mash, it is.'

CHAPTER TWENTY-ONE

Dawson Turner sat in the luxurious leather armchair in the smoking room of his club, the Egerton in Pall Mall, savouring the superb cognac in between draws on his cigar and reflecting on his day. He looked at the ornate clock on the wall and saw that it was almost eight. He should be getting home to his family, a peck on the cheek for his four children in their beds, then a peck for his wife, Emmeline, to whom he would recount the events of the day. Not all of them, of course, but the notable ones. His meeting with Sir Derek Draber, Chairman of the Charity Commission, who'd complimented him on his charitable work and, with a subtle nod and a wink, had indicated that so far the application for a knighthood on his behalf had met with gracious approval. Sir Dawson Turner. He almost salivated at the mere thought of it.

And then, of course, there had been the afternoon of delight with Penelope, snatched secret moments of sheer ecstasy.

'Dawson.' The jovial greeting cut into his reverie. He looked up and recognised the figure of Jefferson Thwaite, a member he hadn't seen for ages. A journalist, he recalled. Someone who might be useful in getting a mention of his name in the court pages of the newspapers just to aid his quest.

'Jefferson.' Turner got to his feet and shook the hand that was offered. 'How are you? It's some time since I last saw you.'

'Yes, I've been up north for the past six months. In Sheffield. I was appointed editor of a new newspaper there.'

'So, you're back in London for a visit?'

'No. I got an offer to become editor of *The Star* here in London. Sheffield was good, but I fancied being back in London.'

'Back in the Smoke.' Turner smiled.

Thwaite chuckled. 'Believe me, Sheffield has smoke enough for two cities.' He grinned. 'No, the offer to edit *The Star* was too good to turn down.'

'I must admit, I don't often catch *The Star*,' said Turner. 'I'm more of a *Times* and *Telegraph* man myself.'

'It's true we're mainly middle market,' said Thwaite. 'But I've been given the brief to change that. Expand our readership. Give them hard facts, not just gossip. Which is why, when I saw you, I thought, "There's just the man."'

'Oh?' asked Turner, curious. 'In what way?'

'You're still on the board of trustees at the Natural History Museum?' asked Thwaite.

'Indeed, I am,' said Turner. 'One of the many trusts to which I'm proud to bring my charitable experience.'

His hope that Thwaite might ask him to enlarge on the other charities to which he was a party disappeared as the journalist asked his next question: 'Then you know about this murder?'

'I do,' said Turner. 'In fact, I was there on the morning the body was discovered. I was in the Grand Hall there, in conversation with Sir Henry Irving and Miss Ellen Terry, when suddenly Bram Stoker – he's the business manager at the Lyceum Theatre—'

'Yes, yes, I know of him,' said Thwaite.

'He rushed in and told us a dead body had been found.'

'Yes, I heard about that. And I also heard – from a source within the police, someone I knew when I was in London before – that they have a suspect.'

'Oh?'

'Yes. One of the trustees.'

Turner's mouth fell open, shocked. 'One of the trustees?' he repeated. 'Who?'

Thwaite gave a grimace. 'That's the problem: he refused to elaborate. Said he'd lose his job if he disclosed the name. My guess is he doesn't know it, so when I saw you, I thought: "There's the man who'd know."'

Turner shook his head. 'No, absolutely not. Until you mentioned it, I had no idea they thought it might be one of the trustees.' He looked stunned. 'To be frank, the idea's unthinkable. I know them. They're all decent people.' He looked earnestly at Thwaite. 'Are you sure about this? I thought the police believed it was connected to the damaged dinosaur skeleton.'

Thwaite frowned, puzzled. 'What dinosaur skeleton?'

'You must have heard about it. The day before the man was killed, a dinosaur skeleton that was on display was found smashed to pieces.' He leant forward and added: 'I heard that it was to do with some financial skulduggery over the purchase of dinosaur skeletons from America.'

'I hadn't heard about that,' said Thwaite. He shrugged. 'But then, a murder tops a broken dinosaur skeleton.'

'But I was under the impression they were connected,' said Turner. 'The damage to the skeleton was the first threat against the museum and the killing of the attendant took it a stage further.'

'More than a stage,' grunted Thwaite.

'I'll tell you what, I'll have a word with the curator's secretary,' said Turner. 'I've always found her very helpful. I'll see what light she can shine on this business of a trustee being a suspect.' He shot a glance at the clock again and gave an apologetic look. 'Sadly, I have to go. Children to say goodnight to. Got to keep in with the family.' He gave a chuckle and added: 'With all my charitable work I sometimes think they might forget who I am.'

The following morning as Dolly and Tess Tilly arrived for work at the Natural History Museum, they found Inspector Feather and Sergeant Cribbens waiting for them on the museum steps. Tess shrank back from the two men, but Dolly took her daughter firmly by the arm, intending to steer her towards the open main doors. However, the two women found their way blocked by the two policemen.

'Good morning,' said Feather. 'We need to ask you some more questions.'

'We're busy,' said Dolly, curtly. 'We've got work to do.'

'We can talk here, or we can take you back to Scotland Yard,' said Feather. 'It's up to you.'

'No,' moaned Tilly. 'Not there.'

The figure of Ada Watson appeared from inside the museum, brought out by Tilly's distress.

'What's going on?' she demanded.

'I'm Inspector Feather from Scotland Yard,' said Feather.

'Yes, I know who you are.' Ada scowled. 'What are you doing upsetting my workers?'

'We just need to ask them some questions.'

Ada Watson shot a look at Dolly, who shrugged.

'It's all right, Ada,' she said. 'We can deal with this.'

Ada looked back at Feather and Cribbens. 'They've got a job to do,' she said.

'So do I, ma'am,' said Feather. 'If you'd prefer me to take them away—'

'No,' said Ada, quickly. She looked at Dolly and Tess. 'You sure you're all right?'

'We're fine,' said Dolly.

Ada gave Feather and Cribbens a last sour look of disapproval before she moved off.

'It would be better inside,' said Feather. 'Too many interruptions if we stay here.'

Dolly marched into the museum, still with a grip on Tess's arm, and walked into the Grand Hall, the two policemen following them.

'Right,' said Dolly, aggressively, turning to glare at Feather. 'What do you want?'

'Raymond Simpson,' said Feather.

'We told you about him yesterday,' said Dolly. 'We didn't know him before he was here.'

'That's not what one of your neighbours says,' said Feather. 'She says that Simpson used to hang around on the stairs outside your home with your son, Tom, and some other boys. In fact, she called the police on them because they were making a nuisance. So, Raymond Simpson used to come to your place to hang around with your Tom.'

'He never came in the flat,' said Dolly.

'But you saw him on the stairs,' said Feather.

Dolly hesitated, then she gave a shrug and said: 'I might have. I didn't know who Tom was hanging about with. I didn't want to know. I didn't like 'em.'

'But Raymond Simpson must have knocked on your door at least once to call for Tom,' pressed Feather.

'Maybe he did,' said Dolly. 'I don't remember.'

'He did,' muttered Tess, in what was barely above a whisper. 'I opened the door. He didn't give his full name. Just asked if Tom was in. He said to tell him it was Raymond.' She looked at her mother in unhappy appeal. 'Remember, you came to the door to see who it was. You told him Tom wasn't in.'

'I can't remember, but I suppose I must have done,' said Dolly.

'But you saw him,' pushed Feather. 'You saw his face. You must have recognised him when he started here.'

'No,' said Dolly. 'The stairs are dark, and there's no gas lamp there; I didn't see his face properly. And I wasn't interested in the boys who used to come calling for Tom. They weren't a good crowd, and I told him so. That's why he left, in the end.'

Ada Watson reappeared. 'You still here?' she demanded crossly of Feather. 'We've got work to do. This place has to be cleaned and got ready for when the people come in.'

Feather nodded to her. 'We're just going,' he said. He turned back to Dolly and Tess. 'Thank you for that. We might need to talk to you again, so please don't go anywhere.'

'Where would we go?' demanded Dolly. 'We're either here, at home or shopping.'

Feather tipped his hat to them in goodbye, then walked off accompanied by Sergeant Cribbens.

'What do you think, sir?' asked Cribbens.

'I don't know,' admitted Feather. 'What they said sounds reasonable, but in this case, it seems to me that nearly everyone's covering up something.'

'Inspector.'

The two men stopped at the sound of the call and turned to see Miss Scott approaching them.

'Miss Scott?'

'I came in early to arrange some things before I travelled to Scotland Yard to see you.'

'Then it's fortunate we are here to save you the journey,' said Feather. 'I assume that Mr Wilson and Miss Fenton have told you about Mr Radley.'

'Indeed, they did. And also about your taking Mrs Tilly and her daughter in for questioning. Although I understand that they were later released.'

'They were, once we received the information about Mr Radley.'

'But I saw you talking to the Tillys just now.'

'We just needed to clarify something,' said Feather.

'And have you clarified it?'

'We have,' Feather confirmed.

'So, everything is satisfactory as far as Dolly and Tess Tilly are concerned?'

'At the moment we are satisfied that Mr Mason Radley should be our main course of enquiry,' replied Feather, diplomatically.

'You're sure it is he who was responsible for the murder of Raymond Simpson?'

'We won't be sure until we get the chance to talk to him,' said Feather. 'And, at the moment, that's difficult. We had a report that he'd left for India, but we can find no mention of him on any passenger lists that have sailed from these shores in the last few days.'

'Miss Scott!'

The booming voice cut through the museum and they turned to see Lady Fortescue bearing imperiously down on them, waving a sheet of paper.

'It looks as if someone else is after your attention,' said Feather. 'We shall leave you.'

'No,' said Scott. 'This is one of our trustees, Lady Elizabeth Fortescue, and what she has to say may have a bearing on the case.'

Feather forced a reluctant smile as they were joined by the obviously angry Lady Fortescue.

'Lady Fortescue, allow me to introduce Inspector Feather from Scotland Yard and his colleague, Sergeant Cribbens. They are investigating the death of young Mr Simpson.'

'And a complete hash they are making of it,' snapped Fortescue. She thrust the sheet of paper at Feather. 'Read this, Inspector. Aloud, please, so that Miss Scott is made aware of the contents. I received it through my letterbox yesterday evening.'

'"To the trustees of the Natural History Museum,"' read Feather. '"This is to inform you that we have taken over the matter of the dinosaur skeletons from Messrs Petter and Wardle. We must advise you that if you do not insist on removing all fossil remains not supplied by the Bone Company of America from your exhibition, personal retribution will result. You have been warned."' He frowned, puzzled. 'It's not signed, and there's no company name on it. Who's it from?'

'That is for you to find out!' thundered Fortescue. 'It is a threatening letter! Personal retribution will result. *Personal!* My safety is at risk!'

'May I keep this, Lady Fortescue?' asked Feather. 'We will examine it in detail at Scotland Yard and see if we can identify whoever has sent it.'

Fortescue hesitated and seemed on the point of reaching out and taking the letter back, but then she gave a disapproving sniff and nodded. 'Very well,' she said. 'But I insist on police protection. I am a widow, and as such I'm in a vulnerable situation.'

'I will certainly arrange that, Lady Fortescue. I assume Miss Scott has your address?'

'Yes, which is why I am here. I assume they can only have got hold of my address and the fact that I am a trustee through the museum. It shows a laxness, Miss Scott, that anyone can find out personal details and send out threatening letters in this way.'

'I can assure you, Lady Fortescue, the information about you did not come from within this museum,' said Scott.

'Where did they get it from, then?'

'The names of the trustees are a matter of public record,' said Scott. 'As most of them are people of high profile I should imagine it would not be difficult to find out their addresses.'

Lady Fortescue was obviously not appeased by this response, as she made clear.

'I find your reply fatuous and wrong,' she said, firmly. 'It is obvious to anyone that the museum must be held responsible for this. And that means you, Miss Scott. I will raise this matter at the next board meeting of the trustees.'

With that, she turned on her heel and marched off.

'Are all the trustees like that?' asked Feather.

'Fortunately not,' said Scott. She looked enquiringly at the inspector. 'What do you think? Do you consider the museum is responsible in any way for this letter?'

'As you rightly say, anyone could easily find out who the trustees of the museum are and their addresses,' said Feather. 'However, there has to be a question as to how they know about Petter and Wardle's involvement. How many people knew about their threatening letter?'

'At the museum, just myself and my secretary, Mrs Smith,' said Scott. 'Then Mr Wilson and Miss Fenton, and the police.'

Feather looked thoughtful. 'This latest letter suggests others were also aware,' he said.

'Well, obviously the people who sent it knew about it,' said Scott. 'This sounds very similar as a threat, so possibly it's the same people again.'

'Yes, indeed,' replied Feather. 'I was just thinking the same thing.'

As Feather and Cribbens left the museum, the sergeant

asked: 'So, do you think it's Petter and Wardle again, sir, up to their old tricks but using a different name?'

'If so, why isn't any name on the letterhead? This sort of extortion only works if people know who to pay.' He shook his head. 'There's something not right about this, Sergeant. In fact, there's lots that's not right about this case.'

'So, what are we going to do about it, sir?'

'There's a possibility that Erskine Petter has sold his scheme to extort money from the Natural History Museum on to someone else. I've known it happen before. So, we need to find out who he might have sold it to.'

'But Erskine Petter's done a runner, and no one knows where he is.'

'But we know where his partner is. I think we need to pay another visit to Wormwood Scrubs.'

CHAPTER TWENTY-TWO

Mrs Smith was at a filing cabinet putting recent correspondence into the correct files, when a tap at the door of her office and the sound of the door opening made her turn. She saw Dawson Turner enter, an extremely worried look on his face. His actions, too, were agitated.

'Mr Turner?' she said, concerned.

'I'm sorry to come here, but . . .' He faltered, and she asked apprehensively: 'Has something happened? At home?'

'With Emmeline?' he shook his head. 'No. I was at my club last evening and I met an old acquaintance of mine, Jefferson Thwaite, who's a newspaper man, and he was asking me about Raymond Simpson's death. According to him, he'd been told by someone he knows in the police that they believe one of the trustees was the person behind it. Is that the case, do you know?'

Smith hurried to the door, hesitated, then closed and locked it. 'I'm sorry, Dawson—' she began unhappily, and Turner, obviously shocked, interrupted to ask: 'Who?'

'Dawson, please. If I knew who it was, I'd tell you. But Miss Scott wouldn't tell me the name, just that there are rumours of blackmail.'

'Can't you find out?'

'I wish I could, but she's keeping it to herself. She's instructed me not to make any comments about it and that all enquiries are to go to her.'

Turner took her hands in his. 'My God, Penelope. This could ruin our plans. You know I have to wait until my knighthood is formalised before we can be properly together. Please, please, I beg you, try and find out who is being mentioned. Our happiness is at stake. We can't have this hanging over us.'

Inspector Feather and Sergeant Cribbens entered the duty office at Wormwood Scrubs and showed their warrant cards to the prison officer on duty.

'Good morning,' said Feather. 'We're here to see Benny Wardle.'

The officer shook his head. 'In that case, I'm afraid you're too late. Him and his brother, Billy, were released yesterday.'

'Yesterday?' echoed Feather.

The officer nodded. 'Every week the governor checks the release dates to see who's due to be let out and if there's anything against them. You know, reports of bad behaviour, that sort of thing, that could mean them being kept in for longer. But there was nothing against Benny and Billy Wardle, so yesterday they were released.'

'Was anyone here to meet them?'

The officer shook his head. 'No. They just put their own street clothes on, collected their belongings and went.'

'Did they say where they were going?'

'Back home, I expect.'

Feather turned to Cribbens, a look of annoyance on his face. 'Right, Sergeant. It's back to Paddington.'

As Daniel and Abigail arrived at the museum later that morning they saw the figure of Dawson Turner departing.

'Wasn't that the trustee?' asked Abigail. 'The one who was here when the body was found, who got the brush-off from Sir Henry Irving?'

'I'd hardly describe it as a brush-off,' said Daniel. 'Bram Stoker hurried them away. But yes, that was Dawson Turner. He was the one who claims he saw Mason Radley. I wonder what he's doing here?'

'Possibly catching up on the latest situation,' said Abigail. 'It's nice to see a trustee who takes their duties seriously. So many sit on boards just to get a step up the social ladder, either to get their hands on a knighthood or a safe seat in Parliament.'

They made their way to Miss Scott's office and found the curator at her desk.

'Good morning,' said Abigail. 'We're on our way to Scotland Yard to confer with Inspector Feather and see if there's any news about Mr Radley or anything else.'

'Inspector Feather was here earlier,' Miss Scott told them. 'He said he had further questions he needed to ask Dolly and Tess Tilly.'

'Oh?' said Daniel. 'What questions?'

'He didn't say,' said Scott. 'But he seemed satisfied with what they told him.'

Daniel and Abigail exchanged puzzled looks, then Daniel said: 'I'm sure, if there was anything amiss, he'll tell us when we see him.'

'There has been another development,' said Scott.

'Oh?'

'Lady Fortescue arrived with a letter that threatened her and the other trustees if the dinosaur skeletons weren't purchased from the Bone Company of America.'

Daniel frowned. 'The same as the first letter, the one from Petter and Wardle?'

'Yes. It even contained the same menacing phrase about retribution.'

'Did Lady Fortescue leave the letter with you?' asked Daniel. 'If so, may we see it?'

'Inspector Feather was here when she arrived, and he took it with him. He'll have it at Scotland Yard.'

'Interesting,' mused Daniel. 'Was that why Mr Turner was here? As a trustee, had he also received a similar letter?'

Scott frowned, puzzled. 'I wasn't aware that Mr Turner was here,' she said. 'He didn't come to see me.'

'We saw him leaving and thought he must have been with you,' said Daniel.

'Perhaps he saw Mrs Smith,' suggested Scott. 'He knows that she's aware of everything that goes on, and rather than disturb me he decided to take the letter to her.'

'Do you mind if we ask her?' asked Daniel.

'Not at all,' said Scott. 'We'll go along there now. But before we do, I have a favour to ask of you, Miss Fenton.'

Abigail looked at her quizzically. 'Of course, Miss Scott. If there's anything that I can do.'

'It's about our presentation on the work of Mary Anning next Wednesday.'

'Yes,' said Abigail. 'I'm very much looking forward to it.'

'The thing is, we'd arranged for someone who actually knew her to introduce the evening, a Mr Jonathan Ewing, but sadly I had a letter from his daughter to inform me that Mr Ewing has passed away.'

'Oh dear,' said Abigail. 'An accident?'

'The accident of passing years, I'm afraid,' said Scott. 'Don't forget, Mary Anning died almost fifty years ago. Mr Ewing was seventy-three and recently fell ill with pneumonia, which took its toll of him. Sadly, most people who actually knew her are also of a certain age, and most aren't willing to make the long journey from Lyme Regis to London. Would you do us the honour of introducing the evening?'

'I'm obviously flattered to be asked, but I'm not sure I'm the right person for this,' said Abigail. 'My area of expertise, as you know, is Egypt and the ancient Middle East. You really need a palaeontologist.'

'We have one, Cedric Warmsley from the British Museum, but to be frank, Miss Fenton, we are looking for what I believe is called in entertainment circles "the name on the marquee". Someone like Mr Ewing would have been of great interest, even if they were just introducing the evening and Mr Warmsley. But with Mr Ewing no longer available, and especially with such very short notice to find a replacement, and as you are here, the fact that noted Egyptologist Abigail Fenton will introduce the evening and act as chair for the questions from the audience after the talk will be a major attraction.'

'I fear you may have an inflated opinion of my reputation, especially if you want someone to be – as you call it – "the name on the marquee". I am not a celebrity.'

'Oh, but you are,' exclaimed Scott. 'And not just amongst the archaeological fraternity. I have heard your name uttered with reverence by academics and historians alike. Indeed, you are a celebrity, and as such there are many of the sort of people we would like to come to the talk who will come because *you* will be there.'

'Well . . .' began Abigail, uncertainly.

'Please say you will,' said Scott.

Abigail turned to look at Daniel and saw that he was smiling, enjoying her embarrassment. He nodded. 'I agree with Miss Scott. I can think of many people who would come here if they knew you were introducing the evening. Remember the old maxim: do not hide your light under a bushel.'

'That's settled, then.' Scott beamed.

Reluctantly, Abigail nodded, but with a glare at Daniel. 'If I am to do this, it would be a good idea if I were to meet with Mr Warmsley to make sure he is in agreement with my appearing at his talk in this way,' she said, still showing her uncertainty about accepting.

'Oh, he is emphatically in agreement,' Scott assured her. 'In fact, it was he who suggested you when I told him that Mr Ewing was no longer available. He knew you were here carrying out the investigation with Mr Wilson.'

'Very well,' said Abigail. 'In that case, I shall call on him at the British Museum and we can discuss the evening, and what he would like me to say.'

'Excellent!' said Scott. 'I shall send him a message to say you agree and that you will be calling on him. And now, shall we go and see Mrs Smith and find out if Mr Turner brought her a threatening letter that he'd received?'

Mrs Smith was at her desk, putting papers into order, when the door of her office opened to admit Miss Scott, Daniel and Abigail. Immediately, Smith rose to her feet.

'Do you wish to use the office?' she asked.

'No, no,' said Abigail. 'Just a question before we go to Scotland Yard.'

'Did Mr Turner happen to call on you just now?' asked Scott.

'Mr Turner?' said Smith, suddenly seeming agitated. 'No.'

Scott frowned and asked: 'He didn't come to tell us about a threatening letter he'd received, as a trustee? Only Lady Fortescue arrived this morning with such a letter addressed to her, and I assume other trustees must have had the same.'

'No,' said Smith. 'He didn't come in here.'

'Strange,' murmured Scott. 'He must have come to the museum for something else.'

As they left the secretary's office, Abigail said, with an apologetic smile, 'Excuse me a moment, there's something I need to check with Mrs Smith. I'll see you downstairs, Daniel.'

With that, she slipped back into the secretary's office.

'We'll go to see Inspector Feather at Scotland Yard and see if there's any news about Mason Radley,' said Daniel. 'At the same time, we'll try and get to the bottom of this latest threatening letter Lady Fortescue received.'

'Thank you, Mr Wilson,' said Scott. 'I must admit, this is all becoming rather more complicated than I thought.'

'Out of curiosity, is Mrs Smith married?' asked Daniel.

'Yes, although her husband is away at the moment and it seems he's going to be gone for a while. He's a sergeant in the army and has been in South Africa for almost a year. Why?'

Daniel smiled. 'No reason. I like to know about other people when I'm on a case. Force of habit, too many years a detective. Though Miss Fenton calls it nosiness on my part.'

They shook hands, and Daniel headed downstairs.

Inside the secretary's office, Abigail approached Mrs Smith, a look of gentle concern on her face.

'Forgive my intrusion,' said Abigail, 'but I couldn't help but notice your distress when Miss Scott asked if Mr Turner had been here.'

'Distress?' asked Smith, nervously.

'Mrs Smith, as one woman to another, I recognise the signs,' said Abigail, again keeping her tone sympathetic. 'For some reason you didn't want Miss Scott to know that Mr Turner had been here to see you.'

The way Mrs Smith looked at her reminded Abigail of a frightened rabbit.

'Was it because he didn't want Miss Scott to think he might be a nuisance to her if he called in to ask how the investigation is going?'

'Yes,' burst out Smith, in obvious relief. 'Yes, that's exactly it. He's such a good man and he knows how busy Miss Scott is . . .'

'And he asked you to keep his visit here secret.'

'For the moment,' said Smith.

'What did he want to know?'

'As you said, how the investigation was going.'

'And were you able to help him?'

Smith shook her head. 'No. I told him there was nothing new, to my knowledge. I didn't know about this latest threatening letter that Lady Fortescue had received until Miss Scott mentioned it just now. Mr Turner certainly didn't say if he'd had one.'

'Thank you,' said Abigail. 'And I can assure you your secret is safe with me. I won't tell Miss Scott that Mr Turner was here.'

Daniel and Abigail both waited until they'd left the museum before they talked about Mrs Smith. It was Daniel who raised the matter first.

'What did you make of Mrs Smith's response when Miss Scott asked her if Mr Turner had called on her?' he asked.

'She lied,' said Abigail.

'And that's why you went back to talk to her?'

'Yes,' said Abigail.

'And what did she say?'

'I gave her an out. I suggested she was covering up for Mr Turner because Miss Scott might think he was a nuisance if she found out he'd called to see how the investigation was going.'

'And she fell on that?'

'With great gratitude. Which made me even surer that there was something else going on.'

'You think she's having a relationship with him, don't you?' said Daniel.

'I do,' said Abigail.

'So do I,' said Daniel. 'Her reaction was that of a guilty person, but one who's not used to lying.'

'I agree. She was caught off guard and got flustered,' said Abigail. 'The question is: is the fact they're having an affair relevant to the murder enquiry?'

'I can't see it is,' admitted Daniel. 'But then, sometimes any investigation is like a jigsaw puzzle. You don't know which are the important pieces until you start to get the whole picture.'

CHAPTER TWENTY-THREE

Inspector Feather and Sergeant Cribbens stood in the small, cramped storeroom behind the grocer's in Paddington and watched Arnold Pinder as he shook his head.

'No, Inspector. I've no idea where Benny and Billy have gone. They turned up to collect some stuff they left here with me when they went away, and that was it.'

'They didn't give any idea where they were going?'

'No.'

'What about their old rooms upstairs?'

'Rented out to a couple of blokes who work on the railway.'

'Nothing of theirs was left in them?'

Pinder shook his head. 'Nothing. They left a suitcase with me which had some clothes in, and I put it in the storeroom here for safe keeping. That was what they picked up when they come here.'

'Were they surprised to find you still had it?' asked Feather. 'Most people would have taken it down the pop shop and got some money for it.'

Pinder gave a grin. 'Only people who don't know Benny and Billy. I gave 'em my word I'd keep it for 'em. You don't want to break a promise to the Wardle brothers; they get a bit annoyed. And when they get annoyed, people get hurt.'

Outside the shop, Feather and Cribbens took stock of the situation.

'What shall we do next, guv'nor?' asked Cribbens.

'If Benny and Billy run true to form, they won't go far,' mused Feather. 'This is their patch. The best thing is for you to go along to Paddington nick, see your old pal there and ask him to keep his eyes and ears open for them. He might even have word about them.'

Cribbens nodded. 'If anyone knows what goes on in Paddington it's Jim Bunn. Are you coming with me, sir?'

'No, I'd better get back to the Yard and report to the superintendent, tell him about this latest threatening letter. I'll see you there later.'

Feather stepped into the police carriage waiting outside the grocer's and headed back to Scotland Yard. A message from Superintendent Armstrong was waiting for him on his desk: *See me*.

Superintendent Armstrong was reading a newspaper when Feather knocked at his office door and walked in.

'You wanted to see me, sir?'

Armstrong scowled and pushed the newspaper aside. 'The papers are getting on our backs about this Natural History Museum killing, Inspector. Accusing us of not doing our job properly because we haven't got anyone in custody. What's happening?'

'I was at the museum early this morning, sir. One of the trustees has received a threatening letter similar to the one the museum was sent, just before the dinosaur skeleton was smashed. It repeats the threat of retribution of some kind unless the skeletons are bought from this Bone Company.'

'Skeletons?' burst out the superintendent angrily. 'We're not concerned with dinosaur skeletons, Inspector. That's not what the commissioner and the public are interested in with this case. They want to know we've caught a murderer. What about this Mason Radley leaving for India? Anything on ship manifests, passenger lists?'

'No, sir. We checked and we've not been able find his name on any ships bound for India.'

'Maybe he didn't go directly to India. He could have got any ship across the Channel and gone from France or Belgium.'

'Yes, sir, I thought of that, so I had Sergeant Cribbens check the passenger lists of all ships leaving Britain for the last three days. No Mason Radley anywhere.'

'He could have used a false name.'

'He could, although my hunch is that he's still somewhere in England.'

'Where?'

Feather gave a sigh. 'If we knew that, sir—'

'Yes, all right,' scowled Armstrong. 'It's not good enough, Feather. If the commissioner asks me for an update and the best I can say is that he's out there somewhere in hiding and we just have to wait till we can lay hands on him, he's not going to be pleased.'

'No, sir,' agreed Feather.

'We need to be doing something while we search for Radley. Something that shows we're looking into it properly and not letting the grass grow under our feet.'

'What do you suggest, sir?'

Armstrong look thoughtful, then he announced: 'I'm still sure there's something in this connected with Wilde.'

Feather looked doubtful. 'With respect, sir, I feel that looking for this Mason Radley would be a better use of our energies.'

'Yes, but it gets us nowhere if we don't find him. We need to be *seen* to be doing something. Something else. Looking at another avenue of the investigation. We know that Simpson tried to blackmail Wilde.'

'He blackmailed other people as well, sir, including Mason Radley.'

'And who's to say he didn't blackmail some other people who were associated with Wilde?'

'He may well have done, sir, but—'

'No buts, Inspector. If I'm asked by the commissioner, I need to tell him something. Yes, we're looking for this Mason Radley, but we're also pursuing our investigations into other possible blackmail victims. We know Simpson was involved with the circle who hung around Wilde, not just because of Wilde himself but the one who killed himself.'

'Tom Tilly.'

'Exactly. Revenge could be a motive, as well as getting rid of a blackmailer. That's the other area I shall tell the commissioner we're exploring.'

'Yes, sir.'

'We need to see Wilde. Get some names off him. Men in his

circle who Simpson might have been blackmailing.'

'I can't see him giving us any of those sort of names, sir.'

'He will if we make it worth his while. By all accounts, he's having a bad time of it in prison. Where is he? Still in Pentonville?'

'Wandsworth, sir. He was moved there in July.'

Armstrong nodded. 'Conditions there are just as harsh. Hard labour. Picking oakum. The treadmill. I've even heard a rumour he may not last his term if his health keeps failing the way it is. Offer him something. Go and see him and tell him we'll make his time in prison more comfortable if he gives us a name or two.'

'Me, sir?'

Armstrong scowled. 'He won't talk to me. He doesn't like me. I think he'd rather die than give me anything. But you, Inspector, he had a different attitude to you. He might talk to you.'

'But, sir—' began Feather.

'Wilde,' repeated Armstrong, firmly. 'Get some names off him. They may not add up to anything, but we'll be seen to be doing something rather than just waiting.'

Feather headed back to his office, a feeling of gloom hanging over him. They were getting nowhere, and this business of going to see Wilde was just window dressing. His gloom lifted slightly as he saw Daniel and Abigail standing outside his office, obviously waiting for him.

'Morning, John,' Daniel greeted him. 'We were informed that you were seen going into the superintendent's office, so we thought we'd wait. Have you got a moment?'

'I have,' said Feather. 'Come in.'

He opened the door, and they followed him in.

'No Sergeant Cribbens and his infamous pipe tobacco today?' asked Abigail.

'He's in Paddington looking for Benny and Billy Wardle.'

'I thought they were in prison,' said Daniel.

'Released yesterday.' Feather sighed. 'I went looking for them earlier after this latest letter came to light.'

'The one about the Bone Company. Yes, that's why we're here. Miss Scott told us about it.'

Feather took the letter from his pocket and handed it to Daniel, who read it and then passed it to Abigail.

'It's very strange,' said Daniel, thoughtfully. 'It doesn't say who it's from. There's no name and address, just the mention of Petter and Wardle, and the Bone Company. If they were asking for money, there's no way it can be paid to them, not with the offices of Petter and Wardle shut up. So, what's the point of it?'

'Which is why I wanted to have a word with Benny Wardle, see if he could throw any light on it,' said Feather. 'As far as I know, according to Miss Scott, the only people who knew about the original threatening letter from Petter and Wardle apart from yourselves were her and her secretary, and Erskine Petter himself. Benny Wardle claimed to know nothing about it when I first saw him. So, whoever sent this letter has inside knowledge.'

'It could be Erskine Petter behind it,' suggested Daniel. 'If he's in hiding somewhere he'll need money, and maybe he's setting something up. Perhaps he's got someone else involved on his behalf on a promise of them sharing the money, but remembering what happened to him before with the police turning up at his office, he's keeping this partner's name and address under wraps for the moment.'

'That's possible,' said Feather, thoughtfully.

'Any news on Mason Radley?' asked Abigail.

Feather let out a heavy sigh. 'The superintendent just asked me the same. The short answer is no. We've checked the passenger lists for sailings in the last few days to India, and there's no Mason Radley,' said Feather.

'He could be using a false name,' said Daniel. 'Or have gone somewhere else before travelling on to India.'

'Yes, we've thought of that, but so far nothing pops up.' He looked at Daniel unhappily. 'Which brings me to the superintendent's latest instruction: Oscar Wilde.'

'What about him?' asked Daniel.

'He wants me to go and see him, to ask him to give up the names of people he knows who might have been blackmailed by Raymond Simpson.'

Abigail and Daniel stared at him.

'That's ridiculous,' said Abigail. 'Raymond Simpson must have been killed by someone who was at the museum early that morning, and so far the person who best fits the bill because he was there at that time, and who we know was being blackmailed by Simpson, is Mason Radley.'

'Agreed,' said Feather. 'But the superintendent has got the commissioner on his back and says we can't just wait for Radley to be found, we have to be seen to be doing something active. And that's to go and see Wilde in prison.' He looked at Daniel, and then appealed to him: 'But I can't see him talking to me. I'm still the police, whatever Armstrong says. But you, Daniel, he might talk to you. You have a way of getting people to talk.'

Daniel shook his head. 'I can't see him talking to me, either, to be honest, John. Why would he?'

'Armstrong wants to offer him inducements. Make his life in prison easier if he gives us names.'

'I don't think Wilde is that sort of person,' said Daniel. 'For all his aesthetic posing, he's tougher than people give him credit for.'

'There is one person he might talk to,' put in Abigail. 'Bram Stoker.'

'Stoker?' Feather shook his head. 'He won't do it, and even if he did, he wouldn't pass on to the police whatever Wilde says. He's angry.'

'He was all right with us,' said Abigail. 'In fact, he was quite complimentary about Daniel.'

'Then why don't we try that?' asked Feather. 'You ask Stoker if he'd go with us to talk to Wilde. I'd have to be part of it so we can get admission to him. He can't just get visitors willy-nilly, he's doing hard labour, remember.'

'What about Abigail?' asked Daniel. 'Stoker seemed very impressed with her. He might do it if she comes.'

Feather shook his head. 'She won't be allowed in. Sorry, Daniel.'

'So, you're suggesting you, me and Stoker go.'

'I have to be there to get us in. Wilde won't talk to me, and I have my doubts if he'll talk to you. He'll definitely talk to Stoker. But Stoker won't come as part of a police party unless *you* ask him and tell him you'll be there. And, emphatically, that Superintendent Armstrong won't be.'

CHAPTER TWENTY-FOUR

William Watling lay between the silk sheets and from his bed admired Elizabeth Fortescue as she pulled on her clothes, the bright daylight sun streaming through the gap in the curtains illuminating her body. God, she was a handsome woman. And ferocious in bed. No wonder her husband had shot himself. Impotent. Couldn't get it up. That's what Elizabeth had told him their first time. He thought he'd been the one doing the seducing, but she'd been an equal party to it. More than equal. On reflection he wasn't sure if it hadn't been her who'd taken the initiative, but in a clever way, making him think she was responding to his overtures. But he couldn't recall making any overtures to her. He'd fancied her, of course, and fantasised about taking her to bed. But then he did that with nearly every woman he met, though most never became reality. But

Elizabeth had been real. Seriously, amorously, ferociously so.

Watling had become alarmed when he discovered that her husband, Lord Fortescue, had learnt about their affair. Who'd told him? He suspected Elizabeth herself had done the deed to rub her husband's nose in the fact that he was a failure as a husband. He remembered thinking: *Was that why he'd killed himself?*

Officially, it had been an accident while cleaning his rifle. Poppycock, of course, because Fortescue knew more about guns than almost any man alive; he'd have treated them with respect. More respect than he showed his wife, certainly. But everyone had done the decent thing, had accepted it was an accident.

And then had come the chilling moment when Elizabeth had murmured to him while they were in bed: 'Well, I've got rid of mine, now it's up to you to get rid of yours.'

At first, he thought she'd meant that she was free as a result of her husband's suicide, but then, as her hints became more outspoken, he began to realise it hadn't been suicide at all. Elizabeth had pulled the trigger that had ended her husband's life. And now she expected him to do the same with Mirabel. Not shoot her, that would never be believed to be a suicide, but some way that wouldn't be suspect.

'I can't do it,' he'd told her.

'I did,' she said. 'I did it for you, so that we could be together. You said you wanted that.'

'I do,' he said. 'But—'

'The "but",' she told him, firmly, 'is that if people suspect that my husband didn't shoot himself, then they will be looking at someone else as the culprit. And that someone else won't be me. After all, I'm just a woman, someone who doesn't

218

understand firearms. But you, William, you are known to be a good shot. My husband used to tell me what a good shot you were. I wonder if he said it to other people?' She'd smiled. 'So much easier if people didn't ask those questions. And they won't ask them of a man who's grieving because he's just lost his wife.'

And so, it had been done. He hadn't needed to pretend at being bereft when Mirabel had died; he'd always thought well of her, in her way. She'd been a useful companion. Not very exciting, but she'd never demanded anything of him. She tolerated his activities outside of their marriage. And now he was to have a new wife, once the decent interval had passed after the deaths of their respective spouses. And providing no one started poking around in their affairs. Which is why he needed to tell Elizabeth about the visit from this Wilson chap and that Fenton woman. She'd need to be on her guard as well.

'I had a visit from that interfering pair Miss Scott has hired to investigate the murder of the attendant,' he said. 'Former policeman, Daniel Wilson, and that arrogant woman who calls herself an archaeologist, Fenton.'

'Abigail Fenton,' said Fortescue as she examined her face in the dressing-table mirror.

'Yes, that's her.' His face darkened as he almost spat out the words: 'They had the nerve to accuse me of being involved in the death of Danvers Hardwicke.'

'No.' Lady Fortescue stopped her ministrations and stared at him, horrified. 'They actually accused you?'

'Not in so many words. They said it was possible his death was deliberate, then added the word "suicide". But I knew what they meant.'

219

'You should sue them for slander. They mustn't be allowed to get away with this. I shall see Miss Scott and register a complaint. I shall insist she dismiss them.'

'No,' said Watling, quickly. 'The police know there's nothing in it. That it was an accident. But the last thing we need is someone stirring things up. Mud sticks, and I can't afford to have people gossiping about me. Especially if we can get rid of Miss Scott. I don't want anything standing in my way when the curator's post becomes free.'

'But we must do something,' Lady Fortescue appealed to him. 'We can't allow these dreadful people to get away with this. Who knows who else they may have talked to? And who knows what they might start digging up?'

Watling nodded, thoughtfully. 'Yes, I will do something.'

'What?' asked Fortescue.

Watling smiled at her. 'Leave that to me, my dear. But I will take action that will stop their filthy, slanderous tongues.'

Bram Stoker studied Daniel from the other side of his desk in his office at the Lyceum, and Daniel could see from his scowl of outrage the indignation the theatre's business manager felt at what he'd just been asked.

'Let me make sure I've got this straight,' he said, his eyes boring into Daniel's. 'You want me to come with you to Wandsworth Prison as part of a police plot to try and force Oscar to give you the names of other people that Simpson may have been blackmailing.'

'Not force,' clarified Daniel, '*ask* if he has any ideas as to the murderer.'

Stoker shook his head, firmly. 'Your suggestion is not only outrageous, it is an insult. You want me to join you and bigots like Superintendent Armstrong—'

'Superintendent Armstrong will not be there,' said Daniel. 'He will have no part in this. It will be just you, me and Inspector Feather.'

'Why do you feel you need me there?'

'Because we consider it more likely that Mr Wilde will agree to talk to us if there is someone there he trusts.'

'So, you want me to betray my friend. Act as Judas for you.'

'We have been advised that we can offer Mr Wilde better conditions while he is in prison if he is able to help us. You have met both me and Inspector Feather, and we hope you agree that we are honourable men who will make sure any promises made are kept.'

'Oscar won't give you any names.'

'That's quite likely,' agreed Daniel. 'But we have been tasked with asking him. The decision whether he helps us will be his. Our hope is that your presence will help to create a less hostile atmosphere between us. You have no need to endorse what we say. In fact, we will be happy for you to make your position clear to him that you opposed the idea of the meeting. He will then know he has at least one ally in the room.'

Stoker studied Daniel, exploring his face for signs of hypocrisy or deviousness. Finally, appearing close to relenting, he asked: 'Can you give me one reason why I should help the police, especially when one considers the way they persecuted Oscar?'

'Because it will give you a chance to visit your friend,' said Daniel. 'I believe tickets granting visitation rights to him aren't readily available. I understand there is a waiting list.'

Stoker fell silent, his eyes fixed on Daniel. Then he nodded.

'You are right, Mr Wilson,' he acknowledged. 'I should have made an effort to visit Oscar, but the idea of seeing him in those surroundings is something I've found difficult to cope with. And I've used the fact that others have already arranged to visit him as an excuse, because – as you rightly say – he is only permitted a very limited number of visitors, and even then at tragically long intervals. I shall accompany you and Inspector Feather.' Then, to clarify, he asked: 'You are certain that Superintendent Armstrong will not be there?'

'I can assure you that he definitely will not be there with us. As I said before it'll be just you, me and Inspector Feather.'

'When do you intend to go?'

'This afternoon. I suggest that we pick you up here at the Lyceum and travel there together. Is that acceptable to you?'

'It's inconvenient because we have a matinee performance this afternoon,' said Stoker. 'Saturdays, you know. However, this way it will save me having to explain my presence to some bloody-minded and obstructive warder if I arrived at the prison on my own. I understand some are being obstructive about letting Wilde see his visitors.'

'Thank you, Mr Stoker,' said Daniel. He stood up. 'I'll see you this afternoon.'

Nora Simpson stood in the empty living room. It wasn't just the living room that was empty, the whole house was bare. Well, that would change as soon as the carters arrived today with her furniture. And if they didn't, she'd go round to Alf Dobbs's house and give him a piece of her mind he wouldn't forget in a hurry.

It was a terrible thing, to be forced out of the home she'd lived in for so many years. It was all the fault of her late husband, George, dying like that and leaving her penniless. It had been fortunate for her that Raymond had been in work at the time and had brought in some money, though only enough for them to get by; there had been no money for little extras. Until one day, Raymond had arrived home with a five-pound note. 'A bonus', he'd called it.

Five pounds. A fortune. Nora hadn't asked what he'd been given the bonus for, she'd just taken it gratefully. And then, at intervals, Raymond had handed over other money he'd received, some as bonuses, others, he told her, were presents. She didn't ask why people were giving him money as presents, that was his business. The truth was that for the first time in her life she was able to afford nice things for the house, good furniture. And new, not shabby second-hand as it had been with George.

And then that policeman had called with the terrible news about Raymond dying. Being killed. Was that because of the presents and bonuses? She'd warned him once when he came home with a particularly large sum of money to be careful. 'Some people might get worried about giving you this money,' she said. 'They might get upset. And upset people can do bad things.'

'Don't worry, Mum,' he'd reassured her. 'I know what I'm doing.'

And now he was dead, and because of that nosey policeman she'd been forced to move home. Luckily, she still had some of the money that Raymond had given her squirrelled away. With Raymond gone, she'd have to be more careful in the future. It did occur to her to find out the names of some of the people who'd given Raymond money. He'd mentioned a few, but she hadn't wanted to ask too much. That way, if things went wrong and he was caught out, she could always deny any knowledge of what he'd been up to. But now things had changed. Raymond was gone, and so was her source of income. It was time to rack her brains for those names he'd mentioned. Only one or two, but if she dug deep she might find out about the others. Then she'd go and see them, tell them that Raymond had told her she was to see them if anything happened to him. It was worth a try.

There was a knock at the door. That would be the carters with her furniture, she thought in relief as she went to the door. When she hadn't heard anything back from Mr Dobbs, she'd wondered if he'd got it organised. He'd been a decent enough landlord, but sometimes he'd struck her as not the most efficient of men. Except when it came to collecting his rent. But then, she had only written to him two days before.

She opened the door and gasped as she recognised the man standing there. That detective inspector from Scotland Yard! And he was with another man, different from the one he'd turned up with at her old house, but this other one was also a policeman, she could tell.

'Mrs Simpson,' he greeted her. 'Detective Inspector Feather from Scotland Yard. We met before. This is Detective Sergeant Cribbens.'

'I've nothing to say to you,' she burst out. She began to close the door, but Feather stuck his boot in.

'We can talk here, or I can have you taken to Scotland Yard,' said Feather. 'In handcuffs if you resist. I can't see your new neighbours being impressed by that, if it happens.'

Simpson glared at him with such hatred that if looks could kill he would have dropped dead on the spot. Instead, she grudgingly opened the door and let them in.

'I hope this won't take long. I'm expecting the carters with my furniture.'

'I also hope it won't take long, Mrs Simpson,' said Feather. 'We want to find the person who killed your son. I'm assuming you want the same thing.'

'Of course I do. He was everything to me.'

'We know he was blackmailing people,' said Feather. 'We need to know the names of his victims because it's likely that one of them may have been his murderer.'

She shook her head. 'I don't know anything about that,' she said, defiantly. 'As far as I was concerned he was a good boy.'

'A good boy to you because he gave you the money to buy all your furniture and everything else,' said Feather, firmly.

'And thank heavens he did!' shouted Mrs Simpson, angrily. 'When my George died he left me with nothing. Absolutely nothing. I was faced with going into the workhouse.'

'Well, let me tell you, Mrs Simpson, that unless you cooperate I'll have all this furniture and everything else you own impounded because it was bought with the proceeds of crime,' said Feather.

'It wasn't. You can't do that.'

'We have proof he was blackmailing people,' said Feather. 'And yes, I can. I'll have this house stripped and you'll end up a pauper, in the workhouse after all. So, what's it to be, Mrs Simpson?'

'If I knew I'd tell you,' she retorted, angrily. 'And not just for the furniture and other stuff, but because someone killed my son. I want justice for him.'

'So, tell me who the people were he was blackmailing.'

'He never told me,' said Simpson. 'He kept his business dealings away from me. He didn't want me to get in trouble.'

'But you are in trouble, Mrs Simpson,' said Feather. 'I can have you arrested for receiving money from the proceeds of blackmail—'

'He never told me their names!' she shouted at him. 'Lately he said that one of them was a trustee at the museum where he worked. He said he had something good on them which was worth a lot of money. And that's the most he ever said. I swear it. You can arrest me and put me in prison, or take everything and put me in the workhouse, but it won't change anything. He never said any names.'

There was a knock on the door. Feather opened it and saw a short man wearing brown overalls standing on the doorstep.

The man beamed. 'Blooms the Carters, with furniture for Mrs Simpson.'

Feather nodded and turned to Simpson. 'Your things have arrived,' he said. 'We'll leave you now. But if you do remember any names, or anything at all, come and see me at the Yard.'

As Feather and Cribbens left the house, Sergeant Cribbens asked: 'Was that right about taking her furniture, sir? I didn't know that.'

Feather shook his head. 'No, and neither does she. I tried that because it's pretty obvious the only thing she cares about is money and her possessions, so it was the only lever I had left.'

'So, one of the trustees, she says. Would that be Mr Radley, do you suppose? The one who's done a runner?'

'Unless he was blackmailing more than one of them. But for the moment, let's be staying with Mason Radley, and let's hope we can lay our hands on him.'

CHAPTER TWENTY-FIVE

Daniel and Inspector Feather sat in the hansom cab as they headed for the Lyceum to collect Bram Stoker.

'I'm surprised you persuaded him to agree to come with us,' said Feather. 'I never thought he would.'

'It gives him the opportunity to see his old friend,' said Daniel.

'Which makes me wonder why he hasn't been to see him already,' commented Feather.

'I think he finds the idea of Wilde in prison in those conditions difficult,' said Daniel. 'How did you get on with Mrs Simpson? Was she there when you went to the house?'

'She was and initially reluctant to talk to me. But she did in the end, although she claimed she didn't know much about her son's blackmail victims.'

'You believe her?'

'I think I do,' said Feather. 'I threatened her with taking her furniture away, leaving her destitute and forced into the workhouse. So, finally, she said the only one Raymond had mentioned to her was a trustee of the Natural History Museum, but he never told her their name. From what we know, he was obviously referring to Mason Radley.'

'Maybe there was more than one trustee who was a victim of his,' suggested Daniel. 'Yes, he was blackmailing Radley, and the fact that Radley's disappeared makes him our main suspect. But Lady Fortescue is also a trustee. Say he found out that she had a role in her husband's death, whether murder or suicide, so he tries putting the screws on her. But she tells her paramour, William Watling, and he kills Simpson.'

Feather shook his head. 'You've got a bee in your bonnet about Watling, Daniel, but nothing to back it up.'

'It's likely he killed Hardwicke.'

'But equally as likely he didn't. That it was an accident, just as he said.'

'He lied about not being able to swim. He could have jumped in and saved him.'

'Into that muck? That's not water in the canal, it's more like a swamp,' said Feather. 'I agree with you it's possible that Simpson may have been referring to some other trustee, but I can't see it being Lady Fortescue. She strikes me as being the sort of person who'd have eaten Simpson alive if he dared to try to blackmail her.' He looked out of the window. 'We're here. Let's hope that Mr Stoker is ready for us.'

* * *

Cedric Warmsley, a tall, thin man in his late twenties, was waiting for Abigail by the reception desk at the British Museum. He looked so delighted at seeing her, so eager to please, that he reminded Abigail of a large puppy one of her neighbours in Cambridge had, who used to greet her with a similar happy expression on his face whenever she arrived on a visit.

'Miss Fenton,' he said and clasped her hand in momentary excitement before releasing it almost apologetically. 'I cannot tell you what a great privilege this is to be working with you. I have admired your work for so very long. Although palaeontology is my area, I have spent so much of my time here at the British Museum in the classical rooms exploring the Roman and Greek, and especially in the Egyptian rooms, so I know all about your work.'

Abigail smiled. 'You flatter me, Mr Warmsley. I was just one worker among many out at the digs, very much an assistant.'

'That's not what I've been told when your name has come up in discussion with archaeologists who were also on those sites.'

'I'm sure they were just being kind,' said Abigail. 'To be honest, Mr Warmsley, I feel a bit of a fraud to be introducing your talk. I am awed by palaeontology, but it is so far removed from my own area of work – by many, many thousands of years and in some cases millions – that I wonder you agreed to my being invited to introduce you.'

'On the contrary,' said Warmsley, enthusiastically, 'when Miss Scott advised me that Mr Ewing was unavailable, because I knew from the newspapers that you and Mr Wilson were at the Natural History Museum investigating this outrage, it was I who had the presumption to ask her to invite you. My reasons were twofold. First, your name would bring in a much larger number of people because I'm sure that more people have heard of you and your reputation than they have of Mary Anning. And secondly, because I was keen to meet you and hear from your own lips about some of your adventures.'

'If it's true what you say about her being not as well known as she should be, then I am delighted if my presence can help redress that situation. As to my own adventures, I doubt if my discoveries from a few thousand years ago can compare with those you have uncovered from far further back in time. When I see the skeletons of the dinosaurs . . .'

'Ah, the dinosaurs,' said Warmsley, with a rueful tone to his voice. 'Alas, my own area is much more akin to that of Anning: marine fossils. I, too, have spent time on the coast of Dorset, following in her footsteps and unearthing the remains of marine creatures from 200 million years ago, and each time I unearth a specimen, especially if it is large and well-preserved, I can't help but feel a tremor of excitement that surges through my whole being. Much the same, I expect, as when you enter into a pyramid for the first time, one that hasn't been opened for many thousands of years, and you are actually touching the distant past.'

'I couldn't have put it better myself, Mr Warmsley,' said Abigail. She became aware that a small crowd had gathered, drawn by Warmsley's excitable manner, and were now watching them as if waiting for this interesting performance to continue. Warmsley also became aware of the watching audience because he gave an apologetic smile to Abigail.

'Perhaps it would be better if we repaired to my office,' he said. 'I share it with another palaeontologist, Jeffrey Withers, but it will afford us more privacy than we have here.' He gestured towards a nearby flight of stairs. 'Please, this way.'

Stoker was silent on their journey to Wandsworth Prison. *He's nervous*, decided Daniel, studying him. *Apprehensive at what we'll find, especially with rumours about Wilde's health in circulation.*

At Wandsworth they were shown into a starkly bare room. Three chairs had been placed in it ready for them. Running across the room was a barrier of iron bars, separating them from the other half, effectively a large prison cell. A lone wooden bench was there, fixed to the flagstones of the floor. A door to one side of this cell opened and two warders appeared, leading a tall, gaunt-looking man in a stained prison uniform. The warders sat the man down on the bench, then stepped back so that they were separate from him but within touching distance.

At first Daniel didn't recognise the man on the bench as Oscar Wilde. But then, he'd never seen the man in person. He looked towards Stoker, who stared at Wilde in a state of shock.

'My God, Oscar! What have they done to you?' he asked, hoarsely, in horror.

Daniel had seen enough pictures of Wilde in the newspapers to know that this haggard wreck sitting behind the bars was vastly different from the popular image of Oscar Wilde, ostentatious playwright, aesthete and man about town. The Oscar Wilde of the newspapers and magazines was large and fleshy, usually seen wearing velvet clothes, his long hair curling over his collar, and his face and hands beautifully and sensitively cared for. The man sitting looking at them was almost skeletal, the sunken hollows of his cheeks made more pronounced by his hair having been cropped in the prison fashion. His ill-fitting uniform hung from his thin frame in folds of cloth. His wisp of an almost beard only heightened the sickly pallor of his face.

'I have been ill,' said Wilde.

'Has a doctor seen you?'

Wilde gave a hollow laugh. As he spoke the once great voice that resonated around theatres, and even in court, was reedy, strained.

'The doctor says there is nothing wrong with me. He says I am suffering from diarrhoea, which is common in here. But then, the food is barely edible.' He forced a smile at Stoker. 'How are you, Bram? It's a while since we met.'

'Yes,' said Stoker, uncomfortably. 'I had intended to arrange a visit, but—'

'The Lyceum and Sir Henry. I understand. I'm sure I would have been the same if our positions had been reversed.'

'No, Oscar, you would not,' said Stoker, firmly. 'I have not been the friend to you I should have been.'

'But you are here now. With others.' Wilde looked quizzically at Daniel. 'I am familiar with Inspector Feather, but you, sir, are new to me. Are you another policeman?'

'I was,' said Daniel. 'My name is Daniel Wilson. I was formerly with Inspector Abberline's squad at Scotland Yard, but now I'm a private enquiry agent.'

'Abberline. The Cleveland Street Scandal. And, of course, the Jack the Ripper investigation.'

Suddenly, Stoker reached out to point to Wilde's hands and exclaimed in horror.

'Your hands, Oscar!'

Wilde looked at his hands with an almost distant expression. His fingers and thumbs were disfigured and scarred with blisters, the skin blackened, his nails broken. 'The price of picking oakum,' he said, wryly. He looked challengingly at his three visitors. 'Have any of you gentlemen ever picked oakum?'

'Yes,' replied Daniel, quietly.

The eyes of the three men turned to Daniel; Stoker's and Feather's faces both stunned, Wilde's curious.

'As a policeman I doubt if you were ever imprisoned. Nor, I believe, did you serve in the navy. You lack the tattoos of most ex-naval men I've met. Therefore, it must have been as a child.' He paused, then asked: 'The workhouse?'

'Yes,' said Daniel.

Wilde rose to his feet and made a bow to Daniel, before sitting again.

'Mr Wilson, you have my greatest respect and admiration,' he said. 'Mr Stoker and I, we came from privilege. Lives of luxury and high company. Why, Bram here even has electric lighting in his house in Bloomsbury. But you, sir, must have fought every inch for the position you've achieved. It will be my pleasure to answer any questions you may ask. I assume that is why you are here.'

'It is,' said Daniel. 'The Natural History Museum has engaged myself and my partner, Miss Abigail Fenton, to look into the murder of a young attendant called Raymond Simpson.'

'Raymond Simpson?' echoed Wilde, and he shot a glance towards Stoker, who nodded and said, 'The same.'

'So, someone has killed him,' said Wilde. 'Everything comes to those who wait. When did this happen?'

'A few days ago, at the museum.'

'Ah, then I have an alibi,' said Wilde, and he indicated the prison walls and the bars.

'We understand he tried to blackmail you,' said Feather.

'He tried,' said Wilde. 'I told him to do his worst.' Again, he looked at his grim surroundings. 'And he did.'

'We feel it's possible that his killer may have been another of his blackmail victims,' said Feather. 'We wondered if you would consider furnishing us with the names of some of those victims. Those that you may know of.'

'Why on earth would I do that?' demanded Wilde.

'To get an easing in the severity of your imprisonment,' said Feather. 'I've been authorised to tell you that if you were able to cooperate with us, there could be a reduction in the hardship you are experiencing.' He hesitated, before enlarging: 'No more picking oakum. No more time on the treadmill.'

'What a pity,' said Wilde, with a wry smile. 'Two of the things that help keep me fit and ease the boredom.' Then he looked at Feather levelly. 'You must know that my answer is, of course, no. Many of my former friends appear to have deserted me, but I would not do them the disservice of having them dragged in for interrogation and their reputations ruined. I have had that experience, and for those who were unfortunate enough to have to hide their true feelings to avoid persecution, I will not be the one who forces them into that hell.' He then demanded: 'Is your next move to offer to increase the severity of my imprisonment if I do not cooperate? If so, I must disappoint you further. I once said that when we are in the gutter we are looking up at the stars. When a man is in here, he looks up and sees no such wonders, just an ugly ceiling.

That will not change regardless of whatever inducements or threats you may throw at me.'

Feather fell silent, mulling this over, then nodded. 'I understand and appreciate your position, Mr Wilde. There will be no threats, I promise you. Your situation will not be made worse as the result of your decision.' And then, to reinforce his words, he looked directly at the warders standing behind Wilde and said clearly and carefully: 'I will make that clear to the governor in my written report on this meeting.'

'But is that your decision to make, Inspector?' asked Wilde. 'Doesn't that rest with your superior, the dreaded Superintendent Armstrong?'

'I give you my word, Mr Wilde, *I* will make the report to the governor, as I have just said.'

Wilde inclined his head to Feather in acknowledgement. 'Then I offer you my thanks,' he said. 'And now we have concluded our official business, perhaps we can indulge in some conversation. I get very little opportunity for genial exchanges in here, and I assume we have little time left to us. The warders here are very precise on the time allotted to visitors.'

Once again, Feather looked directly at the two warders as he said, firmly: 'This is not a social call, Mr Wilde, this is an official visit from Scotland Yard and as such will be terminated when I have decided we have finished this interview.' Daniel saw the two warders, still silent, look uncomfortable at these words, while still retaining their positions of guardianship.

Wilde smiled. 'Thank you, Inspector.' He turned his attention to Stoker. 'So, Bram, it seems we can talk.'

'That's why I came, Oscar,' said Stoker. 'I care nothing for

Simpson, or the fact that someone killed him. I took this opportunity to come because I wanted to know if there was anything I could do for you. Anything I can bring in? Books? Paper? Pen and ink?'

'I am barred from having pen and ink,' said Wilde. 'Similarly, there is a restriction on the books I am allowed to have. So far, I am permitted the Bible and *A Pilgrim's Progress*. I think they are trying to reform me.'

Stoker turned to Feather, angry. 'A writer barred from the tools of his trade,' he snapped. 'And not just any writer, but one of the greatest this country has ever known. Surely, Inspector, you must see that this is the ultimate cruelty.'

'Although perhaps not as cruel as the treadmill or picking oakum,' said Wilde, sagely.

'I will talk to the governor,' said Feather.

'Thank you,' said Wilde. 'I must admit, I do not hold out much hope that the situation will change – others have tried on my behalf – but I do thank you for your sentiment.' Then he looked at them pensively and asked: 'There is one favour I would ask. Lord Alfred Douglas is threatening to publish certain letters of mine to him in a magazine in France.'

Lord Alfred Douglas, Daniel noted, not 'Bosie', the name he'd previously given to his paramour. And the bitter tone in which he spoke Douglas's name suggested that the malicious son of the Marquess of Queensberry was no longer in Wilde's affections.

'It is not just the betrayal that angers me, nor that he is doing it for money and to increase his own publicity, but I have had word from Constance that she has decided not to go ahead with divorce proceedings against me. If these letters appear in public, she may well be persuaded to change her mind.'

'How do you know he intends to publish these letters?' asked Feather.

'A friend, Robert Sherard, was able to visit me recently, and he told me he'd heard about it from an acquaintance in Paris. Things are hard enough with my being here, and with the bankruptcy petition against me.'

'Bankruptcy?' asked Daniel.

'Court costs,' said Stoker. 'Some of us have started a fund to try and deal with them . . .'

'But without as much success as you hoped,' said Wilde ruefully. 'It's nearly four thousand pounds.'

'Surely your plays must have earned you some money,' said Daniel.

'Earned, and spent,' said Wilde, ruefully. 'And now, with my name pilloried everywhere, there is no income for me.'

'I'll see what I can do,' said Stoker. 'I have contacts among some of the magazine publishers. If Lord Alfred discovers he will not only not be paid by these publications but may be liable to charges against him on the grounds of publishing works he does not own, he may well reconsider.'

'Thank you, Bram,' said Wilde. He looked at Feather. 'Is there anything else you wish to ask me, Inspector? I know you said you would decide when this interview would be terminated, but I have to admit to feeling tired. The ambience in here has that effect.'

'Of course,' said Feather. He stood up, as did Daniel and Stoker. 'I thank you for your time.'

'I promise I will come again,' said Stoker. 'And I will write.'

CHAPTER TWENTY-SIX

Their journey away from Wandsworth was in a difficult silence, broken at last by Stoker as he addressed Feather. 'Inspector, I have been wrong about you. I judged you by your association with Superintendent Armstrong.'

'The superintendent was only doing his job, sir,' said Feather, carefully.

'There is no need to be a politician about it,' said Stoker. 'Allow me to compliment you and to say that if I do hear of anything that might help in your investigation, I shall pass it to you.' He turned to Daniel. 'Or perhaps to you, Mr Wilson. The inspector will have no option but to pass anything I say to his superior. You, as a private individual, however, can make your own decision.'

The three men fell silent again, then Feather said, quietly: 'I never knew that about you, Daniel. Your workhouse background.'

Daniel shrugged. 'There was no need for you to have known.'

'Does Abigail know?'

'She does.'

'And how is she with it?'

'It's there, but in the past. However, I would ask that this remains just between us. Some people can be unnecessarily prejudiced.'

'Of course,' said Feather.

Daniel looked at Stoker, who nodded.

'Your history will not be heard about from me,' he said.

'Thank you,' said Daniel.

They dropped Stoker back at the Lyceum Theatre, then Feather asked: 'What about you, Daniel? Is this place all right, or do you want to be dropped elsewhere? Back at the museum, perhaps?'

'No, I'll come with you and we'll compare notes. Not just about Wilde but about everything else we've learnt since this case began. There are so many threads we need to bring together.'

Feather instructed the driver to take them to Scotland Yard. When they arrived, as they stepped down from the hansom, they saw the agitated figure of Sergeant Cribbens running towards them.

'Inspector. Thank heavens you're here.'

'What's happened?'

'Erskine Petter's been found. He's dead. Throat cut.'

'Where?'

'Over in Paddington. I just got a message from Jim Bunn. I was about to go and tell the superintendent when I saw you draw up.'

'Where's the address?'

Cribbens took a scrap of paper from his pocket and thrust it towards Feather. 'Here. It's a lodging house.'

'Right, we'll get over there straight away.'

'What about letting the superintendent know?' asked Cribbens, concerned.

'We'll do that when we come back,' said Feather. 'We need to get there before the scene is messed up by too many people trampling over it, Sergeant.' He turned to Daniel. 'Coming with us, Daniel? An extra pair of eyes is always useful.'

Daniel nodded, and he and Cribbens climbed on board the hansom. Feather shouted the address to the driver, then joined them.

The lodging house was in a narrow street at the back of Paddington railway station. Sergeant Bunn was standing outside, guarding the front door, as Daniel, Inspector Feather and Sergeant Cribbens arrived. Next to Bunn stood an obviously angry middle-aged woman who was unleashing a load of verbal vitriol at him, none of which appeared to have any impact on the man. As Feather and Cribbens walked to the house, Daniel behind them, the woman turned her angry attention towards the new arrivals.

'Are you in charge here?' she demanded.

'Inspector Feather from Scotland Yard, ma'am,' said Feather.

'Don't you "ma'am" me,' she snorted.

'This is Mrs Winship, sir,' said Bunn. 'She manages the lodging house on behalf of the owner.'

'And I've never had anything like this happen in this house in the ten years I've been looking after it,' she said. 'I need to get in there and clean that room up so we can get it rented.'

'We can't do that, there's a dead man in there,' Bunn said to her.

'Well, get him out!' shouted the woman. 'He's dead. He ain't bothered, but I am. That's money being lost.'

'We can't move the body until we've examined the scene,' said Feather, doing his best to calm the angry woman down. 'But once we've done that, we'll be able to remove the body and let you continue. Were you the one who found him?'

'Yes,' said Winship. 'I came to do the cleaning, which is part of the deal, and there he was, dead on the floor with his throat cut. Blood everywhere. It'll take me ages and a lot of scrubbing to get rid of that.'

'How often do you come to clean?' asked Feather. 'Every day?'

'"Every day"?' echoed the woman, scornfully. 'I've got three houses to look after. I can't do them all at once. I go to them every three days.'

'And was Mr Petter here the last time you came, three days ago?'

'He was, and he sat in his chair while I did my cleaning.'

'How did he seem?'

'Normal. He was a quiet gentleman who gave no trouble.'

'The doctor's up there with him,' said Bunn. 'Dr Lynne. He's a local man. Very good. I took it on myself to send for him. I hope that was all right, sir?'

'Indeed, Sergeant. Very commendable,' said Feather. He turned back to Mrs Winship. 'With the doctor here, we should be able to wrap this up very shortly.' He began to go into the house but Winship barred his way, still not content. 'How soon can I get in there?' she demanded.

'As soon as the body's been removed, and we've examined the scene properly and taken away whatever else needs to be removed.'

'You ain't taking things from here without my permission,' she said. 'I'm responsible, I am. Any losses come out of my pocket.'

Feather fixed her with a look. 'This is a murder scene, madam,' he said, firmly. 'We will take as long as is necessary to get the information we require. And I must warn you that if you interfere I shall have you arrested and taken to the nearest police station.'

'You what?' shouted Winship, outraged. 'You can't do that. You've got no authority.'

'I am from Scotland Yard. That gives me the authority.' He looked at Bunn, who was doing his best to stop a smile appearing on his face. 'Sergeant, make sure this woman does not enter the house until I say she can. If she gives you any trouble, arrest her.'

With that, Feather walked into the house, Cribbens and Daniel behind him.

'First floor, sir!' called Bunn.

'And don't make a mess on the stairs,' came Mrs Winship's voice, determined not to be silenced. Then, for good measure, she added: 'I wish I'd never called the police now if I'd known I was going to be treated like this.'

There was a uniformed constable on duty outside an open door on the first-floor landing. He stepped aside to let the three men into the room. A whiskered man wearing a frock coat was stepping back from the dead body on the carpet and wiping his hands on a towel.

'Dr Lynne?' asked Feather. 'Inspector Feather from Scotland Yard. This is my sergeant, Cribbens, and Mr Daniel Wilson, a private investigator.'

They looked down at the body of Erskine Petter which lay on its back on the carpet. His eyes and mouth were open, his skin death-white as the result of blood having pumped out through the gaping wound in his neck.

'The heart carried on pumping after his throat was cut,' explained Lynne, indicating the spread of blood, now dried and clotted. 'Death was a combination of choking on his own blood and massive blood loss from the carotid artery.'

'Any idea of when it happened?' asked Feather.

'From the condition of the blood residues and the state of the muscles, I'd say the day before yesterday. The body had been in a state of rigor mortis, but you'll note that it's begun to return to a flaccid state, which usually occurs after about thirty-six hours.'

'So, he was killed two days ago, on Thursday,' said Feather, thoughtfully.

Dr Lynne nodded.

Feather summoned Sergeant Cribbens over.

'Yes, sir?' asked Cribbens.

'I'm going to check up on a lead at the butcher's shop under Petter's office,' said Feather. 'You carry on the investigation here. The usual things, anything that might point to who did it. Also, arrange for the body to be taken to the morgue at the Yard. Then ask around to see if anyone saw anything suspicious in the last two days. I shouldn't be long, but in case anything turns up to delay us, I'll leave you with the carriage. If you're not here when I get back, I'll see you back at the Yard.'

Cribbens nodded. 'Right, sir.'

As Daniel followed Feather down the stairs to the street, he asked: 'The butcher's?'

'Jones. Petter left a note on his office door saying all correspondence should be left with him. I'm curious to find

243

out whether Petter told him where he'd be hiding out.'

'You think he'd reveal this address?' asked Daniel. 'Surely Petter would have paid him to keep quiet about it.'

'That's true, but he might cough if Benny and Billy Wardle came asking.'

'You're thinking they did this?'

'In my book, they've got a motive. Petter was holding out on them as far as the money went. That's enough to upset them and go looking for him. And they were released on Thursday, the same day Petter was killed. It certainly puts them in the frame.' Then he frowned. 'The trouble is this stabbing doesn't fit with what I know of them. I've never known them use a knife; they've always been fists and boots men.'

'Maybe Petter pulled a knife on them as protection when they arrived,' suggested Daniel. 'They took it off him and in the struggle he died.'

'It's possible,' said Feather. 'Right at this moment I can't think of anyone else who'd want him dead. But then, he was in a shady business; they attract dangerous people.'

It was just a short walk to the butcher's shop, and the first thing they noticed as they walked in was that Jones the butcher was sporting a vivid black eye.

'Who did it? Benny or Billy?' asked Feather.

'Oh, it's you again,' said Jones, sullenly. He scowled. 'If you must know, I fell over.'

'Oh, come on,' scoffed Feather. 'Benny and Billy were let out of Wormwood Scrubs. They came to the office looking for Erskine Petter and found it locked up. They expected that because I'd told Benny that Petter had vanished. Like me, they saw the note on the door saying any post was to be left with you. So, they suspected you might know where he was lying low. Now, when we asked you, you told us you didn't know where Petter was, and we didn't press it. Also, at that stage, we had what we wanted: the firm's papers. But Benny and Billy hadn't got what they were after, which is money that Petter owed them, and they aren't gentle people. Your black eye attests to that. So, I'm asking again, which of them hit you?'

'Billy,' grunted Jones.

'And you told them where he was staked out.'

'I didn't have much choice,' burst out Jones. 'I know what those two are capable of.'

'When were they here?'

'Yesterday afternoon.'

'Yesterday? Not Thursday?'

Jones scowled at him. 'Look at my face. Do you think I'm likely to misremember getting a punch like this? It was yesterday. Friday. But, if anyone asks, I didn't say anything.'

'I understand, Mr Jones,' said Feather.

Feather looked grim as he and Daniel walked back to Petter's hideout. 'So, it wasn't the Wardle brothers,' he said. 'They only found out where Petter was hiding yesterday afternoon.'

'So, who else knew where he was?' mused Daniel.

'One of his old acquaintances, I guess,' said Feather. He swore. 'It would have been so much easier if it had been Benny and Billy. The super isn't going to like this one bit.'

CHAPTER TWENTY-SEVEN

Superintendent Armstrong sat at his desk scowling as he listened to Feather's report about the murder of Erskine Petter.

'Throat cut, you say?'

'Yes.'

'What do you think?' asked the superintendent. 'Thieves falling out? Benny and Billy Wardle feeling cheated because Petter had kept their money from them?'

'That was my first thought, sir, but it doesn't fit with what the doctor says. According to him, Petter was killed the day before yesterday, but we know that Jones didn't reveal his hideout to them until yesterday.'

'The doctor could be wrong,' said Armstrong. 'With death, nothing's that accurate.'

'Dr Lynne seems very good at what he does, sir.

Meticulous. Plus, I had my doubts before Dr Lynne told us that because I've never known Benny or Billy to use a knife. They're strictly fists and boots men.'

Armstrong frowned, then asked: 'You think it could be connected with the murder of Simpson?'

Feather nodded. 'I do. We know that Petter was tied up with the smashed dinosaur skeleton at the museum.'

'And this Mason Radley was seen at the museum the morning Simpson was killed,' mused Armstrong, thoughtfully.

'But I still can't see the connection yet, if there is one,' said Feather.

'How did you get on with Wilde?' asked Armstrong. 'You saw him this afternoon at Wandsworth, is that right?'

'It is,' said Feather.

'And?'

'He didn't give up any names,' said Feather.

'You gave him the offer? Leniency in his treatment?'

'I did.'

'And he still gave nothing?'

'No, sir.'

'How did he look?'

'Ill,' replied Feather. 'In fact, very ill.'

Armstrong looked pensive. 'Maybe you should have taken one of his friends with you. They might have been able to persuade him.'

'I did, sir. Mr Stoker came with me.'

Armstrong stared at him, stunned. 'Stoker? How did you manage that?'

'I asked him. Or, to be exact, Daniel Wilson asked him.'

'Wilson,' burst out Armstrong, angrily. 'You brought Wilson in?'

'Because I thought it might help if a friend of Wilde's was present. It might encourage him to cooperate. But I knew that Stoker wouldn't go with me if I asked him. He feels animosity towards the police. But he seems better disposed towards Wilson, possibly because he's no longer part of the force. And Wilson does seem to be able to persuade the most unlikely people to cooperate.'

'He can't be trusted, Inspector.' Armstrong scowled. 'He's too much of a maverick. A wild card.'

'Yes, sir,' said Feather.

Armstrong fell silent, thinking this over. Finally, he said: 'Well, if that's a dead end, that once again leaves this Mason Radley as the most likely suspect. You think he's still in this country?'

'Unless he used a false name and took a circuitous route to get to India, I think it's highly likely he's holed up somewhere more local.'

'Right. Find a picture of him and put it in all the papers. Offer a reward. But keep looking for the Wardle brothers. There's still a chance it could be them. This way we cover all the bases. The last thing we want is to find for certain it wasn't the Wardle brothers and this Radley character has had the time to get away.'

Daniel and Abigail sat either side of the kitchen range in their home, basking in the glow from the coals, each sipping a post-meal tot: for Daniel it was a whisky, for Abigail, a brandy. Daniel looked up from his newspaper at Abigail immersed in her reading.

'What's the book?' he asked.

'The story of Mary Anning and her work in Dorset,' replied Abigail, showing him the cover. 'She barely left Lyme Regis, but what she achieved was incredible. It's absolutely fascinating.'

'You're cramming in case you get asked any questions?' asked Daniel.

'If there are any questions then Cedric Warmsley will be the one answering,' said Abigail. 'It's just that, as I'm the one introducing the evening, I want to have some knowledge about her at my fingertips in case I'm collared after the talk's over. You know how it can be at these events, people eager to talk about a subject dear to their hearts.'

'Fortunately for me, giving talks to audiences is something I haven't had to do.' Daniel smiled. 'Unlike a celebrity such as your own good self.'

'I'm not a celebrity,' responded Abigail, curtly.

'Yes, you are, my darling,' said Daniel. 'Miss Scott said so. You are the name on the marquee to draw in the crowds.'

'You make me sound like Marie Lloyd,' complained Abigail.

Daniel laughed. 'Now that would be something different, for you to break into a risqué song partway through a lecture on the pyramids of Egypt.'

'Thankfully, I can never see that happening,' said Abigail. She put down her book and said, 'I can sense you have something on your mind.'

'The mention of a risqué song?' Daniel chuckled, archly.

'You are suggesting I have lecherous intentions towards you?'

Abigail smiled. 'I hope so. But no, I can see you're thinking about the case.'

Daniel nodded. 'I am,' he said. His face clouded as he added: 'Recent events puzzle me because they don't add up.'

'You mean this business of the search for Mason Radley?' she asked. She pointed at his newspaper. 'Scotland Yard must have moved with great speed to get his image in the late edition of the paper.'

Daniel frowned. 'It doesn't make sense. I can't see why Radley would want to kill Petter. We know Radley was being blackmailed by Raymond Simpson, but where does Petter fit into that?'

'Perhaps Petter was also blackmailing Radley,' suggested Abigail.

Daniel shook his head. 'I can't see it,' he said.

'Well, someone killed Erskine Petter.'

'Yes, but why?'

'Perhaps the motive is nothing to do with the events at the museum,' said Abigail.

'They're connected, I'm sure of it,' said Daniel, firmly.

'Your policeman's nose again?'

Daniel tapped the side of his nose and nodded. 'Things smell right, or they smell wrong. All this stuff smells wrong. The killing of Erskine Petter feels like someone's putting up a smokescreen. The same with the letters the trustees received, repeating the threat from Petter and Wardle about the fossil skeletons from America, which suddenly came out of nowhere and after Petter had done his disappearing act. It reminds me of those conjurers who deflect your attention to something else so you don't see what they're really up to. A piece of misdirection.'

'Killing someone is a pretty drastic piece of misdirection,' commented Abigail.

'Which means the stakes for someone are very high,' said Daniel. He frowned again as he asked: 'What do you think of Mrs Smith?'

'As a suspect?' asked Abigail, surprised.

'Possibly not as lethal as that. I was thinking more as an accomplice.'

'To whom? The murderer?'

'Not necessarily wittingly. She may have been duped into helping.'

'Helping with what?'

'Those letters, for example. Apart from Miss Scott, Mrs Smith was the only other person we know of at the museum who knew the contents of the original letter mentioning Petter and Wardle and the Bone Company. If she is having an affair with Turner, as we suspect, she could have told him about it. Even shown him the letter.'

'*If*,' stressed Abigail. 'We don't know for certain they are in a relationship. And do you now suspect Mr Turner? I thought William Watling was your suspect of choice. What's brought Dawson Turner into your mind?'

'I don't know. Just a feeling.' He looked at her and smiled. 'Talking of feelings . . .'

She chuckled. 'You are incorrigible.'

'And lecherous, according to you.' He got up from his

chair and walked over to her, took her in his arms and deftly undid the buttons at the top of her skirt, causing it to slide down to the floor. She stepped out of it and let him caress her, before biting his ear and murmuring: 'Bed will be more comfortable, if you can wait that long.'

CHAPTER TWENTY-EIGHT

When Abigail drew back the bedroom curtains the following morning, the world outside had vanished to be replaced with a thick grey and slimy green blanket of fog. Nothing was visible within it. Nor was there any sound, no clattering of horse hooves on the cobbles of the road; the thick fog absorbed everything.

'Fog,' she announced to Daniel as he pulled on his clothes.

He joined her at the window. 'Thick, as well,' he added. Tendrils of oily green rubbed against the windowpane before disappearing back into the thick greyness of the clouds that hid the world. 'A real pea-souper. It's lucky it's a Sunday and most of the places we need to go to will be closed, at least this morning. Do you know it's almost ten years ago that Parliament passed a bill allowing galleries and museums to open on Sundays, but most still remain shut.'

'The Lord's Day Observance Society,' added Abigail. She smiled. 'You know they were founded by a Daniel Wilson. A relation?'

'Absolutely not,' retorted Daniel. 'And they're a very powerful lobby group. They've got the workers on their side because they get a day off.'

'Only those working for big organisations,' Abigail corrected him.

'It's still the majority of working people. And the politicians support them because the Church informs most of those who vote which way to cast their ballot.'

'You sound like you agree with them,' observed Abigail.

'No,' said Daniel. 'If they had their way there'd be no trains running, no postal deliveries, no Sunday newspapers, and even the small shops and establishments that are currently exempt from the law would be forced to close. I prefer people to be given the choice.'

Abigail looked thoughtful. 'I still feel there must something we could do today to push the investigation forward. With each day that passes I feel we lose momentum.'

'There is,' said Daniel. 'Jones the butcher will be open this afternoon. I missed asking him some vital questions. Because John was concentrating on the Wardle brothers as the most likely to have killed Petter, I didn't pursue it and ask who else might have asked him for the information about Petter's hideout.'

'Surely, if anyone else had attacked Mr Jones he would have told you,' said Abigail.

'There are more ways of getting information than by beating it out of someone,' said Daniel.

They spent the morning safe indoors, away from the thick smog that blotted out the city, waiting to see if it would lift. But by the time two o'clock came and there was still no sign of a break in the greenish clouds, they decided to brave the outside. They each tied a large handkerchief around their noses and mouths, keeping it in place with a thick scarf, before setting out. Even through this protection they could taste the acrid smoke of the fog and feel it making their eyes water.

'We might as well walk to Paddington,' said Daniel. 'There'll be no hansom cabs or buses running today.'

Daniel's prediction proved correct, even though as they walked they passed people arguing with the drivers of stationary cabs insisting they be taken somewhere, while the drivers responded that there would be no transport until the fog lifted. 'Too foggy,' the drivers told them, firmly. 'Can't risk the horse. It could stumble and break a leg, then where would I be?'

Even on foot the journey was hazardous, with visibility down to a few yards in some places, and so Daniel and Abigail held hands as they edged carefully forwards, feeling their way with their feet.

After what seemed an age, they arrived at Jones' shop, which was empty except for the forlorn figure of Jones himself in his butcher's apron.

'Hurrah,' he exclaimed as they entered his shop. 'Customers at last.' Then his expression changed as Daniel and Abigail unwrapped their scarves and he saw their faces. 'Oh, it's you again,' he said, grumpily.

'It is,' said Daniel. 'A quiet day for you?'

Jones gestured to the fog that rubbed against his shop window, hiding everything.

'What do you think?' he said, sourly. 'No one's going to be coming out today. Not anyone with any sense, that is.' He looked towards Abigail. 'Unless you've come in for something?' he said, hopefully. 'I've got some lovely sausages. Best quality pork.'

'Thank you, but I'm with Mr Wilson here,' said Abigail.

'I thought you might be,' said Jones, with a groan. His face still bore the bruises inflicted on him by the Wardle brothers.

'We're hoping you might be able to help us,' said Daniel. 'If you do, then it's quite possible we might buy some of those excellent sausages you speak so highly of.'

'Information for a sausage,' snorted Jones, derisively. 'What sort of bloke do you think I am?'

'The sort who divulges information under pressure,' said Daniel.

Jones regarded him warily, then pick up a large meat cleaver from his counter.

'After what happened with the Wardles I've decided to protect myself,' he said, and waved the meat cleaver at Daniel.

'Very wise,' said Daniel, apparently unperturbed. 'But that may be no match for the pistol I carry in my pocket.'

'You've got a pistol?' queried Jones.

Daniel slipped his hand into his jacket pocket. Immediately, Jones put down the cleaver.

'All right, no need for that sort of thing,' he said. 'What do you want?'

'It's something I should have asked you yesterday when I was here with Inspector Feather,' said Daniel. 'Afterwards it struck me that a punch in the eye isn't the only way of getting information. An open wallet is more often a better way.'

Jones looked uncomfortable. 'I don't know what you're talking about,' he blustered.

'Oh, come on, Mr Jones,' said Daniel. 'As I said, I used to be a detective at Scotland Yard. Now, we can have a discussion here that stays here, or I can call in Inspector Feather and he can haul you into the Yard for questioning. Either way, the answer's the same, but the first way will be a lot easier for you. No one'll be looking at you suspiciously like they would if you were taken off to the Yard. So, my question is: who else did you give Erskine Petter's address to?'

Jones fell silent, studying Daniel thoughtfully, weighing things up. Then he nodded.

'It was some toff,' he said.

'Did he have a name?'

'I'm sure he did, but he never said what it was, and I never asked him.'

'When did he call?'

'Three days ago. Thursday morning, in fact. He said he was in the middle of doing business with Erskine and found he'd gone, and it was very urgent he got in touch with him.'

'What did he look like?'

'Like a toff. Good clothes. Good shoes. Nothing cheap.'

'Hair?'

'Ordinary. Dark brown. Cut short, but not too short.'

'Moustache? Beard?'

Jones shook his head.

'Build? Fat? Thin? Tall? Short?'

'About your height, maybe a bit shorter. Not fat, not thin, just an ordinary-looking bloke. Nothing noticeable about him.'

'But well-off,' said Daniel.

'You're telling me,' said Jones, emphatically. 'He offered me twenty quid. Twenty quid!'

Daniel stood, studying the butcher, then he nodded.

'Thank you, Mr Jones. And now we'll take a pound of your sausages.'

As Daniel and Abigail walked away from the butcher's shop, their mouths and noses once again protected by their handkerchiefs and scarves, Abigail asked: 'What was that nonsense with that supposed pistol?'

'It worked,' said Daniel.

'But say he'd challenged you? Gone for you with that meat cleaver?'

'I could see in his eyes he wasn't that kind of person,' said Daniel. 'Anyway, we now have a piece of the puzzle. The person who really killed Petter: a mysterious toff.'

'Which doesn't mean we're much further forward. A mysterious toff with money to spare. There must be many hundreds of them.'

'But not that many associated with the Natural History Museum, and it is the museum thing that links the deaths of Erskine Petter and Raymond Simpson.'

'You're still thinking it could be one of the trustees?'

'I am,' said Daniel.

'Mason Radley?'

'Mr Radley has a very distinctive appearance. Mr Jones described the man he saw as ordinary-looking.'

'But this man may not have any connection with the museum,' said Abigail.

'He may not,' agreed Daniel. 'But I have a feeling about this.'

'And if you're wrong?'

'It won't be the first time,' admitted Daniel. 'But I want to follow it through. Tomorrow morning, we need to go to the museum and make arrangements to get hold of the trustees in one place together. And afterwards we'll go to Scotland Yard and let John Feather know what we've learnt.'

The following morning the fog seemed as bad as ever.

'Another day of walking everywhere,' commented Abigail, looking out at the swirling mist that pressed against their windowpanes.

'The exercise will do us good,' said Daniel.

'The breathing in of the muck it contains won't,' added Abigail.

In Kensington, Evelyn Scott made her way along the path towards the entrance to the Natural History Museum. The fog had been so thick when she left home that she had been unable to find a bus or hansom cab and had been forced to make the journey on foot, blinded for most of the way by the green, evil-smelling smog to such an extent that it had taken her more than two hours to get here, stumbling most of the way, bumping into lamp posts, losing her footing when she came to kerbs. The acrid fog stung her eyes and forced its way into her lungs, despite the handkerchief she held pressed to her mouth and nose. But soon she would be safe inside her office, where she determined she would stay and not venture out again. If necessary, if the fog didn't clear, she might even spend the night at the museum.

She was just level with the tall Doric columns that fronted the museum when she heard a shuffling of feet close by, and suddenly the shadowy figure of what she took to be a man lurched at her from behind one of the columns. His hands were outstretched towards her, and then he was on her, hands grabbing at her clothes, and she screamed.

CHAPTER TWENTY-NINE

'Miss Scott! It's me!'

Scott stared at the figure in front of her, half enveloped in fog. Mason Radley.

'I've been waiting her for you, and when I saw you arrive, I stepped out but stumbled and fell towards you. I'm so sorry I frightened you.'

'Mr Radley. What are you doing here?'

'I've come to hand myself in. To you, Miss Scott, and then I'll go to the police. I want to tell you everything. I swear I'm innocent. I did not kill Raymond Simpson, nor this other man the newspapers talk about.'

There was the sound of muffled footsteps approaching.

'We can't talk here,' said Scott. 'Come inside.'

She was just taking Radley by the arm and guiding him

towards the museum entrance, when Daniel and Abigail appeared out of the fog.

'Mr Radley,' exclaimed Daniel.

'I'm innocent,' Radley burst out, plaintively.

'We're just going to my office,' said Scott. 'Mr Radley says he needs our help.'

'And hopefully we'll be able to provide some,' said Abigail.

The four entered and were met by Herbert Sharp. 'Ah, Miss Scott,' he said, with a smile of relief. 'I wondered if you'd be able to get in with this fog. It's a real old particular.' Then his smile vanished as he saw Mason Radley. 'Mr Radley?' he said, in alarm.

'It's all right, Mr Sharp,' Scott reassured him. 'Mr Radley is here to talk to us.'

'But—' began Sharp, obviously worried.

'I'm innocent, Mr Sharp,' pleaded Radley.

'Did the cleaners manage to get in?' asked Scott, changing the subject back to everyday business.

'They did,' said Sharp. 'Fortunately, they live nearby. As have most of the rest of the staff, although Mrs Smith isn't here yet.'

'Thank you, Mr Sharp,' said Scott. 'If anyone needs me, I shall be in my office with Mr Radley, Mr Wilson and Miss Fenton. Perhaps you could arrange for someone to bring up coffee for us. I'm sure we're all in need of it.'

'Of course,' said Sharp, and he departed.

Once in Scott's office, the curator gestured them to take chairs. 'We'll let you tell your story first, Mr Radley,' she said.

'Thank you,' said Radley. 'To begin at the beginning, Raymond Simpson was blackmailing me. He'd managed to get hold of a document that was potentially lethal for my business.'

'Over the deaths at your plantation in India,' said Abigail.

'You know about that?' asked Radley. When Abigail and Daniel nodded, he gave a groan of misery and added: 'His demands coincided with some unfortunate financial pressures in India. Because of the deaths there have been costs to pay. I'd told Simpson this and said I couldn't pay the extortionate amount of money he was demanding for his silence, but he was adamant that unless I paid up he would publish the incriminating letter. If that happened it would be a disaster: the name of our company would become tainted; a huge amount of business would disappear. Things are hard enough in business as it is.

'I came in early that morning in the hope of striking a deal with Simpson. Tell him that I'd pay, but over time. But then I heard that he was dead, and when Mr Turner said he'd seen me earlier at the museum, which was true, I was sure the police would find out about the deaths in India and make the connection between me and Simpson.'

'So you fled,' said Daniel. 'Your housekeeper told us you'd gone to India.'

'I had to tell her something to explain my absence, but in fact I went to a cousin of mine in Kent, and I've been staying with him while I wondered what to do and how I could prove my innocence.'

'Why did you come back?'

'When I saw my picture yesterday in the national newspaper saying the police were looking for me over the death of this man, Petter, I was concerned that someone in the neighbourhood would report they'd seen me. So, for my cousin's sake, I decided this was the only way. I want to prove my innocence. I can assure you that I never came back to London at all once I'd left the city on the day that Simpson was killed. My cousin can prove it. Please check with him. He'll confirm what I've said is true.'

'Whereabouts in Kent?'

'It's a small hamlet called St Mary's Platt, which is about a mile outside the village of Borough Green. My cousin's name is Dick Cartwright. He's a woodsman and has a cottage in the woods there. Woodman Cottage in Platt Common, which is a lane that leads to Platt Woods.'

There was a knock at the door, then it opened, and an attendant appeared carrying a tray with a jug of coffee, milk, sugar, cups and saucers, and a plate of biscuits.

'Thank you,' said Scott. She waited until the attendant had left before resuming the conversation. 'I'm afraid we'll still need to involve Scotland Yard,' she said.

Radley nodded. 'I understand. But I wanted to explain things to you first.'

'Can I suggest that Miss Fenton and I accompany you to Scotland Yard?' said Daniel. 'We know Superintendent Armstrong and Inspector Feather very well, and there is a chance that they may listen to us.'

'We have some information that may help to back up your plea of innocence in relation to the murder of Erskine Petter,' added Abigail.

'You have?' exclaimed Radley. 'What?'

'Mr Petter was in hiding. On the day he was killed the

one person who knew where he was staying was bribed by a respectable-looking and wealthy gentleman to reveal his secret address.'

'But I'm respectable and considered to be wealthy,' moaned Radley. 'How does that help me?'

'Because the gentleman who got hold of Petter's hideout address can be described as "nondescript". Almost anonymous. With respect, Mr Radley, your appearance is distinctive.'

'Distinctive?' echoed Radley, puzzled. 'In what way?'

'Let's just say, you are once seen not easily forgotten, but in a very nice way,' said Abigail.

'So, you think this anonymous gentleman may be the person responsible for Mr Petter's murder?' said Scott.

'Certainly, that is the suspicion,' said Daniel. 'At the very least, we're sure he is involved in the murder somehow.'

'And you have no idea who he might be?'

'Not at this moment,' admitted Daniel. He hesitated, then shot a look at Abigail, who nodded in silent agreement. 'Miss Scott, would you mind if I stayed here in your office with Mr Radley while Miss Fenton has a private conversation with you?'

'About me?' asked Radley, anxiously.

'No,' said Abigail. 'But we have an idea that may help to prove your innocence once and for all. But for the moment we feel it can only be shared with Miss Scott.'

Scott got to her feet. 'Very well,' she said. 'We shall use Mrs Smith's office. Mr Sharp said she is yet to arrive.'

Abigail gave a look of warning at Daniel, who said: 'There is always the chance that Mrs Smith may arrive during your conversation, and our feeling is that no one else should be involved at this time. So, I suggest I escort Mr Radley downstairs, where we can look at the exhibits together and wait there for Miss Fenton.'

Scott frowned, puzzled, but nodded. 'Very well, if that is your preference.'

Daniel rose and asked Radley: 'Are you ready, sir?'

'I am, and I promise I will not attempt to escape,' Radley assured him.

Abigail waited until the two men had left and the door closed, before saying to Scott: 'We'd like you to send out invitations to all the trustees to the event on Wednesday evening.'

'I'm sure that most of them will be coming anyway,' said Scott.

'Yes, but we'd like to ensure that they all come,' said Abigail.

'May I ask why?' asked Scott.

'There is a possibility that this mysterious gentleman we've learnt about may be one of the trustees.'

'But you don't know who,' pointed out Scott. 'You don't even have a description of him.'

'No, but we do have access to the person who met him and can identify him,' said Abigail. 'The plan is for us to have our witness secreted somewhere in the museum on the evening of the talk and to identify the gentleman he spoke to.'

'You're absolutely sure that this mysterious gentleman is one of our trustees?' asked Scott.

'No,' Abigail admitted. 'At this moment it's just a suspicion of Mr Wilson's, but he's rarely wrong.'

'But he could be,' insisted Scott.

'Indeed, he could be,' conceded Abigail. 'But we both feel this is the best chance we have of discovering the identity of the murderer.'

'The murderer of Mr Petter, but not of Raymond Simpson,' said Scott.

'Daniel feels the two are connected.'

Scott fell silent, thinking this over. 'How sure are you this witness of yours will agree to come to the talk that evening?' she asked.

'He will be escorted here by Inspector Feather,' said Abigail.

'And Inspector Feather agrees with this plan?'

'We haven't yet had a chance to discuss it with him,' said Abigail. 'We came to you first. We'll talk to him about it when we accompany Mr Radley to Scotland Yard and hand him over.'

'You believe Mr Radley to be innocent?'

'We do,' said Abigail.

'And what will happen if this witness identifies one of the trustees?'

'Inspector Feather will take him somewhere for questioning. As we'll be here at the museum, we suggest your office, if you agree.'

'Not Scotland Yard?'

'We may be wrong,' said Abigail. 'The gentleman may be innocent of any crime; he may have wanted to talk to Petter about something else. In which case we'll be able to ascertain that without causing embarrassment the museum.'

Scott nodded, thoughtfully. 'I understand. I'll get Mrs Smith to send out the invitations as soon as she comes in.'

'One other thing,' said Abigail. 'We'd rather you didn't tell her our suspicions.'

'Why not?' asked Scott.

'We'd rather it was kept between us at this moment in case we're wrong. There's a danger that Mrs Smith may inadvertently let something slip to one of the trustees.'

Scott regarded her, quizzically. 'You think there might be something going on between Mrs Smith and one of the trustees?' she asked.

'At this stage we can't make any accusations,' said Abigail. 'It may have nothing to do with the case we're looking into. But we'd rather take precautions to make sure the real reason for the invitations remains only between us.'

Scott hesitated, then said, awkwardly: 'I hope you're wrong about Mrs Smith, but I must admit I've been concerned that lately she seems to disappear from the office at various times. It's often because she has had to go to the British Museum, or on an errand of some sort, but I have begun to wonder if there might be something else happening.'

'An assignation?'

'I don't know,' said Scott. 'But, for the moment, we'll agree to keep the true motive for the invitations between us.'

CHAPTER THIRTY

As they left the museum and stepped into the outside world, Daniel, Abigail and Radley saw that the fog had finally begun to disperse. It still hung ominously above them but at enough of a height from pavement level that meant people were able to once more walk about without bumping into fences or lamp posts, or falling over kerbs. As a result, with cabs once more able to negotiate the streets, they hailed a hansom, which Radley insisted on paying for. Once at Scotland Yard, they made their way to Feather's office and found the inspector and Sergeant Cribbens looking out of the window.

'Yes, John, the fog is lifting,' said Daniel. 'A great relief to all.'

'To all except the muggers and thieves who use the cover to commit all kinds of mayhem,' grunted Feather. He regarded Radley with sudden surprise and recognition. 'Is this . . . ?'

'Inspector Feather and Sergeant Cribbens, allow me to introduce Mr Mason Radley,' said Daniel. 'He's handing himself in and has asked us to escort him here to show his good faith.'

'I didn't do it,' blurted out Radley. 'I didn't kill anyone.'

Feather gave a look of concern to Daniel and Abigail. 'I'm sure this is well meant,' he said, doubtfully, 'but I shall have to bring the superintendent in.'

'Of course,' said Daniel. To Radley, he said: 'It's procedure, Mr Radley. The senior officer in the case has to be kept fully informed.'

Feather turned to Cribbens. 'Sergeant, go and tell Superintendent Armstrong that Mr Mason Radley has handed himself in and is in my office.'

'And tell him that I'm innocent!' Radley called desperately after Cribbens as he left the office.

'Please sit down, Mr Radley,' said Feather, gesturing towards a chair.

'I came here at my own volition,' said Radley, and Daniel could tell from his air of agitation that, now he was actually inside Scotland Yard, he was beginning to have second thoughts about the wisdom of surrendering himself.

'I can assure you that you will be treated fairly by both Inspector Feather and Superintendent Armstrong, Mr Radley,' said Daniel, doing his best to calm the panic that was rising in the unhappy trustee. Inwardly, Daniel thought cynically: *Possibly not as fairly by the superintendent as you will be by John Feather.*

The door burst open and suddenly the bulky figure of Superintendent Armstrong was inside the office, a look of satisfaction on his face as he regarded the unhappy man.

'So,' he thundered in delight. 'The guilty party has handed himself in. Excellent.'

'I'm not guilty,' protested Radley, rising to his feet.

'There is good reason to doubt his guilt, Superintendent,' said Abigail.

'There is also good reason to support it,' retorted Armstrong.

'Tell them about the other man,' Radley appealed to Daniel and Abigail. 'And the fact that I was in Kent.'

'What other man?' asked Armstrong.

'We were just about to update Inspector Feather on something we learnt this morning,' said Abigail. 'A man went round to Jones the butcher on the day Petter was killed and bribed him to tell him where Petter was hiding out. Jones describes him as a "toff", obviously wealthy enough to pay him twenty pounds for the information.'

'A wealthy toff?' said Armstrong. 'That could have been Radley.'

Daniel shook his head. 'I think you'll agree, Superintendent, that Mr Radley is very singular in his appearance. This man didn't have any distinguishing features about him, according to Jones. Except the fact that he was a gentleman.'

'And who is this mysterious toff?' asked Armstrong.

'I don't know,' admitted Daniel. 'But surely it's worth looking into. It strikes me as more likely that this man was the person who killed Petter. The timing fits. He got the address from Jones before Petter was killed.'

Armstrong shook his head. 'It's more likely some dodgy business pal of Petter's who either owed him money or was owed money.'

'And could have killed him,' insisted Daniel.

Armstrong fixed Daniel with a firm glare. 'This is all just chasing shadows. Ifs and buts. Mysterious strangers. Anyway, even if what you say turns out to be true about the murder of Erskine Petter, we're also looking for Mr Radley over the death of Raymond Simpson, and now we've got him.' He turned to Cribbens and said: 'Take him down to the cells, Sergeant. Remanded in custody on my orders.'

'Yes, sir,' said Cribbens, who reached out and put a hand on Radley's arm.

'No!' howled Radley. 'I'm innocent! I didn't kill anyone!'

'That'll be for a judge and jury to decide,' said Armstrong.

With a last hopeless look of appeal at Daniel and Abigail, Radley was hustled out of the office by the sergeant.

'Well done,' said Armstrong. 'I can report to the commissioner we've got our man.'

'We believe there are good reasons to doubt Mr Radley's guilt in this case,' said Daniel. 'Radley insists he didn't kill either Simpson or Petter.'

'Of course he does,' said Armstrong. 'They always deny it.'

'But why hand himself in?' asked Daniel. 'He could have fled. Really gone to India instead of staying in this country.'

'Guilty conscience,' said Armstrong.

'If he had a guilty conscience he'd admit to the killings,' pointed out Abigail.

Armstrong gave a scowl of irritation. 'All right, he's playing a clever game of some sort, trying to make us think he's innocent,' he snapped. 'Who knows? Like I said, it's for a judge and jury to decide. As far as I'm concerned we've got the man we were looking for.'

With that, he swept out of the office.

Daniel gave a heavy sigh and cast a look at Feather. 'Well?' he asked.

Feather returned Daniel's rueful look with one of his own. He sighed. 'Armstrong's the boss.'

'We believe Radley isn't our man,' said Abigail. 'He handed himself in because of his picture appearing in the papers, but we don't feel he committed the killings.'

'You favour this mysterious toff?'

'We do.'

'Who could be anyone. Why would this toff want to kill Petter?'

'Mrs Simpson told you that one of the people Raymond was blackmailing was a trustee at the museum.'

'Yes. Radley. He's admitted Simpson was blackmailing him.'

'But say he wasn't the only one,' said Daniel. 'There's more than one trustee, and I suspect a few have guilty secrets.'

'You're talking about William Watling again,' said Feather, archly.

'Why not?' asked Daniel. 'Or any of the others.'

'You don't know this mysterious toff is a trustee,' pointed out Feather. 'He could be, as the superintendent said, some business pal of Petter's and nothing at all to do with the museum.'

'This all started with the smashed dinosaur skeleton at the museum, which we know Petter was involved with somehow, and the murder of Raymond Simpson at the museum the next morning. For me, that links it with this mystery man looking for Petter just before he died.'

'But you don't know his name or even what he looks like.'

273

'No, but Jones has seen his face, so I suggest we put him in a situation where he's likely to see him again.'

'Where?'

'The museum. There's a talk there on Wednesday evening, the day after tomorrow, about Mary Anning—'

'Who?'

'She collected fossils of prehistoric fish,' said Daniel.

'Sounds fascinating,' said Feather, sarcastically.

'We've asked Miss Scott to send out invitations to all the trustees to get them to attend. We'll have Jones stashed somewhere to watch out as the trustees arrive. And when he points this mysterious person out to us, you move in and arrest him.'

Feather laughed. 'We don't even know this mysterious toff is definitely a trustee. He could be nothing to do with the museum. In which case, the whole thing would be a waste of time.'

'Not necessarily,' said Daniel. He smiled. 'You'll learn a lot about prehistoric fish.'

Feather pondered for some moments before he spoke again. 'All right. We'll do it.'

'Thank you,' said Daniel. 'But in the meantime, what are you going to do about Mason Radley?'

'Keep him in custody,' said Feather. 'We'll talk to him and get his version of events, and then I expect he'll be transferred to Holloway on remand.'

'He's told us his version of events already,' said Daniel. 'He admits he was at the museum when Simpson was killed, but he'd gone there to try and bargain with him. Get time to pay the blackmail.'

'A bit convenient as an explanation,' observed Feather.

'True, but I believe him,' said Daniel.

Feather smiled. 'Sounds like you're getting soft in your old age.'

'At least look into his alibi over the killing of Erskine Petter,' urged Abigail. 'He said he was staying with his cousin in Kent from the day that Simpson was murdered. He was at . . .' She looked at Daniel as she struggled to recall the name of the place.

'St Mary's Platt,' said Daniel. 'It's a small hamlet about a mile outside the village of Borough Green.'

'There's a railway station at Borough Green,' said Feather. 'He could easily have caught a train to London, killed Petter and gone back again without his cousin knowing.'

'Unlikely,' said Daniel. 'For one thing, you've seen him, that red hair and big bushy beard. You think this is a man that Jones would describe as having nothing noticeable about him? At least go and talk to this cousin of his. And check with the railway station staff. If he travelled by train they'd have spotted him.'

'I'm sorry, I can't,' said Feather, apologetically. 'The superintendent's sure he's our man so he's not going to let me go off to Kent just like that, especially when it's outside our area of jurisdiction.'

'Very well,' said Daniel. 'You won't mind if we do? We'll go tomorrow.'

'Not at all,' said Feather. 'And I'm sure you'll find he didn't kill Petter, but the super is certain we can get him for killing Raymond Simpson.'

'Both killings are connected, I'm certain of it,' said Daniel. 'If we can show that Radley didn't kill Petter, it means someone else did, and when we find that person we'll get our link to the killing of Raymond Simpson.'

'And you're convinced that the person who killed Petter is going to show himself on Wednesday at this talk?'

'I am,' said Daniel.

'Talking of people being held on remand, is there any news of Simon Purcell?' asked Abigail.

'He's still being held at Holloway,' said Feather. 'The super wants to wait and get firm evidence about these murders first before bringing him to court. Now we've got Radley in the cells I think that might speed things up.'

'Purcell will still be guilty of conspiracy to blackmail whoever killed Simpson,' pointed out Daniel.

'True, but the super wants to make a big splash in the papers about this whole case,' said Feather. 'The more names the better.'

'With his name the biggest of all.' Daniel smiled.

'He's ambitious.' Feather shrugged. 'What do you expect?'

'I expect that we'll lay our hands on the real killer on Wednesday night at the museum,' said Daniel.

'Let's hope you're right,' said Feather, grimly. 'Especially if I've got to sit through a talk about fossilised fish.'

CHAPTER THIRTY-ONE

The Wardle brothers arrived outside the Railway Tavern close to Paddington Station in grim and determined moods. Everything had gone wrong for them. They had no money, nothing to eat and all their hopes of rectifying this situation had vanished once they'd encountered Erskine Petter. It had been Benny who'd said they weren't just staring at destitution, they were staring at the hangman's rope. They needed to get as far away from London as possible. But to do that they needed money. And not just a pound or two. 'We need real money,' said Benny. 'Ready cash to get us train tickets, boat tickets if necessary.'

'I ain't never been on a boat,' said Billy, doubtfully.

'Scotland might be the answer,' Benny told him. 'We could lose ourselves in a place like Glasgow. But first we got to get there.' He balanced the heavy wooden cudgel in his hand and patted it against the palm of his other hand.

Billy looked at the cudgel he held, of strong oak with nodules studding the length of it.

'It seems a bit of drastic,' he commented, uncertainly. 'I don't like weapons. What's wrong with fists and boots like usual?'

'Drastic times call for drastic actions,' said Benny. 'And right now, we have no money at all. Not a penny. And there's no Erskine to call on for any, nor to come up with a scheme for us to get hold of any. So, it's up to us. People in this area know us and they're frightened of us, and these cudgels back that up. No one's gonna call the coppers on us because they know what'll happen to them if they do.' He hefted the cudgel in his hand and smacked it into his other palm. 'And no one's gonna argue with these once they've seen what we can do with 'em. So, here's the way we do it. We go in and straight away I smash a table. Broken glass everywhere. You grab the nearest bloke and punch him, knocking him to the floor. If he starts to get up, bash him. That'll put 'em all in shock. Then I tell 'em you're coming round with a bag and we want it filled. Money, wallets, watches, whatever they've got on 'em. And if anyone refuses . . .' He grinned and swung his cudgel. 'I'll give 'em a taste of this. And that's all there is to it. We'll be in and out in four minutes.'

Inside the Railway Tavern, Sergeants Bunn and Cribbens sat at a table heavy with pint glasses. Bunn picked up his glass and held it out in a toast to Cribbens.

'Here's to you,' he said, and took a hearty swig.

The third member at the table, Constable Parrot, looked with concern at the glasses on the table, four of which were still filled with beer.

'Shouldn't we be out with the others?' he asked, nervously, referring to the two constables parked just round the corner from the pub in their police van.

'Plenty of time for that,' said Cribbens. He took a puff on his pipe, sending a cloud of thick, dark smoke drifting across the table. 'This is like a conference between Scotland Yard and the local force.'

'Vital.' Bunn nodded. 'Cooperation. Especially at a time like this, with a mad serial killer on the loose bumping people off left, right and centre.'

'I thought there'd only been the two,' said Parrot. 'Erskine Petter and that attendant at the museum.'

'Two we know about,' said Bunn. 'Who's to say there ain't more.'

'Exactly,' said Cribbens. 'That's why we need to swap information, see if we can't get a lead on what's happening and who's behind it. For example, where are Benny and Billy Wardle?'

'There you have hit the nail on the head,' said Bunn, emphatically. 'Not much bad happens in this area without them two being involved.'

'I thought they were locked up,' said Parrot. 'In the Scrubs.'

'They were,' said Cribbens. 'Until the governor of the jail saw fit to let them go.' He shook his head in despair. 'He reckoned they'd served their time, so out they pop to cause mayhem for us who have to patrol the streets.'

'They'll be back behind bars soon enough,' said Bunn, confidently. 'Those two can't stay out of trouble long. And when they do appear—'

It was at that moment the door of the pub burst open, and Benny Wardle rushed in, waving his cudgel, closely followed by his brother, Billy. There was an almighty crash as Benny smashed the weapon down on the nearest table, sending the glasses scattering in a rain of spilt beer. Meanwhile, Billy, following his brother's orders, had grabbed the man sitting nearest to him and punched him in the face, sending him reeling backwards off his chair to fall onto the beer-soaked floor.

'Now, hear this!' roared Benny.

Before he could say any more, there was the ear-splitting blast of a police whistle close by. Horrified, Benny and Billy turned and saw Sergeants Cribbens and Bunn getting to their feet, along with a younger uniformed constable.

'Bloody hell,' moaned Billy. 'The law.'

He turned and was about to run out of the pub, when he found his way barred by two constables who'd responded to the sound of the whistle and come rushing into the scene. Benny stood, helpless, and then he made a run for the door, but before he could get a few steps the young constable had stepped forward, pulling his truncheon from his belt as he did so, and smacking it down on Benny's head. Benny collapsed with a groan and lay still, while Billy was forced to the floor by the two newly arrived officers.

Bunn and Cribbens exchanged very satisfied looks.

'See.' Cribbens beamed. 'Conferencing pays off.' He picked up his glass and took another swig of beer, before putting the glass down and wiping his lips with the back of his hand. 'That's what I call good policing.'

* * *

Daniel and Abigail stepped down from the train at the small railway station that was Borough Green. Or, more properly, 'Borough Green and Wrotham,' said Abigail, reading the station sign.

'It's pronounced Root-ham,' said Daniel. 'Wrotham is another village close by.'

'Another pronunciation mystery of the English language,' said Abigail. She looked admiringly at the hanging baskets and the flower borders that ran along the platform with their proliferation of colour: purples, blues, yellows, reds. 'How lovely,' she said. 'It's a pity they don't do the same with the London stations.'

'They do in the suburban ones,' said Daniel. 'But I agree that this kind of thing would brighten the main stations.' He took a deep breath of the country air, then announced: 'And now we make our way to St Mary's Platt.'

Abigail looked up at the clear blue sky and remarked. 'At least it's good weather for a nice walk.'

'True, but we'll do that on the way back,' said Daniel. 'We'll take a hansom cab to Mr Cartwright's place.'

'I thought you preferred to walk,' said Abigail.

'If we were in London, yes. But this part of Kent is very different. Woods and country lanes, most of them without nameboards. We're looking for a cottage in the middle of the woods up a lane. It could take us hours to find it. Once we've found his cottage and met with Mr Cartwright, I'm very happy to walk back to the station.'

There were two hansoms waiting outside the station ready for passengers from the London train. Other travellers took the first and Daniel and Abigail the second, once the driver had reassured them that he knew the location of Woodman Cottage.

'You obviously know this area,' said Abigail, once they were on their way to the rhythmic sound of the horse's hooves clip-clopping over the stony road.

'I do,' agreed Daniel.

'Is that how you were able to remember what Mason Radley told you? When we were talking to John Feather about where Radley had been staying, my mind went blank. But you knew the whole address. I wondered if that was due to some kind of memory training you did in the police?'

Daniel chuckled. 'No. The truth is I spent some time here many years ago.'

'In the police?'

'No, I came here when I was twelve. '

'Doing what?'

'Hop-picking at a place called Mereworth, which is just a few miles from St Mary's Platt.'

'Hop-picking? Isn't that hard work?'

'No harder than picking oakum, or any other work I did when I was in the workhouse,' said Daniel. 'At that time, I was working different markets in London, helping on stalls. Chapel Street, Inverness Street, Petticoat Lane. There was always work for a willing lad. And one family of stall-owners I worked for told me that every year their whole family decamped to work in the hop fields of Kent, and did I fancy going along with them. There was a promise of good money and a roof of sorts over our heads. As it turned out, our roof was a canvas one, but some of the families had been going to the same hop field for so long they'd built huts for themselves out of old boxes.'

'How long were you there for?'

'Two months. And by the end of it I smelt like a brewery rat. As did everyone else.'

'There was no water for washing?'

Daniel laughed. 'Such luxury. No. But one thing I learnt, when everyone around you also stinks, after a while you don't notice the smell.'

Bert Jugg shuffled down the long stone corridor in a bad mood. He hated being a warder here at Holloway jail. When he joined the prison service the thought he'd be working at Wormwood Scrubs, or Pentonville, or Wandsworth, dealing with proper hardened criminals, people he could boast about to his mates at the pub, telling them how he'd told a well-known murderer or master criminal what to do. But instead he was at Holloway, a mixed-sex prison where most of the inmates were on remand while they awaited trial. It was the women who upset him the most. They had no respect for him, treating him like dirt or laughing at him.

It's because I'm young, he'd decided. *And what's worse, I look young.* He'd applied for permission to grow a beard, but it had been refused, so he had to content himself with cultivating a moustache. But, so far, his moustache wasn't the sort that would give him an air of authority. He had to admit that the few thin strands growing above his upper lip looked more like the remains of a skinny mouse than decent whiskers, which resulted in the women prisoners laughing even more at him. Those who were on remand for things like prostitution and theft, that is. The political women who were here for causing damage as part of their protests either ignored him or treated him with looks of contempt. He wasn't sure which was worse, the open scorn and contempt or the laughter and rude comments.

At least a couple of the male prisoners treated him with the respect he should get. They were the ones who'd never done anything wrong before and were petrified about being in here, and what was going to happen to them. Them, he could wind up. Make 'em scared, especially the younger ones. Like that Simon Purcell. He'd made him cry.

'They hang you for blackmail,' he'd told Purcell. 'I know. I've seen 'em swinging.'

And Purcell had burst into tears.

Good, Jugg had thought, satisfied. *Someone who treats me with respect. Someone I can have a go at and who won't laugh at me or threaten to punch me when they get out. Someone I can have a bit of fun with.* And so, he'd made a point of calling on Purcell in his cell and telling him terrifying tales about what the other prisoners were planning to do to him when they got hold of him in the exercise yard, and the dreadful fate that awaited him after his trial when he'd be found guilty and sent to a proper prison, with hard labour. After the derision and contempt he suffered at the hands of the women, it filled Jugg with satisfaction to watch Purcell shake with fear in his cell. It was payback for what Jugg suffered in this place. Like just now, in the women's block, where that whore Doris Drake had flashed her fanny at him when he opened the Judas window in her cell door and then she'd urinated on the floor, laughing at him all the time. Then she shouted at him, 'Is this what helps you get it up, you creep?'

He'd hurried off, knowing his face was flaming red. As he approached the cell where Simon Purcell was locked up, and where Jugg knew he'd be languishing in abject misery and fear, a new determination filled him to really terrify Purcell with some new stories and predictions about his fate. He'd teach these prisoners who was boss here.

He looked through the window of Purcell's cell and scowled towards the bunk where Purcell could usually be found crouched, a picture of terror. But today Purcell wasn't there.

'Purcell!' shouted Jugg. 'Step out and show yourself!'

But there was no appearance by Purcell from within the cell, or even a sound of movement.

Then he saw a flicker of something dangling from the bars of the window, and a feeling of horror filled him. No. It couldn't be. Not on his watch.

Frantically, with fumbling fingers, he managed to find the key, unlock the cell door and step in. Purcell was naked from the waist upwards, hanging from the bars by his shirt twisted round his neck, his bare feet dragging on the flagstones of the floor.

'No!' yelled Jugg. Then immediately he followed this with a howl of: 'It's not my fault! It's not my fault!'

CHAPTER THIRTY-TWO

Woodman Cottage was a single-storey house of old red bricks, with a roof of red tiles, which was barely visible from the lane because of the cluster of trees that surrounded it.

'A cottage in the woods,' said Abigail. 'It's like an illustration from the Grimms' fairy tales.'

As they walked down the winding path to the cottage, a small man appeared from behind a clump of trees and regarded these visitors suspiciously. He was broad-shouldered, wore a leather jerkin, carried a long-handled axe and walked with a limp.

'Even more like Grimms' fairy tales,' murmured Daniel. 'The woodcutter. Beware of hobgoblins.' Aloud, he called: 'Mr Dick Cartwright? We've come under the direction of your cousin, Mason Radley.'

At the mention of Radley's name, the man relaxed and gestured for them to come nearer.

'Mason's not here,' he said.

'We know,' said Daniel. He introduced himself and Abigail. 'We've come to verify what he told us about staying here with you.'

Cartwright studied them warily before asking: 'Why would you need to verify it? Is this because of what it said in the papers? About some man being killed at the museum?' He hesitated, then added: 'They had a picture of Mason.'

'Yes,' said Daniel. 'Miss Fenton and I are private investigators and we've been hired by the Natural History Museum to look into the tragic event that happened there. I don't know if Mr Radley mentioned it to you?'

Cartwright shook his head. 'Mason turned up and said he was having troubles with his business and he needed to get away from it for a while. Not just the business, London was making him ill. He said he needed somewhere quiet where he wouldn't be bothered by people.'

'He'd been here before?'

'He used to come and stay when he was a youngster. That was when my parents were still alive.' He gestured at the surrounding trees. 'He loved the woods. He loved coming out into them and seeing badgers and foxes and the like. He was always happier in the country than the town.'

'And since he was a youngster?' asked Abigail.

'Not so much,' said Cartwright. 'He'd maybe come down for a few days, then I wouldn't see him or hear from him for a year or two. Then a letter would come from him asking if he could come down for a few days. Up till this time, the last

287

was about two years ago. His business, see. It kept him busy.'

'How did he seem he when he arrived this time?'

'Upset,' answered Cartwright.

'Did he elaborate on why he was upset?'

Cartwright shook his head. 'No. And I didn't ask. That's not my way, and Mason knew that. I never pressured him. I just got on with my work here and let him be. After a day he asked if he could help me, so we worked together.'

'He enjoyed working with wood?'

'I don't know if he enjoyed it,' admitted Cartwright. 'It was harder than the work he was used to, so he was slow at it. But he said he felt better for doing it, which was why he came here. To feel better. Which he did, until Sunday when he walked down to the village and came back with a newspaper. Then he was all upset.'

'Did he show you the newspaper?'

Cartwright nodded. 'We get 'em later here than they do in London. If it's in London's papers on Saturday night, it'll be with us for Sunday morning. The paper had his picture in it. He said, "I've got to go back to London, Dick. They've wronged my name, said I did something I didn't do. I've got to go back otherwise the police'll come here looking for me."'

'Why did he think the police would know he was here? He hadn't told anyone in London where he was really going.'

'Small village,' said Cartwright. 'People here knew Mason. Someone would have reported he was here, especially if they thought there was something in it for 'em. You know, a reward for him. So, he left.'

'When did he leave?'

'Yesterday,' said Cartwright. 'He caught the early train. And

288

I can verify that because I took him to the station myself on my wagon.' He gestured towards a shed partly hidden behind some trees and bushes. 'It's in there. My horse is grazing in the paddock at the back of the house.'

'And when did he arrive?' asked Abigail.

Cartwright thought it over, then replied: 'Tuesday of last week. Sometime in the afternoon.'

'So, he was here for almost a week?'

Cartwright nodded.

'Did he leave here at any time to go back to London?' asked Daniel. 'Before yesterday, I mean?'

Cartwright shook his head. 'No. He was here with me the whole time, here at the cottage. Every morning Mason walked down to the village to get a paper. He liked to know what was going on. And a couple of times we went down to the pub together, which is just a walk down a track. That was all. He didn't even go into Borough Green or Wrotham Heath, just stayed here with me.' He looked at them quizzically, then asked: 'You've come all the way from London?'

'Yes,' said Abigail.

Cartwright looked at them apologetically. 'You'll have to excuse my manners,' he said. 'I'm not used to getting visitors. I should have offered you tea or something. I've got some cider. Home-made. Mason was very partial to it.'

'Tea would be perfect, thank you, Mr Cartwright,' said Abigail.

'You just set yourself down there,' said Cartwright, indicating a wooden table and benches they guessed he'd made himself. 'Mostly I prefer to live outside. I'll be out again as soon as the kettle boils.'

Daniel and Abigail sat and looked at the surrounding trees, watching the birds swooping from tree to tree.

'It's idyllic,' mused Abigail. 'The air's so clean, certainly after London. You've spoken a few times about us living in the country. Is this the sort of place you mean?'

'This is possibly a bit too rural,' said Daniel. 'There'll be no running water here, just a well that runs dry in the summer. And what would I do?'

'Work timber like Dick Cartwright?' suggested Abigail. 'We could do it together.'

'Working timber is a hard and dangerous occupation. Notice the limp. My guess is a falling tree broke his leg at some time. Most people who work with cutting timber end up with some sort of damage.'

'You worked with timber as well?' asked Abigail. 'Another aspect of your life in Kent?'

Daniel shook his head. 'No, it's an observation as a result of interviewing timber workers during my time in the police.' He looked around at the dense woods, savouring the country atmosphere, the lack of noise. 'But it's worth considering. There are plenty of other ways to make a living in the country. And there'll always be crimes to investigate.'

'Yes, but would uncovering sheep stealing or apple scrumping earn us enough to keep us in comfort?'

'There are rich people here. I'm sure that the lords of the manors are just as much in need of good detectives as museums.' He saw that Dick Cartwright had appeared from the cottage bearing a tray with a teapot, cups and saucers, and a milk jug on it. 'Ah, refreshments.'

* * *

'Do you believe Mr Cartwright?' Abigail asked as they walked back to Borough Green.

'I do,' said Daniel. 'Mason Radley didn't kill Erskine Petter.'

To get confirmation, when they arrived back at the railway station, Daniel quizzed the staff to see if anybody answering Mason Radley's description had caught a train to London in the last week.

'"Answering his description".' The booking officer clerk chuckled. 'There's only one man answering that description, with that big bushy ginger beard and that hair. We know Mr Radley and his cousin, Dick Cartwright, well enough, and I can assure you we saw him only twice. On the day he arrived, and the day he went back to London, which was by the early train yesterday morning.

'In fact, old Harry who does the plants on the station lives in St Mary's Platt and he said that Mr Radley never left it the whole time until yesterday.'

'So, there we have it,' said Abigail, as she and Daniel settled down in the train taking them back to London. 'I assume we'll be taking this to Inspector Feather and Superintendent Armstrong?'

'We will,' said Daniel. 'We'll call at the Yard tomorrow.'

'They won't release Mr Radley, though,' said Abigail. 'The superintendent will be determined to hang on to him, to have someone to impress the commissioner. And there's still the murder of Raymond Simpson hanging over Mr Radley.'

'He didn't do that either,' said Daniel.

'Your policeman's nose?'

'That and my reading of people,' said Daniel.

'And you've never been wrong?' asked Abigail.

Daniel gave a rueful sigh. 'Sadly, yes. More than once. But I'm just hoping that this isn't one of those occasions.'

Inspector Feather stood in one of the holding cells in the basement of Scotland Yard. Beside him were two burly uniformed officers, both with their truncheons ready in their hands, because everyone at the Yard knew the reputation of the two Wardle brothers. Although, right now, Benny and Billy didn't look as if they offered much of a threat. They stood as they'd been ordered to, but their postures showed their sense of defeat: their shoulders sagged, their heads hung down and their faces bore the bruises and marks from being beaten in the pub.

'Erskine Petter,' said Feather, accusingly. 'His throat was cut. You went to his room.'

'It weren't us,' burst out Billy. 'He was dead when we got there.'

Benny scowled and threw a dirty look of disapproval at his brother, but then gave a grunt of agreement. 'That's the way it was. Someone got to him before us.' Quickly, he added: 'But we wouldn't have killed him. Not that way, anyway. We've never used knives.'

'Why were you looking for him?' asked Feather.

'He owed us money,' said Benny. 'He said he'd look after us while we was in prison, but he never did. So, we went to get what he owed us.'

'Who killed him?' asked Feather.

Both Benny and Billy looked at him in bewilderment.

'How would we know?' demanded Benny. 'We wasn't there when he got done. By the look of him, he'd been dead for a while.' When Feather didn't answer, he began to step forward, hands held out in desperate appeal. 'Honest, Mr Feather.' One of the uniformed officers stepped forward and gestured him back with his truncheon.

'We didn't kill him,' added Billy, as Benny stepped away from the inspector.

'So, who'd want him dead?' asked Feather.

Benny shrugged. 'I dunno. Anyone he'd crossed. Or taken money off.'

'What about this dinosaur business?' asked Feather.

'What business?' asked Billy, puzzled. 'What's a dino . . . whatever you said?'

'Remember, I told you about it,' said Feather to Benny. 'The letters from Petter and Wardle about the dinosaur skeletons?'

'What's a dinosaur?' asked Billy again.

'Like I told you, Inspector, that was Erskine,' said Benny. 'I didn't know anything about it.'

'Who else was Erskine dealing with?'

'Lately, we don't know,' said Benny. 'We've been in the Scrubs, remember.'

'Before you went in?'

Benny shook his head, helplessly. 'Me and Billy was never involved in who he was dealing with. That was all Erskine. He liked to play things close to his chest. We only got involved when there was money owing. Our job was to put pressure on 'em.'

Feather spent a further fruitless quarter of an hour with the two Wardle brothers, pressing them for the names of any associates of Erskine Petter they knew of, but the two insisted they knew nothing about anything. Usually, Feather would have put their denial down to the pair keeping loyal to the underworld maxim of not informing, but in this case Feather knew it didn't enter their thinking because both brothers were terrified they were going to be charged with Petter's murder. At this stage, Feather wasn't going to inform them that he *knew* they didn't kill Petter, based on the medical evidence and the testimony from Jones about when he'd had his confrontation with the pair of thugs, he wanted them ready to spill any information they had to get themselves off the hook of a murder charge. But no names were offered, nor any other useful information. Erskine Petter really had kept his business arrangements to himself.

With a last warning to them that they were in danger of going to the gallows if they didn't cough up, Feather left Benny and Billy locked in the holding cell and returned to his office, where he found Sergeant Cribbens waiting for him.

'Any joy from the Wardle brothers, guv?' enquired Cribbens.

Feather sighed. 'Not a word. Except to insist they're innocent of Petter's murder. But well done for bringing them in, Sergeant. I'll make sure you get a recommendation for it.'

'Sergeant Bunn from Paddington nick earned one as well, sir,' said Cribbens. 'It was thanks to him that we were in the right place at the right time.'

'I'll make sure his name gets a mention.' He shot an inquisitive look at his sergeant, aware that Cribbens seemed to have something else disturbing him. That was one thing about Cribbens, he thought, his face gave everything away, and his concern about something was very clear. The sergeant would make a terrible poker player, Feather decided. 'Yes, Sergeant? I can tell there's something else bothering you.'

'Simon Purcell, sir. The lad we sent to Holloway on remand on that blackmail business.'

'Yes, Sergeant. What about him?'

'He's dead, sir. Killed himself in his cell.'

'How?'

'Hanged himself from the bars of his cell window, using his shirt as a rope.'

Feather sat down, his expression thoughtful. 'Was he alone in his cell?'

'Yes, sir.'

'So, there's no suggestion of foul play?'

'Not that I've heard, sir. One of the warders found him. No one else involved.'

Feather sighed. 'This case has got one of the highest rates of people vanishing or dying I've ever known.'

'Will you tell his family, sir?'

'As I recall, he's got – had – parents and a couple of sisters in the Holloway Road.'

'That's right, sir.'

Feather shook his head. 'The prison was in charge of him. They can take the responsibility of telling his family. I know how some of the prison staff can be towards prisoners on remand. If there are any questions raised about why Purcell died, I'm making it quite clear his death was nothing to do with us.'

CHAPTER THIRTY-THREE

Daniel and Abigail's first visit the following morning was to Marylebone to talk to Mason Radley's housekeeper. They'd both been aware the last time they'd seen her of her concern for Radley, and they doubted if anyone had bothered to contact her with the latest news of him. When she opened the door to them, they could see that the woman was suffering even greater distress than on their previous visit.

'Good morning, Mrs Walton,' said Abigail. 'May we come in? We have some news about Mr Radley.'

'Please do,' said Walton, making no attempt to hide her obvious anxiety. She led them to the kitchen at the back of the house, saying as they went: 'The kitchen staff are away at the moment, while Mr Radley is absent. There seemed no sense in them being here with no one to serve, though the maids still come in every day to make sure the place is clean for when he returns.'

In the kitchen, she gestured for them to sit at the large and spotlessly clean table. A copy of a newspaper lay on the table, open at the picture of Mason Radley.

'This is dreadful,' said Mrs Walton, pointing at the newspaper. 'They are saying he committed a murder.'

'The reports only say they are looking for him in connection with it,' Daniel corrected her gently.

'It's the same thing,' burst out Walton, angrily. 'And everyone knows it. And it's wrong. Mr Radley would never do such a terrible thing.'

'We agree,' said Daniel. 'In fact, we met with Mr Radley the day before yesterday—'

'You met him? Where?'

'At the Natural History Museum.'

She stared at them, bewildered. 'He is back from India?'

'He never went to India,' explained Abigail. 'He's been staying with a cousin of his in Kent. He returned to London on Monday to hand himself in to the police—'

'The police? Were they at the museum?'

'No. We met him at the museum, and he agreed that we would escort him to Scotland Yard where he would tell his story to Inspector Feather.'

'His story?'

Gently, Abigail related Radley's ordeal as he'd told it to them: the deaths of the workers on his plantation in India, the blackmail by Simpson and fleeing London for fear he would be arrested for a murder he didn't commit. And then the death of Erskine Petter, which the police believed he may also have been responsible for.

'But we know for certain that was not the case,' said Abigail. 'Yesterday we went to see Mr Radley's cousin, and he confirmed that Mr Radley didn't leave Kent at all until his return to London on Monday.'

'The poor man,' said Walton, wringing her hands together. 'What he suffered. Those deaths in India must have distressed him greatly. And he told no one.' Then she looked sharply at the pair. 'But where is he now? You say he came back to London on Monday. It's now Wednesday.'

'He's being held on remand at Scotland Yard,' said Abigail.

'In a cell?' asked Walton, shocked.

'Yes,' confirmed Abigail. 'Unfortunately it was too late for us to go to Scotland Yard yesterday by the time we got back from Kent, but we're on our way there now to tell Inspector Feather that Mr Radley could not have killed the man mentioned in the newspaper because he was in Kent the whole time.'

'And then they'll let him go?' said Walton, her face showing the intensity of her hope.

Abigail shot a look at Daniel, who said: 'We'd like to think so, but the police have their own procedures. They may have to check themselves rather than just taking our word for it.' He hesitated for a second, before adding awkwardly: 'And there is still the fact that he fled immediately after the body of the attendant, who was blackmailing him, was found at the museum, which was why suspicion was cast on him in the first place.'

'But he's innocent,' insisted Walton. 'I know Mr Radley. He couldn't kill anybody.'

'For what it's worth, Mr Wilson and I both feel the same way you do,' said Abigail. 'The problem is convincing the police.'

'And you're going to Scotland Yard now?'

'We are.'

Mrs Walton got up and opened a door that led into a larder. She returned a moment later with a large slab of rich fruit cake, which she brought to the table and proceeded to wrap in pages from the newspaper – although Abigail noticed she was careful not to include the page with Radley's photograph.

'Will you take him this?' she said. 'I'm sure they won't be feeding him properly. Not the type of food he's used to. This is one of his favourites, and it will let him know we're thinking of him.' She looked at them earnestly. 'The greatest gift will be for you to bring him home today, but from what you've said about the police, I suppose that's unlikely.'

'We will do our best,' Daniel assured her. 'But, sadly, I think it may take a little more time. Not much more, we hope. But rest assured, we will be his advocates.'

As they walked away from the house, Daniel looked at the bag Mrs Walton had given him in which to carry the cake for Radley and grumbled: 'On Sunday it was sausages, today it's fruit cake. I'm beginning to feel like a grocer's delivery boy.'

They learnt that Superintendent Armstrong was out when they arrived at Scotland Yard, but Inspector Feather was in.

'So, we'll be subjected to that evil-smelling pipe of Sergeant Cribbens,' commented Abigail as they made their way up the stairs.

Fortunately for them, Sergeant Cribbens was also out, and they found Feather at his desk filling in forms.

'Paperwork,' he grunted, sourly, adding another completed

form to a small pile at one side of his desk. 'These days I seem to spend more time on paperwork than solving crimes.' He looked at the bag that Daniel had placed on his desk. 'What's that?'

'Rich fruit cake for Mr Radley from his housekeeper. I assume he's still here in custody.'

'He is,' replied Feather. 'I'm waiting to see if the superintendent is going to have him remanded.'

'He didn't kill Erskine Petter,' said Daniel. 'He was in Kent the whole time after Simpson died and never left there, according to his cousin and the railway station staff. We went to Kent yesterday to check his alibi. He's in the clear.'

'I agree over the killing of Erskine Petter,' said Feather. 'But that doesn't let him off as a suspect over the Simpson killing.'

'The Simpson killing and that of Erskine Petter are connected,' insisted Daniel. 'The same person is responsible for both.'

'That's just a guess. You can't say that for certain,' said Feather.

'I know it in my bones,' said Daniel. 'But at the moment I can't prove it. I'm hoping we'll get that proof this evening from Mr Jones.'

'We may not,' cautioned Feather. 'This mysterious toff he talked about may be nothing to do with the museum.'

'Let's reserve judgement on that until this evening,' said Daniel. 'Have you got Jones ready? We don't want him doing a vanishing act.'

'I've got a uniformed officer watching his shop and I'm going along to pick him up this afternoon when he closes, and I'm going to hang on to him. He'll be at the museum all right.'

'Thank you,' said Daniel.

'Something else happened,' said Feather. 'Simon Purcell committed suicide.'

'What?' said Abigail, shocked. 'Why? Where was he? I thought he was being held on remand.'

'He was, at Holloway prison,' said Feather. 'One of the warders went to check on him and found him hanging from the bars of his cell window. He'd used his shirt as a makeshift rope.'

'But why would he do something like that?' pressed the horrified Abigail.

Feather sighed. 'Who knows. Usually it's fear. Fear of exposure when his case comes to court, as happened with Tom Tilly. Fear of what lies in store for him when he's sent to prison. Most people know what prisons are like, the harsh treatments that are meted out, by prison officers and other inmates. You have to be tough to survive in places like that. Being physically tough helps but being able to cope emotionally is even more important. Would you agree, Daniel?'

'Sadly, I would,' said Daniel. 'And it's not just in prisons. Any organisation that's run on harsh lines, where physical punishment is a constant threat, the fragile suffer and often take their own lives rather than endure the misery that they know will go on, with each day being as bad as the last, and many times even worse.'

'The army. The navy. Schools,' agreed Feather. 'But in those there's a chance to abscond. There's very little chance of running away from prison.'

Mason Radley sat on the hard bunk in the holding cell, his head bowed, his mind churning. Oh, the misery! He wished he'd never handed himself in now. He should have stayed with his cousin in Kent. But no, common sense told him that sooner or later someone would report his presence in the village to the police, and it would have been even worse for him to have been dragged away in chains. At least he hoped his surrendering himself would be taken as proof of his innocence. Although that depended on Superintendent Armstrong. He didn't like the superintendent. He was callous, short-tempered and indifferent to Radley's protestations of innocence. At least the other policeman, Inspector Feather, seemed sympathetic.

There was the sound of a key in the door of his cell and he got to his feet. He was relieved to see that the man who entered was Inspector Feather, rather than the superintendent.

The cell door was pulled shut by the turnkey in the corridor outside, closing with a dreadful metallic clang. Inspector Feather approached him and held out a small parcel wrapped in newspaper.

'A gift from your housekeeper, Mrs Walton,' said Feather. 'A good-sized slab of rich fruit cake. I believe she is concerned about your health and worried that you might not be getting good enough food.'

'But . . . h-how does she know I'm here?' stammered Radley. 'Have you been to see her?'

'No,' said Feather. 'But Mr Wilson and Miss Fenton have. They wanted to let her know that you are safe and well, although in custody. They also wanted to tell her that they'd been to see your cousin in Kent and confirmed that you couldn't have been in London killing Erskine Petter in that time.'

'That's what I told you,' said Radley, excitedly. 'Does that mean I can go?'

'I'm afraid not,' said Feather. 'The superintendent is still conducting enquiries into the death of Raymond Simpson.'

'I did not kill him,' burst out Radley, in despair.

'I'm afraid, until we find a suspect who's seen as more likely, the superintendent will insist you stay here.'

Radley fell back down on the hard bench with a groan and buried his face in his hands. 'How long must this dreadful nightmare go on?' he moaned.

As Feather looked at him he thought of Simon Purcell and how alike the two were. Yes, Purcell had been a blackmailer, but he'd been a fragile figure, not a hardened criminal. Radley, too, was fragile. Incarcerated in a jail cell for the first time and desperately fearful of what fate awaited him. A man out of his natural element; a man lost and helpless.

'Rest assured, Mr Radley, there are people working on the case even as we speak, looking into other potential culprits. I know this is hard for you, but there is hope. There is always hope. If you are innocent, as many believe, then I promise you, you will be released. I have never sent an innocent man to the gallows, and I do not intend for that to happen now.'

Feather handed him the cake, then walked to the door and banged on it to be let out. As the cell door swung shut, through the gap Feather saw Radley breaking off a piece of the cake. His last look at Radley seemed to show that the man had perked up just a little. He hoped it had been his few words of comfort, but he reflected that it was more likely to be the fruit cake. Whichever it was it didn't matter. Whatever happened, while Radley was in his custody here at the Yard, Feather was set on making sure there was no repeat of what had happened to Simon Purcell at Holloway.

CHAPTER THIRTY-FOUR

Evelyn Scott and Mrs Smith stood at the back of the Grand Hall and watched as people filed in and took their seats. On the temporary platform that had been erected at the front of the rows of seats, Abigail and Cedric Warmsley sat together facing the display of large illustrations depicting Mary Anning, along with many of the various fossils she had discovered during her short career. There was a buzz of anticipation among the audience, an air of quiet excitement.

'It's a very good attendance,' murmured Smith.

Scott smiled. 'It is indeed. With some very famous faces, which will make this quite a society occasion: Herbert Wells, William Gilbert, Bram Stoker, and I see George Bernard Shaw is here as well. And it looks as if nearly all of the trustees have turned up. Although there'll be no Mr Radley, of course.'

'It was his own fault, really,' said Smith. 'If he hadn't run away as he did . . .' She stopped. 'I see William Watling is here, accompanying Lady Fortescue.'

They watched as Watling and Lady Fortescue made an entrance full of pomp and self-important grandeur, sweeping down to the front row and the seats that had been marked 'Reserved for trustees and guests'.

Scott cast a look at the clock. 'Almost eight o'clock,' she said. 'I think we can begin.' She was about to raise a handkerchief and wave it in a prearranged signal to Abigail telling her to begin when Smith stopped her.

'One moment,' she said. 'Mr Turner has just arrived. Do let him take his seat.'

Scott waited until Turner had hurried to the last remaining empty seat at the end of the front row and sat down, then flourished her handkerchief.

Abigail rose and as she moved to the front of the stage, there was a round of applause from the audience. Abigail acknowledged it with a smile and a bow.

'Thank you for that lovely reception, and for coming here tonight to what I know will be a wonderful presentation from Mr Cedric Warmsley of the British Museum. When Miss Scott invited me to open this evening's talk I felt rather a fraud. I was flattered because I have long been an admirer of this woman's wonderful work, but palaeontology is not my particular area of expertise. However, fortunately you will not have to hear me lecture on it as many of you here have far greater knowledge than I on the subject, but instead it gives me the greatest of pleasure to introduce Mr Warmsley, himself a noted palaeontologist and also an expert on the life and work of Mary Anning. My lords, ladies and gentlemen, I present Mr Cedric Warmsley.'

Abigail gestured for Warmsley to step forward, while she retreated to a chair at one side of the stage.

At the back of the Grand Hall, Daniel and Inspector Feather stood beside Jones the butcher.

'Did the man you spoke to arrive?' asked Feather.

Jones nodded and pointed towards the front row. 'That's him all right,' he said.

Feather moved quietly down the side of the audience to the front row and knelt down beside Dawson Turner.

'I'm sorry to disturb you, Mr Turner,' he whispered, 'but I'd be grateful if you would come with me.'

'Now?' Turner frowned.

'If you would, sir. Without a fuss, if you please.'

Turner got up and accompanied the inspector to the back, where they joined Daniel. Jones the butcher had made a hasty exit from the scene and was now in the reception area in the company of a police constable with orders to keep an eye on the man in case he was required.

Feather ushered Turner out of the Grand Hall and towards the stairs that led to the first floor. Daniel was about to follow them when he was stopped by Miss Scott.

'What's going on?' she asked. 'Why has the inspector taken Mr Turner out?'

'Because we have evidence that it was Mr Turner who was responsible for the murder of Erskine Petter,' Daniel told her. 'We feel it also implicates him in the killing of Raymond Simpson.'

Scott stared at him, horrified. 'Mr Turner?' She gasped. 'No, that's impossible.'

'I'm afraid not,' said Daniel. 'We'll be talking to him in your office if you are still in agreement with that.'

'Of course,' she said. 'But—'

'Rest assured, there'll be no trouble. Nothing to disturb the evening,' said Daniel. 'I'll let you know once we have confirmation.'

As Scott stared after his departing figure, she was aware that Mrs Smith had joined her, and her secretary appeared to be in a state of nervous agitation.

'What's going on, Miss Scott?' she whispered. 'Where are they taking Mr Turner? And why?'

'Prepare yourself for a shock, Mrs Smith. The police say that it was Mr Turner who killed Raymond Simpson.'

Smith stared at her in horror. 'No,' she burst out. 'That's impossible. It can't be.'

'If it's not so, I'm sure Mr Turner will be able to reassure them, but I understand they have convincing evidence.'

'What evidence?'

'I'm not exactly sure, but I believe they'll be presenting it to Mr Turner for him to answer.'

'Where are they taking him?'

'I've said they can use my office.'

'But—'

'Ssh,' said Scott, putting a finger to her lips. 'We don't want to create a disturbance.' And she turned her attention back to the stage, where Cedric Warmsley was pointing to a large drawing of a very young Mary Anning, portrayed as a tiny girl wearing a slightly shabby dress.

'Mary Anning was born in May 1799 in Lyme Regis in Dorset,' said Warmsley. 'Her father, Richard, was a carpenter who also earned money by collecting fossils from the fossil beds close to the town and selling them to tourists, which is how young Mary came to get involved in fossil-collecting. Mary's parents had ten children, but most of them died during infancy. Just Mary and her brother Joseph survived, and Mary only survived thanks to luck. In 1880, when she was just fifteen months old, she was at a show of horsemanship being put on by a travelling company. She was being held in the arms of a neighbour who was watching the show along with two other women, when suddenly lightning struck the tree under which they were standing and all three women were killed instantly. Fortunately, the infant Mary was alive, but unconscious. She was rushed home and plunged into a bath of hot water, where she was revived.'

In Scott's office, Dawson Turner sat, silent, his eyes darting backwards and forwards between Daniel and Feather. It was Daniel who was doing most of the questioning. Or, to be more exact, instructing Turner on what had led them to him.

'You made two major mistakes, and both were linked to your attempt to point to a dispute over the fossils as being the motive for the killing of Raymond Simpson and so divert attention away from the real motive, which was about blackmail.

'You killed Erskine Petter as part of the plan to persuade everyone that the bones were the motive for the killing. But very few people knew where Petter was hiding out. In fact, as far as we can find, the only person Petter had confided in was Mr Jones, the butcher. Mr Jones was at the meeting tonight, watching out with us, and he pointed you out as that person who'd paid him for Erskine's address.

'Your other mistake was sending out those letters to the trustees and mentioning Petter and Wardle. The only people, apart from the police and Erskine Petter himself, who knew the original letter was from Petter and Wardle were Miss Scott and Mrs Smith. And you and Mrs Smith have been lovers for some time.'

'Even if it were true, which it's not, that's irrelevant,' said Turner, curtly.

'Is it?' asked Daniel. 'My guess is that Simpson had found out about your affair with Mrs Smith and was blackmailing you. You're in line for a knighthood, I believe, which would be at risk if your adultery was discovered. So, you had to get rid of Simpson. There were just two trustees here when Simpson was killed: you and Mason Radley. I believe you didn't know that Radley was going to be at the museum at that time, but when you saw him you leapt at the idea of putting suspicion on him. And it might have worked, too, if you hadn't overdone it by killing Erskine Petter.' He looked quizzically at Turner. 'Would you like to fill in some of the blanks? I'm sure I've left some important points out.'

'I refuse to answer any of your questions,' said Turner, sharply. 'If you wish to charge me do so, and I'll have my lawyers deal with it. You have no proof of anything.'

Daniel shrugged. 'Very well. If that's to be your attitude. But we're giving you the chance to answer the accusations against you in an informal setting, rather than Inspector Feather taking you to Scotland Yard and charging you formally.' He paused, then added: 'We're sure that when we talk to Mrs Smith she'll help us add some details.'

'Leave her alone,' snapped Turner. 'She had nothing to do with anything.'

'With the murders, or the threatening letters to the trustees?' asked Daniel.

Turner glared at him. 'I'm saying nothing,' he said, firmly.

Scott climbed up the stairs in pursuit of the agitated Smith.

'I know you said it's urgent, but I'm sure whatever it is can wait until the talk ends, Mrs Smith,' she protested.

'No, it can't,' insisted Smith. 'It's in my office. It's vitally important.'

She opened the door of her office and hurried in. 'It's here,' she said, pulling open one of the drawers in her desk.

Scott joined her, looking down at the open drawer. 'Where?' she asked.

'Here,' said Smith, and suddenly she pulled out a pair of scissors and thrust the sharp points so that they pressed painfully against the flesh of Scott's neck.

'Mrs Smith. What are you doing?' asked the shocked Scott.

'I'm saving my lover.'

With that, she grabbed hold of the back of Scott's blouse and tugged sharply on it, exposing the woman's neck even more.

'Now,' she ordered, 'we go to your office and you do what I say when we get there. Otherwise, I'll kill you.'

They left Smith's office and Evelyn Scott allowed herself to be ushered towards the door of her own office and the uniformed police constable standing on guard outside it. Smith held Scott's blouse in such a tight grip that the front of her blouse collar pulled against the front of her neck, forcing her head back. She could feel the sharp point of the scissor blades against her skin

310

just behind the bone of her chin. One sharp upwards thrust and the point would go through her soft skin, up through the roof of her mouth and into her brain.

'You don't need to do this,' she whispered, desperately.

There was no reply from Smith; her attention was fixed on the constable, who stared at the two women in shocked amazement.

'What's going on?' he demanded.

'Open the door,' hissed Smith.

'What?' said the constable, stupefied by what he was seeing.

'Open the door or I'll kill her.'

'B-b-but . . .' burbled the constable, bewildered.

'Open the door,' echoed Scott, as calmly as she could.

The constable opened the door, and Smith forced Scott through, the scissors still digging into her neck.

Daniel and Inspector Feather turned in their chairs at the sound of the door opening.

'I said no interruptions—' began Feather, angrily. Then he stopped and rose slowly to his feet, as did Daniel. Dawson Turner sat staring at Smith and Scott, stunned.

'Let him go or I'll kill her,' said Smith. 'Let him go and he and I will walk out of here with Miss Scott. We'll let her go once we're clear.'

Daniel and Feather stared at the two women, not believing what they were confronted with. Turner got up.

'Penelope, don't do this,' he appealed.

'We're in this together, Dawson,' said Smith. She looked at Daniel and Feather, challengingly. 'One push is all it will take and she's dead. Now, let him go.'

Scott saw the hesitation and uncertainty on the faces of the two men. *If they let him go, what will happen then? There's a chance she'll still kill me. I can't let this happen*, she decided. *I'm a strong woman. I will not let everything end for me here.*

'Mrs Smith,' she began. 'Penelope . . .'

'Quiet,' hissed Smith.

Because Smith's attention was fixed firmly on Daniel and Feather, with occasional glances towards Turner, she didn't notice that Scott was very slowly raising her right hand towards the hand that held the scissors. Suddenly, Scott's fingers closed on Smith's wrist and pulled downwards, just enough to take the point of the blade away from her skin. Daniel and Feather saw this and immediately threw themselves at Smith, grabbing the arm that held the scissors and wrestling the secretary to the floor. Daniel dropped on top of Smith while Feather tore the scissors from her grasp. Then the two men rolled Smith onto her front, and Feather produced a pair of handcuffs from his pocket which he shackled around Smith's wrists. But as soon as Smith was released from their grasp, she leapt to her feet and threw herself at the two men, biting and kicking, spittle flecking from her lips as she screamed 'No! No!' at them, before she was pulled off them by Scott, who grabbed Smith by the hair and forced her to her knees. Feather lifted Smith up and pushed her onto a chair, where he held her.

'Do you have any strong string?' he asked Scott.

Scott went to her desk and took out a roll of string, which she handed to Feather. The inspector tied Smith's ankles to the legs of the chair. Smith's head hung down and she panted heavily, emotionally exhausted. Turner looked at her in anguish.

'Penelope,' he said, 'there was no need for this.'

'Yes,' said Smith. 'There was. They have evidence.' Then Smith looked up at Feather and Daniel, her glare defiant.

'It was me,' she said. 'I killed that man Petter. Dawson had nothing to do with it.'

'And Raymond Simpson?' asked Feather.

As she hesitated, Turner's resolve crumbled. 'I did it,' he admitted. 'I killed Simpson.'

'*We* killed him,' said Smith. 'Together. It needed both of us to wrap him in that cloth.'

'Quiet, Penelope,' Turner warned her.

Feather strode to the door and opened it. At first the corridor looked empty, but then a constable appeared on the run, accompanied by two others.

'I'd gone to get help, sir,' said the constable, out of breath.

'It's all under control,' said Feather. 'But from now on, make sure no one comes in.'

Feather returned to the room, then closed the door. Turner had resumed his seat next to Smith and had his hand on her arm. Daniel was standing with Miss Scott, examining the area of skin beneath her chin.

'The skin's not broken,' he said. 'You are a very brave woman, Miss Scott.'

'The instinct of self-preservation,' said Scott. To Feather, she said: 'I assume I am now part of this, Inspector.'

'Very much so,' said Feather. 'It's only right that you know everything that happened. And I can only endorse what Daniel has already said: you are an incredibly brave woman.'

313

CHAPTER THIRTY-FIVE

Feather had brought in other chairs and he, Scott and Daniel had taken their places opposite Turner and Smith. She seemed to have recovered her usual composure, although Daniel was aware of the anger that burned in her eyes.

'Penelope – Mrs Smith – had nothing to do with anything,' said Turner. 'I killed Raymond Simpson. I killed the man Petter.'

'That's not true,' said Smith. 'He's just saying that to protect me. We killed Raymond Simpson together.'

'Who strangled him? You or Mr Turner?'

'Does it matter?' asked Smith, dismissively. 'It took two of us to roll him in that cloth. We did it together.'

'And Erskine Petter? We know Mr Turner went to the butcher's and got the address of the lodging house where Petter was hiding out.'

Smith nodded. 'Yes, he got the address, but it was me who went to see Petter. Dawson was worried that the investigation was looking into blackmail as the motive for Simpson's death. I told Dawson we needed to get it back to the threat to the museum, which started with the smashing of the dinosaur skeleton, and so get people's minds off the blackmail idea.'

'You told him about the letter from Petter and Wardle.'

'Yes. I said if we could get Petter to write another threatening letter it would do the trick. We would have paid him to do it, but then we learnt that he'd gone into hiding. So, I asked Dawson to find out where he'd gone, and I offered to talk to him. But when I tried, Petter became abusive. He ordered me out. He threatened me with a knife. Luckily, he was drunk, so I was able to overpower him.'

'And you killed him.'

'Because I knew we had to do something. If he wouldn't write the letter, then if his dead body was found it would make the police think his murder was connected to the museum and turn them away from the blackmail motive.'

'So, you slit his throat?'

She nodded. 'Yes.' Bitterly, she added: 'I didn't think it would take so long before his body was discovered. I thought he'd be found straight away.'

In the Grand Hall, Warmsley had just finished, taking his bow as the audience rose to their feet in a standing ovation, cries of 'Bravo!' being heard amidst the applause. Abigail moved across the temporary stage to join him.

'Well done,' she congratulated him. 'That was most excellently done. A real credit to her memory.' She looked towards the audience and saw many of them were heading towards the stage. 'It looks as if there are some questions for you and also, I suspect, many wanting to express their congratulations. I'd better leave you to your audience and report on the evening to Miss Scott.'

'Yes,' he said, looking around. 'Where is she?'

'I believe something urgent came up which took her away,' said Abigail.

At that moment the first of the crowd arrived, eager hands reaching out to shake Warmsley's.

'Magnificent,' boomed one large man, earnestly.

William Watling and Lady Fortescue watched as Abigail manoeuvred her way through the throng and headed for the stairs.

'She'll be on her way to Miss Scott's office,' grunted Watling. 'It's time for us to get ready for her and Wilson.' He and Fortescue headed for the museum entrance and the outdoors.

'You're taking care of Fenton?' asked Fortescue.

'I am,' said Watling. 'And I've arranged for someone to deal with Wilson. He's waiting outside for us.'

'He knows what he has to do?'

'Shoot him,' said Watling.

'Good,' said Fortescue.

'The thing is we want to make sure he shoots the right man, so I need you to point Wilson out to him.'

Fortescue stopped and glowered at him. 'I don't like the sound of that,' she snapped. 'Why can't you do it?'

'Because I shall be busy dealing with the Fenton woman.'

'Surely you could have pointed Wilson out to him before this,' seethed Fortescue.

'I intended to, but there's been no chance,' Watling protested. 'For some reason, Wilson's been tied up with the police since halfway through tonight's event. And Fenton will be leaving the museum at any moment, so I have to make sure I'm there ready for her.'

'Very well,' said Fortescue, sourly. 'But I'm not happy about it. It's dangerous. I don't want to be associated with this.'

'You won't be,' Watling assured her. 'I haven't told him my name, and I most certainly haven't told him yours. We're anonymous, which suits him. All he's interested in is the money.'

'Where is he?'

Watling led her outside and gestured towards a short man dressed in slightly ragged clothes who was hovering a short distance away.

'There,' said Watling. 'Now, I'm off to intercept Fenton. I'll come to you later and we can celebrate.'

'I still don't like it,' complained Fortescue. She looked towards the small man, who was watching them. 'He looks seedy.'

'He is seedy, but he'll do what we want,' said Watling. 'I've got to go. I expect that Fenton will be coming out any second now.'

He moved off. Fortescue glared after him. The small man, on seeing Watling depart, sidled towards Lady Fortescue.

'That bloke said you'd point out who's to be topped,' he said.

'"Topped"?' repeated Fortescue, with distaste.

'Offed,' said the small man. He pulled a revolver from his jacket pocket.

'Put it away,' said Fortescue, sharply.

The man slipped the weapon back in his pocket.

* * *

Abigail walked along the corridor towards Miss Scott's office and found a uniformed policeman guarding the door.

'Are Mr Wilson and Inspector Feather still busy?' she asked.

'They are, miss. They've ordered me to make sure they're not disturbed.'

Abigail nodded. 'I understand. When they finish, let Mr Wilson know that Miss Fenton will be waiting for him outside the main entrance.'

Abigail then headed back down the stairs to the Grand Hall and deliberately chose a circuitous route towards the main entrance that avoided most of the crowds, who were still gathered and chatting animatedly about the evening's talk. Right at this moment, she didn't want to be distracted from concentrating on what answers Daniel and Inspector Feather were getting from Dawson Turner. Did they have enough to charge him?

She walked out into the evening air and found her way barred by the figure of William Watling.

'Miss Fenton,' said Watling, curtly.

'Mr Watling,' responded Abigail, equally curt, and made to go past him, but again found him barring her way.

'You will walk to my carriage,' he said.

'Why on earth would I consider doing that?' retorted Abigail.

Watling pulled back one side of his coat and revealed a pistol that was pointed directly at her. 'Because, if you don't, I will shoot you right here,' he said.

Abigail stared at the pistol, stunned. 'This is nonsense,' she snapped.

'No, this is reality,' said Watling. 'You and your partner have been a thorn in my side, and now I'm dealing with it. Now, walk to my carriage.' He gestured towards the waiting vehicle.

'And if I refuse?' demanded Abigail.

'Then I will shoot you.'

'The sound of the shot will draw attention to yourself.'

Watling shook his head. 'I will say we were talking when a shot rang out and you fell to the ground. No one will suspect an eminent person like myself of having committed the crime, especially when my coachman will back up my story. Now, walk.'

I have to go along with this and play for time, thought Abigail. *Look for an opportunity to get away.*

Abigail headed towards the carriage where a coachman sat on the driving seat, the reins for the black horse in his hands.

'Step down, Jeffers,' said Watling.

The coachman climbed down from his driving seat.

'Tie her wrists together,' ordered Watling.

'Yes, sir,' said Jeffers.

He'd obviously been expecting this instruction because he had a length of cord ready.

'If you attempt to resist, or try anything, I will shoot you,' Watling threatened Abigail.

She stood, her hands thrust forward, and allowed her wrists to be tied. She'd taken the initiative of pushing her hands in front of her to hopefully prevent her hands being tied behind her back, which would have made her situation more precarious, and fortunately the coachman and Watling seemed happy to accept this. Her wrists tied, Watling gestured for Jeffers to return to the driving seat.

'Get in the carriage,' ordered Watling, brandishing the pistol at Abigail. To his coachman, he called up: 'The wharves at Chelsea Creek.'

Abigail climbed inside. Watling waited until she was settled in her seat before getting in himself, pulling the door shut and seating himself on the opposite bench. There was the muffled call from Jeffers to the horse, and then the carriage began to roll onward over the cobbles. *Chelsea Creek*, thought Abigail. *Why there?*

CHAPTER THIRTY-SIX

Daniel and Feather stood with Miss Scott outside her office, watching as Turner and Smith were led away by uniformed police officers.

'Where will you take them?' asked Scott.

'Scotland Yard,' replied Feather. 'They both seem eager to talk, mainly to protect the other, so I think we can safely say this closes the case.'

Scott shook her head in bewilderment. 'I still can't believe it,' she said. 'Mrs Smith always seemed so . . . ordinary.'

'Many ordinary people do extraordinary things in certain circumstances,' commented Feather. He turned to Scott, his hand extended. 'Goodbye, Miss Scott. I'll go with them and fill in the paperwork so we can start processing them.'

'Goodbye, and thank you, Inspector,' said Scott, shaking his hand.

'I'll see you, Daniel,' said Feather. 'Say goodbye to Abigail for me and give her my apologies for missing the talk.'

Daniel smiled. 'I'm sure she'll understand. Don't forget, Miss Scott and I missed it too.'

Feather turned to the constable on duty outside the office. 'I think we can safely say you're relieved, Constable,' he said. 'You'd better come back to the Yard with me and give your statement about tonight's activities.'

'Yes, sir,' said the constable. 'I was just waiting to pass on a message to Mr Wilson from Miss Fenton.'

'A message?' queried Daniel.

'Yes, sir. She said she'd be waiting for you outside the museum entrance.'

'Thank you,' said Daniel.

'I have to say again, Miss Scott, how brave you were,' said Feather. 'I'm not sure I would have been as brave.'

'Tut, Inspector,' said Scott. 'I wouldn't have put you down as a flatterer.'

'It's not flattery, ma'am,' said Feather. He tipped his hat to them before he and the constable headed off.

'He's not a flatterer,' said Daniel. 'He meant it. As I do. This museum is lucky to have someone as brave and tough as you, Miss Scott.'

'We were also lucky to have you and Miss Fenton here to solve the case,' responded Scott. 'Perhaps if you both are able to come in tomorrow, we can fill in the paperwork. Sort out your payment.'

'Thank you, Miss Scott,' said Daniel. 'And now, I think I'd better go and find Miss Fenton and discover how the evening's talk went.'

'I would imagine very successfully,' said Scott. 'So, two successes in one evening.'

She and Daniel shook hands, and he made his way down the stairs and headed for the entrance. Most of the audience had now left the museum, with just a few still milling around talking. Cedric Warmsley also seemed to have left, and the staff was already at work dismantling the displays that formed the stage. Daniel headed for the street outside, looking forward to catching up with Abigail and relieved that the case had ended successfully.

Fortescue watched the crowd leaving the museum and soon afterwards spotted Daniel. He'd paused on the front steps of the museum and was looking about him. Searching for the Fenton woman, Fortescue guessed.

'That's him,' Fortescue told the small man, pointing towards Daniel. With that, she left.

Daniel stood on the steps, looking around. There were still a few people left and he wondered if Abigail had got caught up in conversation. If so it wasn't taking place out here because she was nowhere to be seen. He was just about to turn and go back into the museum when a small man in ragged clothes appeared beside him.

'Don't shout or I'll shoot you right here,' he said, his voice quiet and calm.

Daniel looked down at him, startled, and saw the pistol in the man's hand.

'There's a horse and cart by the kerb,' said the man. 'Walk to it.'

'What's going on?' demanded Daniel.

'Don't waste time. Walk,' said the man.

As they walked along the path towards the horse and cart, Daniel's mind was racing. Why was this happening? It couldn't be to do with Dawson Turner; he was in custody and no one had tried to free him as far as Daniel knew. And then there was the fact that Abigail hadn't been where she said she'd be. Had she been abducted? If so, who by? Was she on the cart?

Daniel looked at the waiting cart. It was a flatbed vehicle, and as far as he could see there was just one person on it already, the driver. So, where was Abigail?

'Where are we going?' Daniel asked.

'For a ride,' said the man. And he gave a little chuckle.

It was the chuckle that made Daniel's mind up. He wasn't going anywhere. At least, not alive. Once he was on the cart the gun would go off and he'd be driven away for his body to be dumped somewhere. The cart was still a short distance away. Was the driver also armed? If so, Daniel couldn't afford to wait before he made his move; he had to strike now.

He stopped suddenly.

'Move,' growled the small man.

'I've got something in my shoe,' said Daniel. 'A stone.' And he began to bend down, reaching for his shoelaces.

'Get moving,' snarled the man, and he prodded Daniel with the barrel of the pistol.

Obligingly, Daniel stood up, and as he did so he swung his right hand down hard on the man's wrist, knocking the gun to one side, while at the same time smashing his left fist hard into the man's throat.

The man dropped the gun and fell to the ground, clutching his throat and making dreadful gurgling noises.

Daniel scooped up the fallen pistol and aimed it at the driver of the cart. The driver had obviously been keeping close watch on Daniel's and the small man's approach because he snapped his reins and the horse began to move, hauling the cart away from the kerb. Daniel was torn between staying with the fallen man or chasing after the cart. He decided to stay rather than risk losing both his possible abductors. He considered shooting at the driver, but the cart was well on its way, and there was always the danger of accidentally hitting some innocent bystander.

His assailant was now trying to push himself off the ground, but he was still choking. He reached up and tried to grab the pistol back, but Daniel kneed him in the face. As the man went down, Daniel smashed the gun on his head and his would-be assassin sank to the ground with a groan.

CHAPTER THIRTY-SEVEN

Abigail sat, her wrists tied, and regarded Watling coldly. The pistol in his hand remained firmly aimed at her, despite the rattling of the carriage as it rumbled over the cobbles.

'You won't get away with this,' she told him, defiantly. 'Daniel Wilson will find us.'

'I doubt that. At this moment, your friend Wilson is at the bottom of the River Thames with a bullet in his head. And shortly you will be joining him. When they recover your bodies and the pistol, the authorities will put it down to murder followed by a suicide. Wilson shot you, then killed himself.'

'Why on earth would they believe that?' demanded Abigail, coolly, though inside, calm was the last thing she felt. Her heart was racing with a mixture of terror at the sight of the pistol held very firmly in Watling's hand and the thought of Daniel being killed. Surely he'd been able to escape. He'd have fought back against whoever tried to kill him.

Watling smirked. 'Because I will tell them that we saw you arguing after the event at the museum and Wilson actually threatened you with a gun.'

'That's preposterous. No one will believe you.'

'There will be other witnesses to the incident,' said Watling. 'My coachman was with me and he'll testify to the fact.'

'I assume this is because we were getting too close to proving that you killed Danvers Hardwicke.'

The smile vanished from Watling's face at this. 'It was an accident,' he burst out angrily.

'Nonsense,' retorted Abigail. She'd decided that the only way she was going to get out of this situation alive was to keep him talking while she looked for an opportunity to launch some sort of attack on him. But first, she had to get the pistol off him. 'You and he were bitter rivals. Or, at least, you were the bitter one, and you were determined to get rid of him and take his job as curator. You took the opportunity of being by the canal to throw him in, after first striking him on the head to make sure he drowned.'

'No!' raged Watling and he repeated: 'It was an accident!' Then he scowled at her as he added: 'I admit we argued and I pushed him, but I didn't mean for him to fall in the canal.'

'And your wife, drowning in her bath?' demanded Abigail. 'And Lord Fortescue conveniently shooting himself?'

Watling glared at her. 'You can't prove anything.'

'Can you be sure of that?' asked Abigail.

Watling fell silent, looking at her with a haunted look. 'It

327

wasn't my fault,' he bleated. 'It was Elizabeth. She shot her husband and then forced me to get rid of my wife. I had no choice. She would have ruined me otherwise. She said that I'd be blamed for her husband's death, not her.' Then he gave a vicious smile. 'Not that knowing that will do you much good. You and Wilson made a serious mistake when you decided to go after me. You, especially, Miss Fenton. You seem to think you are equal to us men. You are not. Women never will be, certainly not in a confrontation like this. Women do not have the strength of a man, and not just physical strength but the grit and the guts to be ruthless. A woman can never be a warrior.'

'No?' said Abigail, archly. 'Boudica? Joan of Arc?'

'Nonsense,' sneered Watling. 'Legends and folk tales.'

Suddenly, the carriage gave a jolt as the wheels ran over something in the road, causing both Abigail and Watling to slither on their seats, Abigail tumbling to the floor of the carriage. Watling recovered, bringing the pistol back to bear on her.

'Get up,' he snapped.

Abigail pushed herself up off the floor, and as she did so she threw herself forward towards Watling and smashed the bony ridge of her forehead into his face. Watling shrieked in pain, blood spurting from his broken nose. He waved the gun blindly and fired, the bullet going through the ceiling of the carriage. Before he could recover himself, Abigail kicked him hard in the groin, and this time Watling shrieked and dropped the gun to clutch himself with both hands.

Abigail snatched up the fallen gun and brought it down hard twice on Watling's head. He crumpled to the floor.

The carriage had pulled to a halt at the gunshot, and Abigail heard the driver dismounting and calling out, 'Is everything all right, sir?' Jeffers opened the door and stared in shock when he saw Abigail pointing the pistol at him.

'Step in,' said Abigail. 'If you try anything I will shoot you. And I warn you that I am a deadly shot.'

Jeffers stepped in, fear showing on his face. He looked nervously down at the unconscious Watling.

'You will untie my wrists,' ordered Abigail. 'And remember, the whole time you're doing it, that this pistol will be close to your belly and my finger is on the trigger. If you try anything—'

'I won't,' burst out Jeffers, fearfully.

With trembling fingers, the coachman set to work to untie the cord from Abigail's wrists. When that was done, she kept the pistol aimed at him as she ordered: 'Now, tie Mr Watling's ankles and wrists together behind his back. And tie them tightly.'

Jeffers did as she instructed.

'Now, you're going to drive us to Chelsea Creek,' she said. 'But I shall be next to you on the driving seat, with this pistol in your side. If you attempt any trickery, such as going somewhere else . . .'

'I won't!' Jeffers assured her in a begging tone.

Abigail gestured with the gun, and Jeffers got down from the carriage.

'Stay there until I'm in the driving seat,' ordered Abigail.

Jeffers nodded and stood waiting obediently as Abigail climbed down from the carriage. His pose of obedience had lulled her into feeling in control, which is why she wasn't prepared for him to leap at her as he did, striking at her hand that held the pistol.

BANG!

Jeffers gave a scream of pain and fell to the ground, rolling and thrashing about, clutching his foot in agony where the bullet had torn through the leather of his boot when the pistol went off involuntarily. Abigail felt a sense of shock and revulsion at the fact she'd shot someone, albeit accidentally, but she knew she had to maintain the pose of sheer ruthlessness if she was going to get Jeffers to drive them to Chelsea Creek. And she needed to get there. Her only hope was that Daniel was still there too, still alive.

'Get up,' she snapped.

'You shot me!' howled Jeffers. 'My foot's broken!'

'Get in that driving seat or the next bullet goes in your head,' barked Abigail.

Jeffers looked up at her, at the grim, determined look on her face and the way the pistol was held in her firm grasp, pointing straight at his head.

'You're an evil witch,' he sobbed.

'I'm an evil witch with a gun,' she said, curtly. She climbed up to the driving seat, keeping the pistol pointed at Jeffers the whole time. When she was in place, she said: 'Climb up here and take the reins.'

'I can't,' moaned Jeffers. 'My foot's busted. I can't climb up.'

'You've got another foot and two good hands,' said Abigail, coldly. 'Now, get up here. If you can't you're no use to me, and I might as well finish you off.'

'That'll be murder,' said Jeffers, tearfully.

'It'll be self-defence,' said Abigail, flatly.

Accompanied by agonised moans of pain the coachman struggled to his feet, then hopped to the carriage and hauled himself up to the driving seat, using two hands and his one good foot.

'Right,' said Abigail when he was settled. 'Chelsea Creek.'

'Where were you to take Mr Wilson's body after you'd shot him?' demanded Armstrong.

The superintendent sat in the leather chair in his office and glowered at the shabby man sitting handcuffed across the desk from him, the would-be assassin, Thomas Carthy. Daniel and Inspector Feather stood either side of the desk, their eyes fixed on him. A uniformed constable stood behind Carthy, but if Carthy was supposed to be intimidated by this show of police strength he wasn't showing it.

'I keep telling you, I wasn't going to shoot him,' insisted Carthy. 'I just told 'em I'd kill him so I'd get the money, but I wasn't going to. I'm not a killer.'

'What were you going to do?' demanded the superintendent.

'I was going to knock him on the head, put him on the cart and then dump him. They wouldn't have known the difference.'

'You keep saying "they",' said Armstrong. 'Who were "they"?'

'I told you already, I didn't know their names. Nor the name of the bloke who was driving the cart. We were all strangers to one another. All I know is the bloke was paying, and that was good enough for me.'

'You said a man paid you, but it was a woman who pointed out the intended victim.'

Carthy nodded. 'That's right.'

'Describe them.'

'Well, they were both very posh. Upper class. It was the way they spoke.'

'What did they look like?' demanded Daniel, impatiently. Then he shot an apologetic look at Armstrong for the interruption. Armstrong nodded, sympathetically, aware of Daniel's concern for Abigail.

'Yes, come on. What did they look like?' snapped Armstrong, the menace in his voice making Carthy recoil in his chair.

As the small man described the pair, Daniel nodded in recognition. Seeing this, Armstrong rose to his feet.

'Constable, keep an eye on him,' he barked, then gestured for Daniel and Feather to follow him outside into the corridor.

'Well?' he demanded.

'William Watling and Lady Elizabeth Fortescue,' said Daniel.

Armstrong frowned. 'Are you sure?'

'Yes,' said Daniel. He turned to Feather. 'You met Lady Fortescue.'

'Yes,' said Feather. 'That description certainly sounds like her.'

'But what would a titled lady be doing getting involved in something like this?' demanded Armstrong in bewilderment.

'Because she and Watling knew we were on to them for a murder. Possibly three murders.'

'Three?'

'Can I explain the details to you later?' Daniel appealed to the superintendent. 'Right now, it's my belief that Watling has got Abigail and we need to know where. Regardless of what Carthy says, their plan was to kill me, and I'm sure they mean the same

332

for Abigail. We need to go after Watling and Fortescue.'

Armstrong nodded and turned to Feather. 'Inspector, go and bring in Lady Fortescue. My guess is she won't come easy so take three constables with you. Be prepared for rough stuff but be careful. Anything to do with the aristocracy is always messy.' To Daniel, he said: 'I'm guessing you know where Watling lives, Wilson. So, take Sergeant Cribbens and a couple of constables and go and pick him up. But you're only there in an advisory capacity, you're not an official, so if there's any rough stuff leave it to the officers.'

CHAPTER THIRTY-EIGHT

Lady Elizabeth Fortescue paced around her drawing room, unable to settle. William should have been here an hour ago. All he had to do was kill the woman and dump her body in the river. Her own part of the action had been over and done with long ago: she'd seen the grubby little man take Wilson away at gunpoint, and that had been enough. There'd been no reason for her to wait. The exact opposite, in fact: if anything went wrong when the man shot him, some interfering busybody becoming involved, then it was vital that she was nowhere near the scene. Even if things did go wrong and the grubby little man was caught, there was nothing to link herself and William to it. William had assured her that no names had been mentioned. Providing Wilson was dead – and she had little doubt of that, after all the man had been holding the pistol pressed into Wilson's side with no chance of missing –

she and William were in the clear. No further investigations into their business by that dreadful pair. The Museum Detectives, the newspapers called them, she thought scornfully. Well, not any more. When their bodies were found they'd be known as the Dead Detectives, and rightly so. That would teach them not to poke their noses into people's personal lives.

The sound of the doorbell made her stop pacing. At last! She'd given her maid, Effie, the night off and informed her housekeeper, Mrs Penton, that she could go and stay with her sister overnight, because she had private business to conduct. She smiled to herself as she hurried to the door and thought of how she'd be celebrating her private business. Very noisily, and frequently. First, in the hallway, followed by a roister in her drawing room, before finally taking William to the bedroom.

She jerked open the door and stared at the four men who stood there on her doorstep. Not William, but three uniformed police officers and a man in an overcoat who she vaguely recognised. Of course, the detective from Scotland Yard, the one who'd taken that threatening letter. Was that what this was about? A sense of fury and indignation filled her. Of all times to call. At this late hour when she was expecting her very special visitor.

'Lady Fortescue?' said the man in the overcoat. 'We met before. My name's Inspector Feather—'

'Yes, I know who you are,' snapped Fortescue. 'What do you mean by calling at my home at this hour?'

'I have a warrant for your arrest on a charge of conspiracy to commit murder,' said Feather, producing a sheet of paper which he held out towards her. 'You will please come with me.'

Fortescue stared at Feather, her mind in a whirl. 'How dare you!' she thundered, angrily, at last. 'Do you know who I am?'

'Yes,' said Feather. 'You're a woman accused of conspiracy to commit murder.'

Fortescue stepped back and began to slam the door shut, but Feather stopped the door from closing with his boot.

'I must advise you that if you resist—'

In response, Fortescue snatched up a walking stick from a stand in the porch and began to strike out at the inspector, but Feather – who had anticipated some action like this – grabbed hold of the stick and jerked it sharply towards himself, pulling Fortescue off balance. As she stumbled, Feather ordered the uniformed officers to take hold of her. 'Handcuff her and take her to the van,' he ordered. 'And if she kicks, put shackles on her ankles.'

The driver pulled the carriage to a halt at Chelsea Creek.

'I'm dying here,' he moaned. 'My foot's busted.'

'Shut up,' snapped Abigail. She surveyed the area. There was no sign of anyone. There were a few barges moored at the actual wharfside, but they all appeared to be empty. No cargo, no people. The wooden buildings, similarly, all seemed to be empty and locked.

'Where is he?' Abigail barked at Jeffers. 'Where's Mr Wilson?'

'I don't know,' Jeffers appealed. 'All I know is what I was told to do, which was drive you and Mr Watling here.' He looked at the dark waters of the Thames. 'I suppose they put him in already.' Then he cringed in fear beside her as he realised what he'd said. 'But I had nothing to do with it. I didn't! I swear! Please don't shoot me!'

And then, before she could stop him, the coachman had hurled himself off the driving seat. He hit the ground with a thud, screaming in pain as his injured foot smashed into the wooden surface of the wharf, before flopping and laying still.

Oh my God, thought Abigail.

She climbed down from the driving seat and approached the fallen coachman warily, expecting him to launch an attack on her, but there was no movement from Jeffers. Cautiously, she moved nearer to him. He seemed to be out cold, but she remained suspicious. She poked his injured foot with her own shoe. There was no reaction; he was unconscious.

'Damn.' She scowled. She needed to get help. She needed to find out what had happened to Daniel. Was he dead, his body dumped in the Thames as Watling had said? She wouldn't be able to cope with that. To have found the one person who filled her life with love and to lose him like this. Her eyes filled blindingly with tears at the thought, and she sank to the ground, the pistol still clenched in her hand.

Daniel forced himself to fight against the rage and frustration that welled up inside him as he, Sergeant Cribbens and the uniformed officers walked away from William Watling's house and returned to their police van. There had been no sign of Watling. According to his housekeeper he'd left some hours ago to attend a talk at the Natural History Museum. He had advised her that it was unlikely he would be home at all that night and told her he would see her at some time the next day. Sergeant Cribbens and Daniel had used the arrest warrant in their possession to search the house, but to no avail. Sergeant

Cribbens instructed the two uniformed officers to wait on guard outside the house and arrest Watling if he returned, while he and Daniel made their way back to Scotland Yard.

'We'll find her, Mr Wilson,' said Cribbens, noticing Daniel's obvious distress and trying to reassure him. But Daniel wasn't reassured.

Platitudes, he thought angrily. It wasn't the sergeant's fault, but that was all they had so far. His only hope was that Watling had taken Abigail to Lady Fortescue's house and Feather had found her there. If Watling wasn't there . . . It didn't bear thinking about. It meant she was still in his clutches, in mortal danger. Then helplessness filled him at the thought that if Watling was at Fortescue's, but with no sign of Abigail, then he'd already killed her.

I'll kill him, he vowed silently. *I don't care if they hang me for it, because if he's killed her I'll have lost the one person who makes this life worthwhile, which means I have nothing to live for. I cannot bear the thought that she's been snatched away from me before we've really begun to live our life together.*

As he and Cribbens mounted the stairs to Armstrong's office he began to silently pray that Watling would not be there. If he wasn't it meant there might still be a chance that Abigail was alive.

As he neared the superintendent's office, he saw John Feather walking along the corridor accompanied by Thomas Carthy and he burst out: 'Have you found her, John?'

'No, nor Watling,' said Feather. 'But we've got Lady Fortescue. She might know where they are.'

Daniel felt weak and had to force himself to stop from collapsing.

'We'll find her, Daniel,' said Feather. 'While Watling's out there, there's a chance she's still alive.'

That's what Daniel had told himself, but a large part of him felt it was just wishful thinking. *Please don't let her be dead*, he begged, fervently.

Feather gestured at Carthy. 'The superintendent's sent me to get him to identify Fortescue. Hopefully, once that's happened, she'll reveal where Watling's gone to protect her own skin.'

'I didn't do any murder,' Carthy reminded them. 'Nor was I ever going to. I was just stringing 'em along.'

Feather ignored him and knocked at the superintendent's door, then pushed it open and ushered Carthy in. Daniel and Sergeant Cribbens followed.

Lady Fortescue was sitting bolt upright in a chair across the desk from Superintendent Armstrong. Her handcuffs had been removed. Both she and Armstrong looked up as the visitors entered.

'No sign of Watling at his house, sir,' reported Sergeant Cribbens. 'I've left officers on duty there in case he returns.'

'This is all nonsense,' sneered Fortescue.

Armstrong looked at Carthy. 'Is this the woman who pointed out to you the man you were to shoot?' he asked.

Carthy looked at Fortescue, then nodded. 'That's her,' he said.

'This is an outrage,' blustered Fortescue. 'Who is this man? I insist on seeing my solicitor.'

'If you give me his name and address, we'll send someone to fetch him,' said Armstrong. He turned to Cribbens. 'Take Mr Carthy down to the holding cells, Sergeant.'

'Yes, sir,' said Cribbens, and he guided the small man out of the office.

'You're making a very big mistake, Superintendent,' snapped Fortescue. 'I'll have your job for this.'

'And if Mr Watling has harmed Miss Fenton I'll have your head and his in a hangman's noose,' retorted Armstrong. 'Your only chance is telling us where he's taken her.'

'I have no idea what you're talking about,' said Fortescue, sternly. 'Mr Watling and I attended a talk at the Natural History Museum this evening. There were plenty of people who can verify we were there. Afterwards, I made my way to my house. I assume Mr Watling did the same. The fact he was not at home when your officers called is neither here nor there. It's certainly nothing to do with me. This man you produced who claims I ordered him to shoot someone is obviously either lying or is deranged. I shall be making my complaints about this travesty, this outrage, to the Commissioner of Police, who was a close personal friend of my late husband, as well as to the Prime Minister, whom I also have an acquaintance with. I insist you return me to my home at once. The longer you keep me here, the more you compound the situation. Not only will I ensure you are dismissed from the police service, and without a pension, but I will make sure you are jailed for the appalling way you have treated me. Invasion of property, wrongful arrest – these are just the start of the legal proceedings you will face. Furthermore—'

She was interrupted by the door bursting open and Sergeant Cribbens rushing in out of breath.

'She's here, sir,' he gasped. 'Here!'

'Who's here?' demanded the bewildered Armstrong.

340

'Miss Fenton, sir. She's outside on a carriage.'

'On a carriage?' repeated Armstrong, trying to make sense of what he was being told.

'Yes, sir. She's driving it.'

Armstrong looked towards Daniel and Inspector Feather, but they had already rushed out of the office. Armstrong rose to his feet and gestured towards Lady Fortescue, who seemed to have shrunk at this sudden news. Certainly, her face showed a mixture of fear and panic.

'Keep an eye on her, Sergeant,' said Armstrong to Cribbens. 'If she gives you any trouble, handcuff and shackle her to the chair.'

CHAPTER THIRTY-NINE

Abigail was climbing down from the driver's seat of the carriage when she heard Daniel cry out, 'Abigail! Thank God!' She turned and saw him running towards her, closely followed by Inspector Feather, and she broke into a run, then she and Daniel threw themselves into one another's arms.

'Daniel! I thought you were dead,' she gasped.

'I thought you were dead too,' said Daniel, taking her in his arms and hugging her tightly.

Feather stood and looked at the carriage and the horse in awe. 'You drove this?' he said.

'I had no choice,' said Abigail.

Superintendent Armstrong appeared. 'Miss Fenton,' he exclaimed. 'God be praised. You're alive and well.'

'I'm not sure about being well,' she said. 'In fact . . .'

Suddenly, Daniel realised that Abigail was slipping down in his arms, then she collapsed to the pavement.

'Abigail,' said Daniel, dropping to his knees beside her and lifting her in his arms.

'It's just . . . just a bit of a headache,' said Abigail. She passed her hand over her eyes. 'I've never headbutted anyone before. I didn't realise it would hurt as much as it did. It was all right while I was rushing around and then driving the carriage, but once I relaxed . . .'

'Headbutt?' asked Daniel.

'You *really* drove the carriage?' said Armstrong, looking in awe at the black horse.

'I had to,' said Abigail. 'The driver was unconscious.'

She began to push herself to her feet but Daniel eased her back down again. 'Don't try to get up yet,' he said.

'Where's William Watling?' asked Feather. 'We went to his house, but—'

'He's inside the carriage, along with his coachman. They're both tied up, but the driver's been injured.'

'Injured?' asked Armstrong. 'Badly?'

'Yes, I'm afraid so,' said Abigail. She hesitated, then admitted: 'I shot him.'

'Shot him?' The men stared at her in horror.

'Just in the foot. And it was accidental. I was holding the gun when he attacked me, tried to knock it out of my hand, and in the struggle it went off.'

'You had a gun?' said Armstrong, stunned.

'It was Mr Watling's. He was going to shoot me with it, and I took it off him.'

'My God,' said Feather. 'Abigail, you never cease to amaze me.'

'And me,' muttered Daniel. 'We need to get you to a doctor.'

'No,' said Abigail. 'Right now, I just need something to drink. I've got a thirst on me like you wouldn't believe. I'm sure it's just a nervous reaction, but . . .'

'No problem,' said Armstrong. 'I'll get someone to brew you a good strong cup of tea.'

'Tea?' said Abigail, derisively. 'I've been abducted, fought for my life, shot a man and driven a horse and carriage halfway across London. What more do I have to do to merit a brandy?'

CHAPTER FORTY

It was around lunchtime the following day that Inspector Feather arrived at the house in Camden Town to catch up with Daniel and Abigail, where he found Daniel making cheese and ham sandwiches.

'I'd come to take you to the pub for lunch,' he told them, 'but I can see you're producing your own gourmet repast.'

'With pickled onions.' Daniel beamed.

'Which Daniel assures me are a rare delicacy,' said Abigail. 'I have yet to put that to the test.'

'I can assure you they are,' said Feather. 'And, just in case this was the situation I encountered, I brought some supplies.' And he opened a bag and took out three bottles of beer. 'If beer is all right, for you, Abigail?'

She picked up one of the bottles and examined it. '"Best stout",' she read. 'Does this mean that I am now an honorary copper?'

Daniel finished making the sandwiches, while Abigail opened the bottles of beer and poured the dark brown liquid into three glasses.

'I thought you'd be interested to know we have the men who damaged that dinosaur skeleton in custody,' said Feather.

'What? How?' asked Abigail.

'Luck,' admitted Feather. 'Fred and Ray Brown, cousins of Benny and Billy Wardle. They boasted to a barmaid about how they'd done this job at the Natural History Museum and never been caught. Smashed up a fossil and got paid for it. The barmaid told the local beat copper, they were brought in and admitted everything. Including the fact that it was Erskine Petter who paid them.'

'So, the last part of the jigsaw,' said Daniel. 'Congratulations.'

'On luck?' asked Feather. sipping at his beer.

'It's as much a part of the copper's armoury as anything else,' observed Daniel.

'True,' agreed Feather. 'I've also come to give you advance notice of a press conference the superintendent is holding this afternoon, so you'll be seeing reports in the papers tomorrow.'

'In which he will have personally solved the murder at the Natural History Museum.' Daniel smiled.

'And the murder of Erskine Petter, and those of Danvers Hardwicke, former curator at the museum, Lord Fortescue, and Mrs Mirabel Watling.'

'My heavens, he has been busy.' Abigail chuckled. 'I sense a knighthood is being pursued. I assume there is no mention of our involvement?'

'Yes and no,' said Feather. 'Which is why I decided to come round and alert you before it all appears in print.'

'But there is a "yes"?' enquired Daniel.

'His statement reads that Scotland Yard, under his direction, solved the cases and brought the culprits to justice, with the assistance of some members of the public, for which he is grateful.'

'Did he name these members of the public?'

'No, although I believe that some of the reporters present were able to hazard a guess. Your old friend Joe Dalton from *The Telegraph* was there, and he asked if these members of the public were the famous Museum Detectives, Daniel Wilson and Abigail Fenton. To which Armstrong said it would be unfair to single out individual members of the public who'd helped, and he'd like to remind everyone that it was the proper procedures carried out by the Metropolitan Police that had resulted in the successful conclusions to this case.' He raised his glass to them. 'It would not surprise me if you got a visit from Joe Dalton to ask for your version of events.'

'And we shall tell him that the real detective hero of this case is Scotland Yard's Inspector John Feather,' said Abigail.

'Please don't, not even as a joke.' Feather shuddered. 'The superintendent can be very sensitive.' He turned to Abigail and said: 'I have to ask, Abigail, had you ever driven a horse and carriage before last night?'

'No,' replied Abigail. 'But I felt I was left with very little option other than to attempt it. However, I reasoned that I had ridden a camel when I was in Egypt and the principle might well be similar. Pull the reins either to the left or right to steer it. And, very importantly, let the animal know that you are in charge and that you mean it no harm. I also remembered watching how cabmen controlled their horses.'

'Astonishing,' said Feather.

'Yes, she is,' said Daniel, and he took a bite from his sandwich. 'So, how are the various accused reacting? Watling and Lady Fortescue, and Turner and Mrs Smith?'

'Very differently,' said Feather. 'Turner and Smith each insist that they were the real guilty party and that the other was merely caught up in it but it wasn't their fault. Whereas Watling and Fortescue are busy blaming the other for everything and protesting their own individual innocence. As a result, with Watling and Fortescue working so hard to protect their own skins, I feel confident we have all the evidence we need to convict them.'

'Providing the Establishment goes along with it,' said Abigail. 'They won't be keen to see two of their own being hanged. And Lady Fortescue has friends in some very high places, as she was very keen to let everyone know.'

Feather sighed. 'True. We'll just have to wait and see. As for Turner and Smith, that becomes more difficult with each admitting guilt. It's possible they'll both hang. However, the good news is that Mason Radley is back at home, exonerated. To the delight of his housekeeper, Mrs Walton.' He smiled and added: 'I delivered him home personally, and if ever there was a woman with lovelight in her face, it was in hers when she opened the door to us. If the man's got any sense, he'll propose and get his life sorted out.'

'Talking of proposing and getting lives sorted out . . .' said Abigail. She stopped and looked towards Daniel.

Feather regarded them quizzically, then asked: 'Who proposed to whom, and when is the happy day?'

Daniel laughed. 'As with Dawson Turner and Mrs Smith, we each take the blame. As to the date, to be fixed, but soon, though at the moment we're keeping everything quiet. The reason we're telling you is because I'd be most grateful if you'd act as my best man.'

'Me?' said Feather, stunned.

'There's no one else I'd want at my side on the day Abigail and I marry,' said Daniel.

'And the same goes for me, too,' said Abigail. 'Please say yes, John.'

'I'm flattered and grateful,' said Feather. 'And, of course, yes.' He drained his glass and smiled. 'This calls for more beer!'

ACKNOWLEDGEMENTS

I'm delighted to have the opportunity to thank the superb team who worked with me creating this book and this series (The Museum Mysteries, featuring Daniel Wilson and Abigail Fenton): my wonderful publisher at Allison & Busby, Susie Dunlop, my brilliant editor, Kelly Smith, and my agent, Jane Conway-Gordon, who have all inspired and worked with me in creating this series and these characters. It may be my name on the cover, but without those three these books would be far less in many ways and may possibly have not existed at all. I have no doubt it's thanks to them that we have now reached book number five in the series. Thank you Susie, Kelly and Jane; and thank you, dear reader. You and your comments are the other vital ingredients of this team.

JIM ELDRIDGE was born in central London towards the end of World War II, and survived attacks by V2 rockets on the Kings Cross area where he lived. In 1971 he sold his first sitcom, starring Arthur Lowe, to the BBC and had his first book commissioned. Since then he has had more than one hundred books published, with sales of over three million copies. He lives in Kent with his wife.

jimeldridge.com